T0130226

# IGNITION

*Inception of Christian Faith*

PAUL OSHIRO

WESTBOW
PRESS®
A DIVISION OF THOMAS NELSON
& ZONDERVAN

WestBow Press books may be ordered through booksellers or by contacting:

WestBow Press
A Division of Thomas Nelson & Zondervan
1663 Liberty Drive
Bloomington, IN 47403
www.westbowpress.com
1 (866) 928-1240

ISBN: 978-1-9736-6919-7 (sc)
ISBN: 978-1-9736-6918-0 (e)

Library of Congress Control Number: 2019910338

Print information available on the last page.

WestBow Press rev. date: 9/3/2019

# I

# Introduction

*I was alive and yet not alive. I was lost in the lonely wilderness of life.*
—Shi'mon Bar Jonah (Peter)

The black ink of darkness surrounded me as I made my way forward. Seeing nothing, I steadied myself with my left hand on a wooden rail. My clothes were sticky with humidity, and the air was heavy with the strong smell of sea salt. I was alone. Not a sound. Not even the wind called to me.

Then out of nowhere there came a "Boom!" It was the sound of a hundred hammers hitting metal all at once. Then came the shriek of hysterical men. The screaming was so loud I had to cover my ears.

My brother, Andrew, yelled, "Lower the sail, or we will all die!" I couldn't see anything in front of me. Flashes of white light from lightning came so close to us that we had to cover our eyes from the searing-white light. Then rumbled the thunderous boom. It was so loud that it left a ringing in my ears. Then it started again—white flashes blinding us, followed by ear-shattering booms.

Huge waves crashed over the sides of our small boat, smashing into us and tossing everyone around. I strained to count our crew of five. It was hard to see in the near darkness between the crashing waves and flashing lightning. We were rocking back and forth like a small leaf caught in the wind. No, not five of us on board. Only four! Whom had we lost?

Then I heard it in the distance. A pleading voice yelled my name, a desperate and guttural scream filled with fear and panic. And I could almost hear the coughing and choking in her screams as water filled her lungs.

"Shi'mon! Shi'mon! Help me! Shi'mon!" And then nothing. Just blackness filled with roaring thunder, blinding flashes of white light, and cold waves battering us.

I bolted up, screaming. Sweat covered my body. My hands were shaking.

Silence. No wind, no waves, no thunder or lightning. Only silence. I looked over, and my brother Andrew was staring back at me with concerned eyes. The rest of the crew went about their business as if they hadn't heard my screaming or witness my thrashing about like a mad man with seizures. Would my nightmares never go away? I was alive and yet not alive. I was lost in the lonely wilderness of life.

This is my story. I am Shi'mon Bar-Jonah (Son of Jonah), a simple fisherman who lost everything and then found eternal life.

Like my father and his ancestors before him, I was a fisherman sailing the local waters of Galilee. My father had taught me everything I knew—from fishing the waters and handling the crews to selling the fish and speaking many languages to deal with the buyers, the local laborers, and the horrid tax collectors. He always told me, "Shi'mon, it's a rough world. Work hard and keep your head straight, and all will be well." My father had a lot of one-liners and taught me many good life lessons, always with the underlying message that it's a harsh world. Disease, hunger, war, greed—they bring out the worst in people trying to survive, and it was up to us to protect our family and friends. Here, where the death penalty was levied for the smallest of crimes, including speaking out against Rome, we learned to respect and fear the soldiers and the government.

For all the harshness and cruelty of life, they all melted away once I jumped on the boat. There all seemed right; there was a peace about being on the waters. And life was simple. My duties included checking and rechecking that all the nets were on board, making sure the fish baskets were empty and ready, anticipating the catch, and ensuring we had a few goat skin sacks of water, a bit of cooked fish for a snack, and some bread. The days were long and exhausting, even with a full crew of five to work the boat. We worked hard with two on the oars or the sail and two to help with the nets. And of course, I made five and did a bit of everything.

Fishing was a never-ending cycle. Always there was something to do or to fix. Fishing mostly occurred at night; we used torches to attract the schools of fish close to the boat within netting range. A good plan was using torches; it was a big sea, and the torches didn't cast much light into the waters, which made for a lot of long nights of moving from place to place, throwing nets, bringing them in, removing the catch (if there was something in the nets), and then throwing the nets again. Mornings brought no relief since the fish needed to be brought on shore, sorted, counted, then sold off. The nets were then cleaned and mended for the next night's ventures.

It was a young man's profession to run a fishing boat. One had to be on top of one's game all the time, especially when selling the fish. The cost depended on so many factors: what was caught that day by everyone else, the time of the year, other crops that provided food for the community, even the holiday season. One had to process it all in the head to bargain effectively with the wholesalers. There were over twenty types of fish in the waters; the big three were musht (tilapia), biny, and sardines. The musht were considered the best fish; they were medium sized, good tasting, and great for the frying pan. They were often caught in large schools, even in the shallow areas. Bings were also a good catch. They were hardy fish much larger than the musht; they were a favorite for the Sabbath feasts. Sardines were the low fish of the catches, being the smallest of the fishes and considered unclean by the locals. Still, all in all, sardines were a very tasty fish that could be sold to the Gentiles. They liked it, and I had no issues with making a little extra money wherever I could. Since I was a practical man, fishing was a business, and there was no time for getting too caught up with the ideas of the learned men about what was acceptable to eat and what wasn't and who we should sell fish to and who we should not. Words didn't feed the family.

Our fishing grounds were the Sea of Galilee. Surrounded by mountains on all sides—three to four parasa wide (eight miles, thirteen kilometers) by five parasa long (thirteen miles, twenty-one kilometer)—the sea was a spectacular sight when I was in the middle of the waters on a calm day.

Glimmering and shimmering still waters were surrounded by beautiful mountains that rose gently from the water's edge. Fleets of boats, docked for the day, awaited the night of fishing, and some others tried their luck on the seas for the odd school or line fishing for larger fish.

Life was a never-ending routine, simple and hard. Little was I to know how much more life had to offer, and it initially came through my brother Andrew.

"Keep your ears open and your mouth shut" Andrews always said. Ever the listener, he had learned a lot while trading and selling. The people weren't happy. But when was anybody ever happy these days with the high taxes, low wages, and the ever-brutal laws from the Romans? There was a law for everything and ever-increasing punishment, unless of course you had money to bribe the soldiers. After scraping for the next meal, finding a roof over your head, and looking for firewood for cooking and heat, there was nothing left.

Recently things had become different; unrest and even clashes with the soldiers were increasing. Andrew had heard Rome was bringing a new official to clean up the mess. We were the mess. It didn't sound good; all the better to keep out of the big cities and stay on the water. The Romans were beating and imprisoning anyone voicing his or her ungratefulness to Rome. The other day there had been a big clash over the new taxes. The situation got out of control, and people died. The Romans needed a head, and who better than the loudest mouth in the community, Barabbas?

I felt sorry for Barabbas, not that he was a good man by any stretch of the imagination. But he did everything with zeal, including lots of fighting. Looks like he did it this time, though; and now he was in prison for killing someone. Andrew hadn't heard whom Barabbas killed; maybe one of the tax men? If so, it was a crime, of course, one born out of frustration, a feeling we all had but never expressed physically.

Tax men were the lowest of the earth. Imagine cheating your own people, gouging us for more and more. And how did the tax men improve our lives? Did they grow food? Did they craft furniture, heard animals? Did they make anything at all? No, they took our money and pocketed what they wanted. When Rome asked for more, instead of giving some of their share, they made us pay more. It was enough to make one join up with Barabbas and fight them all. Could anyone or anything ever make a difference? Was our fate always to be under the yoke of oppression? There were others in the community who were teaching a different way than violence and force.

John the Baptist was one of those prophets who preached in a different way. Andrew kept pushing me to go with him whenever John was in town. John preached to us to get ready for the coming Messiah, to straighten out our lives, and to refrain from drinking and being obsessed with worldly things. He ate no meat or bread. He drank no wine. He lived off locusts and honey, and he wore clothes made from camels' hair. That was such a hard life to follow.

It was hard not to believe in John the Baptist; he was a pure man untainted by the attractions and trappings of the world. If I could have been like him, I would have tried, but it was hard. My heart was there, and I did believe in a better time for all of us, a day when there would be less suffering in this world, a day when equality would be spread among God's people once again and we would be rid of the yoke of our oppressors. When would John the Baptist's Messiah come? Our Messiah. Would it happen in my lifetime? That was what he was saying; I prayed he was right. We needed someone to lead us to freedom. John gave us hope for a better future, one filled with love, spiritual power and freedom, and forgiveness of our sins. I prayed that God would help me to be strong for the day of the coming of our Lord. So much had happened over these last few years. The last few painful years. The lost years.

It seemed just like yesterday when we had been so in love. Just married, we had done everything together. We knew each other from early childhood, and Sarah was the love of my life. She was always full of energy. She had long black hair and a quirky grin that lit up any room. Always playing jokes on me and Andrew, she was no typical girl; she was the outgoing, hands-on type in a good way. We lost track of each other for some years when Andrew and I went to work for our cousins' (James and John's) father, Zebedee. It was the way of our fishing village. We were boys turning into men, fishing the waters as our families had done for generations. It was funny that, just moving to the opposite shore of our small sea and during that short separation, I didn't see anyone again from my childhood village.

One early morning we were bringing the boat in from a particularly good night of fishing. Our boat was full of musht, some of them a foot and a half long. There must have been over two hundred of the large fish in the catch, flapping in the baskets; the boat seemed to even ride a bit lower in the water, and the oarsmen strained a bit harder on the way back to shore. Of course, they did all this with big smiles, knowing we had just made a month of wages each. Yeah, at times like these, it was good to be a fisherman.

On the shore the people were oohing and aahing at all our fish. We gave the catch to the women, who sorted them out for taxes and sale at the market. Then I saw her in the distance, with her long hair, big green eyes set in a dark-tanned face due to days in the sun. With a wide grin, she saw me and shouted, "Nice catch, pasty face."

Well, I liked the nice-catch part at least. A few months on night duty tended to wash away a nice tan pretty easily. Her wide smile and the twinkle in her eyes said it all, and it was great to see her as well. I couldn't help but stammer out a reply. "Uh, yeah, great to see you too, Sarah." Not exactly world-class stuff, but she got the message.

My thoughts reeled back the years to a much simpler time. Our formal schooling had been working for the family business, in which case for me had been the fishing trade. There was still a lot of work to do even as a youth, but there was time for playing games, skipping rocks off the water, and wandering around town with carefree, uncluttered minds only the young possess. When she came closer, her glow magnified a hundred times, and I was struck that the little girl was now a woman, the most beautiful woman to grace this piece of shoreline.

The years apart evaporated in seconds, and it was as if we had never parted. My best friend from long years past had returned to me, and from that day on, we were never apart. It wasn't long after that, and we were married. We talked every night about our future, what our children would look like, even their names. My life was fulfilled. What more could a man ask for? The seasons and a few years passed by quickly with no great events, a comfortable life of fishing, family, and friends in our little community sheltered from the harsher parts of life. As I had come to learn the hard way, all things, good or bad, never last. Another of my father's sayings.

A long winter storm hit us. Days and days of rain and bitter-cold weather. Heavy fog rolled over the sea during the cold days and made it harder at night with choppy seas. Cold sea spray jumped over the boat's edge just enough to give anyone about a fine spray of ice-cold water with irritating regularity. Pitch, roll, and spray all through the night. It wasn't rough enough to hold us back from fishing, just enough to make us so cold from the metronome of never-end rocking, sea spray, constant rain, and even ice rain at times. It was enough to cut straight through to our bones. We were prepared as could be for the cold, but our cloth tunics held the water like wet blankets. At least they kept the wind from cutting through.

Sarah was by my side through it all and didn't want to hear of me going out without her. It was just like Sarah, loving to a fault, never one to take no for an answer. Strong of both mind and body, she always helped out wherever she could—from mending the nets to getting the nets ready. Being on the boat wasn't a woman's place, but Sarah aptly states she could do everything a man could do and better. Not the brute physical part, but she had the knack for finding fish. It was a gift that spread quickly through the small community. God had blessed Sarah with a sense of where the schools were, and her success belied any of the crews' misgivings about bringing a woman on board. So much for the male ego. When money got into your pocket, it seemed like a lot of ego went by the wayside, and the crew liked having Sarah aboard. Her presence calmed everyone down; her laughter and bright smile were an infection no one was immune to.

Without warning, a huge wave came up suddenly and hit high the boat directly on the side, tilting the boat sideways and almost dipping the boat into the wave. Then the white water washed over the side, an icy froth shooting cold daggers into everyone, pushing and tossing the baskets, nets, and crew about. We were all disoriented for what seemed like hours as the boat continued to toss around the waves, everyone holding on to whatever he or she could that was anchored to the boat. The torches went out, the sky laden heavy with clouds. No moon or stars shone through; everything went pitch black. Then on the distant horizon, the small twinkling of village lights appeared. Thank God there was no fog. Sails were down from the high winds; shouts to man the oars were given to turn the boat toward the village lights, which were barely winking in and out in the distance.

Smoldering embers from a clay pot were brought out, and dry torches were lit. Netting and tools were everywhere tangled to one side of the boat. Calmed by the torches and seeing the shore lights in the distance, we regained our bearings. A quick shout-out to count the crew. Male voices shouted out one by one. Everyone accounted for, everyone except Sarah. Panic hit me, and I grabbed a torch.

We scrambled through the netting. *Lord, protect Sarah.* She must be tangled up. The deck was laden with flapping fish, nets, turned-over woven containers, clay water jugs, and spears. Seconds seemed like hours with no trace of Sarah. Fear grew to despair; we searched the boat and rowed and rowed through the frothy sea, everyone with a torch in his or her hand, yelling for Sarah.

Grabbing a rope, I secured one end to the mast and the other to my waist. I gave my torch to Andrew, and before he could stop me, I leaped off the side of the boat into the black waters. Darkness enveloped me, and all I could see were the whites of the choppy waters glimmering faintly by the torches on the boat. On and on I treaded water, barely holding my head up over the froth waters. My legs grew weary, and I felt the cold seeping in. Hearing shouts from the boat of her name, I couldn't remember whether it was their voices or mine that I heard echoing in the darkness. When my legs finally gave out, the sea cold, a gentle tug caught me, dragging me closer to my fate.

"Shi'mon! Shi'mon!" My brother Andrew's voice echoed softly at first, then louder. My head felt like it was splitting open, and I was retching my stomach out on the boat. "Thank God, Brother. When we dragged you on the boat, we thought you were dead."

"Not dead in body, Brother," I replied. Two more times that night, I jumped off the boat in search of Sarah, and two more times I was dragged back onto the boat. Two more times our Lord didn't see fit to take me home to be forever with Sarah.

The night turned to day, days into nights, and I searched for months. No fishing, just rowing by myself. The water that gave us life had taken mine away in a moment.

They say you know when you hit rock bottom because there is

nowhere lower to go. I lost track of time. What did any of it matter anymore? A few too many drinks, a few fights. My only constant companions were hopelessness and despair. I was still living life and working the boat but now without any passion or emotion. How could life be so perfect one moment and then, just like that, you could have everything taken away? What was God thinking? Did He hear my cries? Did He even care? Why take Sarah from this life? From me? All our plans were gone, never to be. Was there really a God? Could He be so unfeeling and cruel? Or was I just too small for Him to care about my life and those in my life? My questions were never answered, and over time I resigned myself to stop questioning the things I couldn't change. They say time heals all wounds, and the days turned to weeks, the weeks into months, and the months into years. I was never fully healed; the monotone of daily activity drew out the years and dampened down life's expectations. Who could have known it would all change?

# 2

# Hope

*And the God of all grace, who called you to his eternal glory
in Christ, after you have suffered a little while, will himself
restore you and make you strong, firm and steadfast.*
—SHI'MON (PETER) (1 PETER 5:10)

The morning was bright and sunny, not a cloud in the sky; the sea was glimmering and so calm, the reflections so perfect that one couldn't tell where the sky and mountains stopped and where the sea began. Soft, white, puffy clouds drifted slowly by like sentinels, ever watching us, never staying, moving on to the next village and town. It wasn't so cold that there was the need for a heavy tunic; nor was it so hot that one had to strip off for a day of fishing.

The small seaside birds, gulls, and even from time to time vultures circled the boat, singing their songs to us in the hope of joining us, catching some of the fish the sea had to offer. It was a perfect day, a day just like this three years ago when Sarah had walked backed into my life; now it was a year since she was gone. Fishing wasn't a pleasure anymore, just work. It was work to care for the family and take care of Sarah's family as well. Not six months after Sarah's passing, her father joined her, taken by a terrible accident. Her mother moved in with our family. My mood was turning sour again.

A gruff hand clamped hard on my shoulders, shaking me out of my darkness. "Brother, a beautiful morning, isn't it?"

Andrews bright eyes looked sharply into mine with a sad expression,

11

seeing the utter lack of emotion on my face. Nothing needed to be said, for a brother knows the other as no one else can. "The rabbi is here in town today, giving a sermon at noon in the town square. Let's go and listen to him."

My response was quick. "Rabbi?" More words. I had been to the Sabbath lectures and heard our esteemed learned ones spouting off rules and regulations from the book, wise sayings from men who haven't toiled in the fields or on the boats, laboring hard for a meager life. These were men who filled their lives with words and no deeds, living off our hard work. Were they no better than the tax collectors?

Knowing my thoughts, Andrew blurted out, "You know this man is different, Shi'mon. Come and see. He has come from far away to speak to us." For some reason no one knew, he had never come into the towns before, preferring to live and preach only in the wilderness areas.

"I will not go. Brother, I am busy today."

"Busy?" Andrew's eyebrows lifted. "You haven't been busy for the last six months. Come, Shi'mon, and I will ask no more of you." Andrew's eyes, full of sorrow, looked straight at me again. No more words. Just a penetrating look. Not pity but sorrow for a brother who had lost so much.

"Okay then," I said. "We will see this preacher. Then you will leave me to my work."

It was just as they had said. The rabbi John the Baptist wore an old tunic made of camel hair and used a big leather rope for a belt. Skinny as a rail with wild hair and a bushy beard, he walked barefoot. Had this man ever lived anywhere except in the wild? He sure looked like it; he was a pitiful sight. He wouldn't have lasted a day on a fishing boat, but it was those deep, brown, penetrating eyes set in his dark skin with an easy smile and a look of utter peace that shook me. He seemed to have nothing, yet his peace was more than I had ever had, at least for as long as I could remember.

He stood in the center of the village square on a rock so all could see him. It looked like the whole village had turned out. Hundreds gathered around, intent on hearing what this rabbi had to say. Some said he was Elijah reborn, and others even said he was the Messiah come to save us all. His name was John, better known as John the Baptist. Every day he preached on the southern shore of Galilee, where the waters turned into the Jordan River. He preached and then baptized people by dunking them in the water. Doing this for years now, he had a large following, and from all over they came to John to be baptized.

From as far off as Jerusalem and beyond, they came to him to experience what we had lost, our faith. A faith lost from hundreds of years of captivity beating down generation after generation, taking away our will, passion, and faith. Not all at once but slowly. So ever slowly that one didn't notice that we had lost anything at all. We had just learned to survive from day to day, trying to make a living, our focus on food and shelter for the family. They became the only priorities in life. Sickness, hunger, long days, and the whip were the realities of life for most of our people. Our rabbis kept telling us to live by the rules cast down over us by our overlords, the Romans, telling us to work hard and give any extra we had, even what we didn't have, to the temple as an offering to God. The big festivals and holidays of Lent, Passover, and others were further burdens on all of us. No one could afford them, and yet we had to go, had to give, and had to sacrifice what we had so our God would be pleased with us. Or that was what the rabbis taught us.

But this John was different. Standing before us, he talked for hours about our God, a God of righteousness, love, and compassion. A God who cared for each one of us individually. A God who cried with us in our sorrow. A God who was there by our side in both good times and bad. A God who required us to give to the holy Pharisees or Sadducees, even if that meant we went hungry ourselves, having nothing left to provide for our families. No, this last part wasn't of God.

John cried that this was injustice and even yelled at our supposed holy men, cursing that they were vipers in sheep clothing preying on us; they were doing not the will of God but the will of men. They were men bent on keeping us away from our true God, enslaving us to our Roman masters, and never freeing us to become what God had envisioned for our lives; to be people of passion, love, energy, and freedom; to be able to pray directly to our Lord; and to provide for our families without the burdens imposed by our learned rabbis. This was giving to God out of our love for Him and not out of obligation, not out of rules imposed by men.

Wow! I had never heard such powerful words. As he spoke, it was as if he talked to us individually, welling up what had been lost for generations. What was it? That mysterious spark that ignited in me a long-forgotten flame? Yes, it came to me. It was hope. Hope for a better life. Hope in a God who truly cared for us. A God who was different from the God of the Torah, who wiped out villages and towns, who required us to sacrifice for Him at the expense of our families. He spoke of the same God of our fathers yet who was different at the same time.

After speaking for hours, John walked to the water, calling out, "Come and be baptized in the name of our God." Then he said something all the more curious. "I baptize you with water. But one who is more powerful than I will come, the straps of whose sandals I am not worthy to untie. He will baptize you with the Holy Spirit and fire." Who could this man be whom John was speaking of? How could anyone, any rabbi, be of greater passion or truthfulness than John? He shouted, "Repent for the kingdom of heaven has come near."

There, that perfect day. That morning so beautiful that it made me forget for a moment all my sorrow and pain. I found anew what was lost, and John baptized me. Zebedee John's brother, James, was also baptized, and the two of us became followers of John the Baptist.

Life from that day on for me wasn't the same. I no longer felt that God had completely abandoned me, that my life was to be only that which I toiled at during the days and nights. There was more to come. More to do. What that was, I was unsure.

John left and went back south to the Jordan River to Bethany and to the wilderness areas to continue his preaching. We often journeyed to see John, and he always lifted our spirits. Andrew and I split our time on the fishing boat so one of us could be with John. It wasn't often; there were times when Andrew and I went to be with John together. Those were truly good days.

# 3

# First Encounter

*The time has come; the kingdom of God has come
near. Repent and believe the good news!*
—JESUS, THE CHRIST (MARK 1:15)

It was Andrew who saw Him first. He was in Bethany, walking with
John the Baptist, when John the Baptist got excited and exclaimed
at the top of his voice for all to hear, "Look, the lamb of God who takes
away the sins of the world! This is the one I meant when I said, 'A man
who comes after me has surpassed me because he was before me.' "I saw
the spirit come down from heaven as a dove and remain on him. And I
myself did not know him, but the one who sent me to baptize with water
told me, 'The man on whom you see the Spirit come down and remain
is He who will baptize with the Holy Spirit.' I have seen and testify that
this is God's Chosen One."

Thunderstruck at this, Andrew and his friend were dumbfounded.
There before them stood a strikingly handsome man of about their
age, not handsome as a man with perfect features but handsome in a
charismatic and magnetic way, dressed in an off-white linen tunic with
a brown rope belt. The ends of his tunic were frayed near His feet, a sign
of a lot of walking. He was a head taller than most, His eyes sparkled
in the sun, His face and arms dark brown. He was lean yet not unfed, a
wiry frame of sinewy muscle that held strength. His wide grin set inside
a short beard shone brightly with both happiness and true joy, all framed
by flowing long hair colored brown from long days in the sun. Following

the charismatic man for a time, the man turned to them and said, "What do you want?"

Andrew replied, "Rabbi, where are you staying?" He beckoned them to follow; Andrew and Zebedee John spent the entire day with Him.

A week after that day, Andrew found me. Where else would I be? Coming off a long night of fishing, I felt cold in my bones. The night waters had given up sardines, three full baskets of them. Not bad for a night's work. The local people wouldn't touch them; however, sardines were good-tasting fish, and the Gentiles paid well for them.

Running up, out of breath, he called, "Brother!"

Before he could get another word in, I blurted out, a bit irritated, that I had been left this week to fish on my own. "Andrew, just in time to help me with the catch. Let's go to the market."

Andrew stood there, staring at me for what seemed like an eternity with a smile a mile wide. It almost became a bit awkward, and I gave up my irritation to see his smiling face. At least someone was happy.

"Brother, you look as if you found a treasure. Did you finally find a companion on your journeys with John the Baptist?"

"Even better than that. Much better than treasure or a lady."

"Hmm, then what did you find there?"

"John introduced us to the One he keeps talking about, the One whose sandals he is not fit to touch. The Messiah, Shi'mon! He is here now, walking this earth. Come and see."

My curiosity was piqued, so to Bethany (beyond the Jordan) we went. Bethany was located twenty-four parasa (one parasa is approximately two and a half miles or four kilometers) south of the Sea of Galilee or three parasa north of the Dead Sea. It was a hard three days' journey by foot. So impassioned was Andrew that his excitement filled me with that same nervous energy I had felt that day when we saw and heard John for the first time. Could this man really be Him whom our people have been waiting for since the time so long ago when we had our own country? Was He here to free us? Then we wouldn't be enslaved by anyone, a strong country unto ourselves, not under the tyranny of any. Finally, we would be a free people again with our own king. Or was this even more so than that? If John the Baptist's words were true and this man was the Messiah, then He was even greater than David, greater even than

Moses or Abraham, the true Son of God Himself made flesh in man. A warrior, a king, a miracle man. Why was He here now? What would He do? The questions were endless.

I tried not to get my hopes up too high. I had lost so much before, and only now did I feel my life was getting back on some normal track. And yet there was always something missing, a feeling that there was more to this life. God had bigger plans for me. What they were and when they would come, God had never answered those questions. On the way to Bethany, hearing Andrew talk about this Teacher, this Son of Man, my heart welled up.

*Yes* was the only thought my mind said when I heard his words. *Yes, your questions will be answered about all the things left undone in your life, and yes, the great void in your heart torn from you by the loss of Sarah will be healed.* No more lonely nights with my only companions, no more dreams of a better past, no more unfeeling presence, nor an unknown future devoid of hope. Yes, I heard Him calling. I heard Him say He had come to fill that which was not in my life. To overfill the cup of my soul. To ignite in my heart that which was lost.

Andrew stopped and looked at me curiously for a moment with a word so faint at first that I couldn't hear what he had said. A whisper. Then louder: "Yes, Shi' mon. He said it to me as well."

"What did He say to you, Brother?"

Andrew's eyes widened ever so slightly, and with a slight tremble in his voice, he reverently whispered, "Jesus looked at me and said, 'Yes.'"

Bethany (beyond the Jordan), a Roman town, was a fair-sized village of more than five hundred homes and structures. Nestled between the Jordan River to the west, a thick belt of trees, and bushes called "the jungle of Jordan" to the east, Bethany was a quieter town than its much larger neighboring city of Jericho to the west. East of "the jungle," the landscape changed dramatically to a soft, chalky, white barren area the people called "the wilderness."

A place full of history for the Israelites, Bethany was known by many names, Beth-Abara or Bethabara, which means "house of the crossing," referring to Joshua's and Elijah's crossings of the river. In the Old Testament, the same area is also referred to as Beth-Barah, the place where Gideon defeated the Midianites and slew two of their leaders.

17

These same fords across the Jordan are thought to be the place where Jephthah, the Gileadite, seized these fords during his battle against the Ephraimites; most of all, the hill at the heart of Bethany was revered as a holy site, a place where Elijah had sought refuge upon God's command and where the ravens had fed him meat and bread. Bethany also held the spot from which Elijah ascended to heaven.

Daily life was different from what we were used to in their fishing villages along the Sea of Galilee. Work life focused on farming the land around the Jordan River; the land was blessed with temperatures higher than other areas, allowing for year-round farming. The long history in the area also brought in a lot of travelers stopping over to pay homage to esteemed ancestors—in other words, tourists. Life was different and yet the same. Homes had stairways to roofs; main streets of pebbles helped to control dust and mud during the rains, but they were a sore spot for the people since dropped coins were impossible to find. Local carpentry, metal working, pottery, cloth making, and other local stores brought the area to life; the area was buzzing during the days.

It was always an exciting feeling to walk less-familiar streets, taking in the sights and sounds, the chattering of the locals about the happenings in the community. In Galilee life was all about fishing: who caught what or what the weather would be like that night. Everything revolved around the sea. In Bethany life was about the crops: who was growing what, how the crops were, and how the various cattle were doing. All in all, it was the same. Talk was about who was getting married and who wasn't, family members who had fallen ill, and the general happenings common to any village life. And there were the same undercurrents, whispered grumblings of high taxes, abuses, even killings in other towns and villages by our Roman masters. Here in Bethany, home to John the Baptist, there was an air, a feeling different from Galilee. It was on their faces, a look somewhat different from the solemn, stern demeanor of Galilee and the other small towns we passed on the way here. It was a look of expectation, a feeling that something was coming. Something great. Was it John the Baptist? Or even more, was it that man John the Baptist was proclaiming as the Messiah?

Homes were clustered together, and large ovens were located outside in the inner courtyards just like the Galilean towns. Smells of the open-air wood fire stoves wafted into the streets; fires were started early in the morning and roared all day. Mixed in were the smells of donkeys in the streets and farm animals. The temperature was much hotter and dryer. There was no large sea to blow cooler winds from the water onto the land; there was something else a little different.

When one wandered down the street, it all looked the same: the shops lined up, people trading for goods and wares. There were sounds of haggling and donkeys hee-hawing, never happy at being tied up outside without any shade or water and agitated by the constant crowd of people. They were always wearily staring at any passersby with those big, round, sad eyes. Get too close, and there was more hee-hawing; it was louder with a touch of panic. The boys must have known this instinctively since they purposely ran up to the poor donkeys from behind to get their prize of a loud cry and curses from nearby shop owners.

At the public square, rabbis held open teachings to small groups of people under a thatched shade next to a small temple. How did they keep their clothes looking so new? There was never a spot of dirt or any smell. In the other corner of the square were the retched tax collectors with their tax tables, taking from the poor and giving to the rich. And wafting around everyone were the ever-present smells, heavier than the Galilean towns. Instead of fish mixed in with the donkeys, the air was filled with the musky, heavy smells of farm animals grazing just beyond to the east. Even the wispy smoke from the courtyard stoves birthed heavier gamy smells of cooking meat and vegetables. The air was heavy with it. Without the wide-open expanses of a sea next to the village, the smells and smoke tended to linger, hovering overhead like a low or thin cloud before slowly dispersing into the hot, dry air.

Approaching the square, Andrew and I spotted John the Baptist in the center surrounded by a few people. As they drew near, they heard a voice preaching to the gathering crowd. More and more people approached, and we lost sight of John the Baptist. I said, "Brother, who is that man? That's not the voice of our teacher, John the Baptist."

"That is the man I spoke of. That is Jesus."

Getting closer was difficult since the crowd grew larger. People seemed drawn to Him as if He held a special power. Even the people who had been listening to the rabbi approached the square, leaving the rabbi to himself with a sour look on his face. The man in the center stood on a small stool so He could see over everyone. He called out, "John, I see our friends in the back corner next to the carpenter's store. Bring them over here."

A few minutes later John the Baptist escorted us (Andrew, Zebedee John, and I) to the center. Curious eyes looked at us, and people wondered who we were that the teacher would ask for us by name. Not wanting to draw more attention, I didn't return the stares. Jesus came down from His stool and immediately embraced Andrew and John (son of Zebedee). Then He turned to me, His smile so wide; He grinned at me with a mirthful look of a boy looking at a best friend after not seen him in a long time. It was a look of pure, innocent joy, and there were those unusually twinkling eyes.

So pure was His face that I couldn't hold His stare and looked away for a second, embarrassed by the rush of feelings for this man I had never met before. He was a person I had never even said a word to in my life, and yet in that brief gaze, my heart quickened, and a nervous sweat broke out.

He grasped my shoulders, looked upon me, and said, "You are Shi'mon [he who listens to the word of God], son of Jonah. From now on you will be called Cephas [Peter, the rock]."

We listened to Jesus for the rest of the day. Utterly transfixed by His words, even John the Baptist didn't say anything; he just listened to words of love and forgiveness. It was talk of our God, who require anything from us but what we had lost, a deep love of our Father in heaven. The message was about a willingness to bring Him into our lives every day, not just on the Sabbath or during the holidays; our God was a God who wanted to be part of everything we did.

The next day Jesus left for Galilee. We stayed behind a couple of days to be with John the Baptist and help him with his water baptizing. Then we also headed back to Galilee, our hearts full of excitement and even more, a stirring of hope that this man Jesus may be more than just a teacher, possibly more. As we walked, I asked Andrew how Jesus had known my name.

Andrew had to think about my question for a moment and, turning to me, said, "I didn't tell Jesus, John the Baptist, or Zebedee John that

I would return with you to meet him." There was no good answer. A lot of questions and no answers. And why had Jesus changed my name to Peter? I had been called many things in my life—zealous, loud, hotheaded, emotional, erratic—but never a "rock." Maybe Jesus knew how thickheaded I was. Then I guessed "rock" seemed fitting.

It was good to be back in Galilee with the cool air from the sea and the familiar sights and sounds. Not three days had passed since we met Jesus, and we had already heard from our prophet of Bethsaida upon arriving in Galilee that Jesus had found more followers, Philip and Nathanael. Nathanial swore to me that Jesus had known him before they first met. He said Jesus had known where he was resting far away when Philip called him to meet Jesus. There was no way Jesus could have seen him resting under the fig tree that far away from any road or footpath. Who was this Jesus?

# 4

# First Miracle

*What is impossible with man is possible with God.*
—JESUS, THE CHRIST (LUKE 18:27)

It was fall, and the temperature was cooling down. It was the perfect time for celebrations, and what could be more festive than a wedding party? Preparations for this wedding had been going on for some time now, and it was expected that there would be a lot of people there. The whole marriage process was very long. *Too long,* I mused, remembering the labored and long process Sarah and I had gone through.

I'd had to go to Sarah's father's house to negotiate for Sarah's hand in marriage. Of course, we'd both known each other since Sarah and I grew up together in the same town many years ago, and I remembered Sarah's father as an honest, hardworking man, always looking after the family welfare and devoted to Jewish traditions. But he was a bit stern. I never really thought her father looked on me with favor since I was a fisherman's son. Being rough and ready with more zeal than common sense at times got me into more trouble than I cared to remember, and I hoped Sarah's father didn't remember that as well; this visit was about money negotiation, and I had a boat of my own now and could pay the price (mohar) for his daughter.

The haggling was quick; I paid the price he'd asked, which brought perhaps the first smile I'd seen from him or at least the first smile ever directed at me. The price paid sealed the covenant between Sarah and me, and we were officially married. The next day a rabbi came over to Sarah's house, a few relatives gathered, and the rabbi said a brief betrothal benediction and gave us a cup of wine. I proposed a toast, and we drank together from it. After the ceremony, I returned to my house, and as our custom required, we spent the next twelve months apart to allow Sarah time to prepare for married life and for me to prepare a room in my father's house for us. We sneaked in times when we bumped into each other at the marketplaces or at the fishing shores, where our boats were docked. There were chance meetings our friends helped arrange.

On the twelfth month to the day we had our covenant seal, we had our wedding ceremony. It was early evening, the sun just setting over the mountain to the west, a fiery orange-red glow fading to brilliant turquoise and deep purple to the east. Twelve of my best friends were my escorts. We lit the torches, each taking one, and then walked the five miles or so to Sarah's house. As per tradition, Sarah didn't know what time I would arrive. It was supposed to be closer to midnight; we started early.

As we approached, the lead escort, my brother Andrew shouted, "Make ready for the coming of the groom." He blew the shofar, a trumpet made from a ram's horn, so loudly that it echoed for miles. At the doorstep of her father's house stood Sarah with her twelve female attendants, each holding an oil lamp that shone brightly as twilight turned to evening. We met together at the doorstep, all embracing each other; we turned and walked together back to my father's house, where the guests were waiting for the bride and groom to arrive, and the ensuing party lasted all night. A good memory indeed. My mind shook it off; back to the present and someone else's wedding.

The whole town of Cana was abuzz. In addition to the bride and groom's family, Jesus's mother, Mary, had been invited, as was Jesus; and by extension His new disciples followed along. There were seven of us now with the Teacher: me; my brother Andrew; James and John (the sons of Zebedee); Phillip and Nathaniel; and John the Baptist (John the Baptist). John the Baptist was back in Bethany with his ongoing baptismal work, so there were only six of us as Jesus's guests at the wedding. At least we hoped no one would mind that we'd tagged along with Jesus.

Cana was about two parasa just northeast of Nazareth and about ten parasa west of Capernaum, with an elevation difference of one-quarter parasa. It took two to three days of normal walking to make the journey, but the trip was well worth it. By the time we got there, it must have been midway through the wedding week. Traditional Jewish wedding festivities lasted a week with a dinner party every night; this was definitely one of them.

We arrived in the early evening, and there was live music, dancing, and lots of great food. We were famished from the journey. After a quick washup, we joined the festivities, laid our hands on cups of wine, and checked out the long table of food: endive salad with olives, dolmas (stuffed grapevine leaves), rack of lamb with spicy mint sauce, sweet millet fruit balls, and platters of melon balls, raisins, and dates. We piled on the plates as high as we could get them and sat in a corner to enjoy the food, wine, and entertainment. The wine was okay but not the best; what could one expect after day three or four of a seven-day feast?

We finished the delicious supper and went in search of more wine. When we asked the servants for wine, they responded with nervous looks. I wasn't sure whether it was nervousness or despair on their faces. Jesus's mother, Mary, passed by quickly without saying hello and went to the far corner of the banquet room. There she moved past a few people to a man talking to a small crowd. It was Jesus.

We followed Mary to Jesus, and as we approached her, her hands were in the air with a distressed looked on her face. Pointing to the kitchen area, she said, "Jesus, they are out of wine. Please go and help them."

"Woman," Jesus replied, "why do you involve me?" But Jesus knew the distress of His mother, and she took Him by the arm and went to the kitchen. We, of course, followed behind out of curiosity. Why was Mary asking Jesus for help? What would He do? Give money to the servants to buy more wine? It would take a day or more to get more wine barrels to the party. What would the guests drink tonight?

Mary said to the servants, "Do whatever my Son tells you to do." In the corner were six stone water jars; each could hold about five baths (one bath equaled six gallons or about twenty-four liters).

"Fill the jars with water." Jesus said. Then, approaching the jars, He briefly bowed His head in prayer, beckoned the servants over, and told a servant to dip a cup into one of the jars and take it to the master of the banquet. We watched as the servant dipped the cup in, drawing out a cup of the water, and we followed him back to the main banquet hall.

The servant gave the cup to the master of the banquet, who took a long drink. Immediately he stood up and clapped his hands loudly, calling for silence to the music band and all in the hall. There must have been over a hundred people in there. They all looked at him, as did we. Knowing he had just drunk water after asking for wine, we waited nervously for the reprimand to follow. Running out of wine halfway through the wedding festival week was a big embarrassment.

Straightening his robe, he said, "Everyone brings out the choice wine first and then the cheaper wine as guests have had too much to drink, but you have saved the best till now." He proceeded to sit back down and continue drinking from the cup the servant had just given him. We hastily went back to the kitchen with the servants and dipped our cups in a different water jar. It was wine—and not just wine. It was the smoothest- and richest-tasting wine we had ever drunk. We looked back at Jesus, and He was talking to guests as if nothing had happened. But He had just turned water into wine!

After the wedding banquet was over, Jesus, His mother, and His brothers returned with us to Capernaum for a few days of vacation. It was always special to spend time with Jesus. He taught us so much about the true nature of God. Just being in His presence lifted our spirits. Jesus and His family then returned to Nazareth, and we spent the rest of the fall and winter season going about our business. Andrew and I were back on the boat, fishing. When we could, we went down to see John the Baptist in Bethany. We told him about what Jesus had done by turning water into wine. Of course, by this time he told us he knew of the event from others, but we had actually been there and saw it. We also went to Nazareth to see Jesus and continue our discipleship with Him. John the Baptist didn't mind us spending less time with him because of Jesus. He told us, in fact, that we should spend less time with him and more time with Jesus, since Jesus was also his Teacher and so much more. Why learn from a fellow student? Go and see the One who is Master of all.

# 5

# Journeys

*Very truly I tell you, no one can see the kingdom*
*of God unless they are born again.*

—Jesus, the Christ (John 3:3)

The winter season passed without much excitement, and the time for Passover approached. We met Jesus in Nazareth and then journeyed on to Jerusalem. Every Jewish male must make the trip to Jerusalem every year as he was able to do so. During Passover only, unleavened bread was eaten for seven days. On the fourth day, an unblemished lamb was chosen, slaughtered, and eaten on the fifth day. It was time to remember the night when the angel of darkness had come over the people of Egypt and taken the lives of every male firstborn except those who had painted their door sills with lamb's blood. It was the last of the plagues Moses had brought on Pharaoh in the name of God for not freeing our people from over four hundred years of bondage. And now we had been under the scourge of the Romans for nearly one hundred years.

From Nazareth it was about thirty-six parasa (ninety miles or 145 kilometers) to Jerusalem; depending on the route, it normally took up to five days of walking. The six of us—me, my brother Andrew, James and John (the sons of Zebedee), and Phillip and Nathaniel—met Jesus in Nazareth and began our walk toward Jerusalem, stopping by multiple villages along the way. There were several ways to travel from the Galilee area to Jerusalem. The fastest way was to pass through the Herodian royal estates in the Jezreel Valley to Ginae, the last city in Jewish territory;

this route could be made on the first day of our journey. From there it was a walk across the rolling hills and valleys of Samaria to Anuathu Borcaeus, the first Jewish city of Judea, or farther if daylight and weather permitted on the second day. The third day was spent walking along the ridge route of the mountains of Judea up to Jerusalem.

The direct route through Samaria wasn't, however, the only way from Galilee to Jerusalem. It was also possible to follow the Jordan River to Jericho, then ascend the Jericho road to Jerusalem. This route was not only over eight parasa (twenty miles or thirty-two kilometers) longer; it was also considerably hotter, with a steeper ascent to Jerusalem. The steep road wound through a desolate wasteland of barren rock with twisted canyons and cliffs. Some said the road through Samaria was dangerous, full of bandits and thieves; of course, what else would one think of the barbarian Samaritan people?

The route through Samaria was much faster, and it seemed Jesus preferred this way, saying there was nothing wrong with the Samaritans; rather, we were those who were the problem. So it was the Samaritan route for us. There were also stories of hungry wild animals roaming the desolate hill areas of Samaria. Jesus never mentioned the wild animals. Somehow, we never gave danger a second thought while in the company of the Teacher.

In every Jewish village, it seemed like the news of Jesus's coming preceded us since there was always a crowd gathered as we approached. Everyone had heard about the miracle of the water changing to wine, and people brought the lame and sick to Jesus, hoping for a miracle to happen to themselves or their loved ones. And in amazing fashion, Jesus laid His lands on them and cured whatever aliments people had. In traditional fashion we stayed over at a local resident's house. There was never a person unwilling to have the Master sleep over at his or her house, except for our Jewish rabbis, of course. Was it anger, fear, jealousy, or a combination of all? The rabbis always rebuffed Jesus, calling Him a fake or worse, a blasphemer.

We walked long hours each day and made it to Jerusalem in four days. Jerusalem was the big city that never slept. It was full of large temples, marketplaces, and eateries. People from faraway lands came here for business and trade. If you were a Jew, you made the journey several times a year for the various celebrations. We approached the main temple. So grand it was and almost unimaginable that people had actually constructed this modern wonder. The enormous trapezoid area of the Temple Mount was one hundred forty-four thousand square meters. Its wall lengths were 280 meters (south wall), 460 meters (east wall), 315 meters (north wall) and 485 meters (west wall). The mount was ten stories high, designed to host more than one hundred thousand visitors during the holidays.

It was always busy with traders and money changers, especially during the big celebrations. Walking to Jerusalem was hard enough, taking multiple days each way. Many people couldn't afford to have donkeys and carts to bring the required sacrifices and temple offerings Jewish Law required. That's where the traders came in. Filling the temple courts were all manner of stalls filled with cattle, sheep, doves, and so much more for the pilgrims. It was far easier to carry money while on the journey to Jerusalem and then buy the offerings. Add the money changers haggling with lines of people everywhere to the mix, and it was a madhouse of noises, smells, and general chaos.

Walking through the throngs of people, we couldn't even talk to each other without shouting, adding to the overall frenzy. Jesus's demeanor changed immediately as we walked. He picked up cords, tied them together, and made a whip. Then all at once, standing in the middle of all the merchant tables, He gave such a yell that everyone froze in place.

Taking the rope, He then whipped the animals, driving them toward the temple doors. Jesus proceeded to overturn the money changers' tables, scattering coins. His eyes were aflame with rage; turning to the dove merchants, He yelled at them to move those foul cages from "My Father's house!"

After all the animals and doves were gone, there was a silence. Merchants and people stood around the overturned tables, a wide circle with Jesus at the center of it all. We there with Him, feeling very uncomfortable because of all the stares. But not all the stares at us were angry. It seemed that some of the merchants looked on us not with anger but with embarrassment, for they knew in their hearts that it wasn't right to trade in the house of God.

Chaos tuned to silence. Then there was a shout at us. They knew or at least had heard of the man standing in front of them. They'd heard the stories of His miracle at Cana and the healings. They'd heard of His radical teachings about a God who was different from what the rabbis taught. The people's shouts weren't angry; they were more a question. "Who are you to do this? What miraculous sign can you show us to prove your authority to do all this?"

Jesus's reply was completely unexpected. "Destroy this temple, and I will raise it again in three days."

General laughter from the merchants ensued. "It has taken forty-six years to build this temple, and you are going to raise it in three days?" The merchants by this point clearly wanted to beat us, yet they held back since the people around them were awed by Jesus's words, His pure zeal and passion for what everyone knew was righteous.

They pulled back a path for us, and we briskly walked on out of the temple area, disappearing in the crowds. We walked for a short time and stopped by a deserted courtyard. Jesus looking on us with a glow about Him, no longer with the fiery eyes we had just witnessed but with a look that was calm and gentle. We were about to ask Him what He had meant back there about rebuilding the temple. In three days, no less? Jesus, knowing our thoughts, instead spoke to us and said we would understand in time all things He was saying.

Jesus continued to preach and heal the sick, more and more crowds gathering each time. Word quickly got around Jerusalem of the Nazarene who performed miracles and continually rebuffed the Pharisees and Sadducees—to their great frustration, I must add.

The Pharisees were the most popular rabbis with the people since they were down to earth; they were the people's rabbis, who related more to the worker and slave, preaching the oral Law (written in the Talmud) that God had given to Moses at Sinai along with the Torah (written law). The Pharisees also maintained that an afterlife existed and that God punished the wicked and rewarded the righteous in the afterlife. They also believed in a Messiah who would herald an era of world peace. The smaller sect of rabbis were the elite Sadducees, who maintained the priestly caste and insisted only in literal interpretations of the Torah, the written law, which didn't speak of an afterlife or a Messiah. It seemed the Sadducees' lives revolved around the temple rituals far removed from the common people. Both the Sadducees and Pharisees served in the Great Sanhedrin, which served to interpret civil and religious laws.

During that week, one of the Pharisees came to us one night while we were having dinner. It was a bit odd for one of the rabbis to seek out Jesus. Where he had come from, we didn't know. He just appeared out of nowhere. Well, I guess if I had been him and been in his position, I would have been afraid that someone would see me around us as well. His name was Nicodemus, and he was no ordinary rabbi; he was a member of the ruling council.

He sat with us around the campfire. We chatted, and he ate and drank with us. He was a very kind and curious man, who seemed to sincerely revere the Master; his intrigue with Jesus bordered on the suspicious, since he knew everything about the Teacher: where Jesus had grown up, who His parents were, the miracle at Cana, His healings, and all His preachings. He knew too much. Yet Nicodemus didn't seem to know who we were. Thank God for that!

The Pharisee asked Jesus a lot of questions and seemed to enjoy listening to the Teacher. At the end he said, "Rabbi, we know that you are a Teacher who has come from God. For no one could perform the signs you are doing if God were not with him."

Jesus replied, "Very truly I tell you, no one can see the kingdom of God unless they are born again."

Andrew nudged me. "A standard Jesus reply, way over my head. I wonder if old Nicodemus knows what Jesus is talking about." Staring at Nicodemus, we saw his face twist from a contented smile from giving praise to Jesus to a look of confusion at the Master's reply. Jesus proceeded to tell Nicodemus and us, as we listened in utter confusion as well, that "no one can enter the kingdom of God unless they are born of water and the spirit. The flesh gives birth to flesh, but the spirit gives birth to spirit."

Jesus continued His teaching, but the more He spoke, the more confused everyone became. His words were far beyond our comprehension, and Nicodemus was just as lost as we were; yet for all our incomprehension of what Jesus was talking about, we knew He spoke the truth. At the end when the Pharisee got up to leave, he bade us farewell and looked on us; the expression on his face said it all. It was a mixture of joy from the time spent with Jesus and sorrow because his time was ending. Nicodemus didn't want to leave; he wanted to become one of us, disciples of the Master. We were all too familiar with feelings of both joy and sorrow at the same time from those long periods when we too had to part from the Master's company to work and attend to family matters. But not now. Not this week. This time was ours with Jesus, and we soaked it all in.

After Passover week, we headed north back to Galilee and stopped in Judea at Aenon near Salim since we had heard that our first teacher and fellow disciple, John the Baptist, was there baptizing. Aenon, located north of Jerusalem with an abundance of water flowing in local streams, was ideal for baptizing.

Located in a wide valley with copious springs about thirty miles (forty-eight kilometers) north of Jerusalem, just north of Salem, Aenon was set in a valley with a towering white limestone hill to the north and a gentler sloping hill to the south with a wide stream in between. At the base of the rock cliffs, crevices exploded with spring water, connecting to the main stream like branches from a tree. Aqueducts further branched off the life-giving water to feed local houses set close by each other in small clusters along the valley floor. In the center of each of the cluster of houses, smoke rose, fully bringing smells of cooking lamb and vegetables.

Sheep grazed lazily on the ample grassy plains extending a mile wide on both sides of the main stream. Fig trees shaded both sides with the meadows beyond, a true paradise. There was nowhere better than Aenon in the springtime. The sun rained down on the valley all day as it crossed from east to west, showering the grassy plains and the river with warm beams of light. At this time of the year, it was warm enough to walk about without any heavy clothing—better yet, to lie down and nap on a cloudless afternoon.

John the Baptist had been there for some time, and people came every day in droves to be baptized. It was a family reunion, and we had a great time sharing our stories of adventures in Jerusalem with him. John nearly fell off his chair with a loud cheer when hearing the stories of Jesus's zeal in throwing out the merchants from the temple, his open preaching and healing of the sick, and the night when one of the council members ate with us. All these and so many more things we saw Jesus do in words and actions solidified our growing closeness with Jesus. For

John the Baptist it seemed this was further proof of what he had told us that first time he introduced us to Jesus.

Jesus was more than a teacher, more than a man. John the Baptist looked on Jesus as the Messiah, the Savior, and even more, the Son of God. Of course, Jesus was a great teacher, a prophet even. Was He the Son of God as John thought? Andrew and I spoke of this from time to time; we couldn't yet get our heads wrapped around Jesus as the Son of God. It was unimaginable that God had been made into a man just like us—eating, drinking, getting tired, sleeping, laughing, crying, and doing all the things we did, and yet He was the Son of God? And if He was God, then why hang around a group like us? Local fishermen from nowhere Galilee? If He truly was God, I had so many questions. Was there truly life after death? I wanted to ask Him about Sarah. How was she? Was she in heaven with God? What was the purpose of suffering? I had done many things wrong in my life; were my grievances so many that God needed to punish me and take what I loved most in life? Ah well, knowing Jesus, if I asked Him, He would respond with an intense preaching I had no chance of understanding.

We all stayed with John and his new disciples in Aenon for a few days. It was a comfortable house set on the peak of a low hill about thirty meters above the edge of the river and about 150 meters away. A cluster of five houses was on the hill surrounding a central courtyard, where most of the cooking and central activities of the families took place. It was a standard small community layout—and what a view! The whole valley floor spread out in all directions from the houses with the large, white rocky mountain to the north and the high rolling hill to the south. The two mountains elongated the valley, stretching in each direction and funneling the sunlight all day as it moved from east to west. To the east and west the valley opened up again like a ladle on both ends of a spoon. The soil was rich, and many vegetables were planted all year-round, fed by the fresh waters flowing from the mountain springs to the north and south. Multiple clusters of houses were spread throughout the valley floor, some even nearer the mountains in the distance.

In the morning we woke early with John to help with the village works. Waking up at dawn, we moved the animals from the pens to the grazing grassy areas for the day, gathered fresh water from the nearby streams in buckets, and pulled weeds between the vegetable fields. We made a point that although we were there to spread the good news of our Teacher Jesus, we weren't to be a burden to the people who had graciously opened their doors and hearts to us. Even Jesus Himself was with us doing the chores and manual labor works. The villagers took notice of our Master and remarked that they had never seen their esteemed religious men of the cloth, the Pharisees or Sadducees, ever doing anything more than giving lectures. And here was the man who could be the Messiah Himself with His disciples, all working happily side by side with the villagers and with great cheer, doing the manual work of even the lowest laborer.

Jesus, all the while working, talked about the glory of the kingdom of heaven, His Father's love for all people, His grace and favor to all, and His undying forgiveness of all sins. He spoke of how He had come to show them the Father's love and His plan for salvation. Not once did Jesus speak of the need for offerings, money, physical sacrifices of lambs, special holidays, or such. He preached belief in our Lord God, speaking directly to Him, not by temples or the learned men but by living pure lives from sin, loving others, and caring for others. These were what was needed to attain the glories of heaven.

With the morning works done, we ate a small lunch and headed to the river for baptisms. By the early afternoon, crowds gathered by a wide, shallow bank area at the river, where one could wade up to chest deep in calm waters. There were two such places near each other, separated by about thirty meters or so. John the Baptist and his disciples would be at one area with Jesus, and we would be at the other. The crowd started off at about an even amount; soon afterward, as word spread that Jesus and His disciples were just around the corner, the crowd migrated from John's area to our area. By midafternoon we were all in the water, baptizing hundreds. Late in the day, the crowd subsided, and we took our leave, knowing the new influx was on their way for the next day.

That evening we all had dinner together with Jesus and the disciples of Jesus and John the Baptist. It was a big group of us. John's disciples complained to us that with Jesus here, hardly anyone had come to them to be baptized. They weren't angry, more disillusioned with John the Baptist and their abilities to baptize the way they had done in the past.

Hearing their complaints, John spoke up. "Friends, we have been together for a long time. A person can receive only what is given to them from heaven. You yourselves can testify that I said, 'I am not the Christ but am sent ahead of him.' The bride belongs to the bridegroom. The friend who attends the bridegroom waits and listens for him and is full of joy when he hears the bridegroom voice. That joy is mine, and now it is complete. He must become greater; I must become less." John went on to explain that our Lord and Savior Jesus was among us, and it was He whom John the Baptist had prophesied. "The Christ is amongst us now. And here in this very place with us! Let us not be sad at the waning of ourselves but rejoice in the greatness of our savior and Lord."

I looked at John, and there was such great peace in his eyes and a smile on his face. We had some time alone since it had been a while since I spoke with John, being a disciple of him only a short time; so much had happened that it felt like a lifetime. In our quiet talk, John's smile and joy faded some, and a sadness came over him. I asked him what was troubling him. He said to me that to be with the Messiah this day was a great blessing and that whenever he was near Jesus, his heart could scarcely contain itself in his chest, wanting to explode with joy; in a dream he had been having lately, his time on this earth was drawing to a close. As Jesus grew in His ministry, John's time had come to move on.

"Move on to where?" I asked.

John's simple reply was that the path of our Lord Jesus was one of faith, and for some that would mean sacrificing everything. He stared at me intently when he said this to me. A cold chill ran down my spine, and my hands grew clammy and cold. I had thought about this for a while now. I still had my fishing business in Galilee, and of late we had been spending more time with Jesus and His journeys to minister. Was John the Baptist alluding to the fact that we would have to give up everything to be full-time disciples of Jesus? This wasn't a new thought, and I had spoken with James, Zebedee John, Philip, Nathaniel, and Andrew about this matter often, especially of late; there was more to John the Baptist's voice, more to his tone and his intent stare.

"For some the calling of Jesus, to serve him will require giving up of everything." His stare pierced my heart, and the joy mixed with sadness in his voice when he emphasized "everything" jolted me like nothing I had ever experienced. Perhaps once long ago, I'd had that same feeling. A panic hit me and a fear I hadn't known since that fateful night when I lost my wife. I weakly nodded my understanding to John, and yet I didn't understand his meaning then. I would come to find out what he had meant soon enough.

# 6

# Keepers of the Law

*If you knew the gift of God and who it is that asks you for a drink, you would have asked him and he would have given you living water.*

—JESUS, THE CHRIST (JOHN 4:10)

A s the days passed, we baptized more and more people. Too many. The news spread quickly to the larger neighboring villages where the Pharisees had a full-time presence in the larger Jewish temples. Jesus called us and said it was time to leave and depart back to Galilee. Heading out the quickest way meant to continue to the north and travel through Samaria. There were a great many Samaritans, by some accounts over one million living in the area. That was almost one-third of the total number of Jewish people. It was sad that we, the Jewish people, considered the Samaritans as second-class citizens. We shared the same ancestry and belief in the Torah, and we worshipped the same God of Abraham.

In Hebrew we called them *Shomronim*, which meant "Samarians" (inhabitants of Samaria); the Samaritans preferred the Hebrew term *Šamerim/Samerim*, Guardians/Keepers/Watchers (of the Law/Torah).

The schism between the Samaritans and the main population of the Jewish people had started many years ago. The Samaritans believed their worship was the true religion of the ancient Israelites prior to the Babylonian captivity, as opposed to Judaism, which the Samaritans said was a related but altered and amended religion, brought back by those returning from the Babylonian exile.

Ancestrally, Samaritans claimed descent from the Israelite tribes of Ephraim and Manasseh, the two sons of Joseph (son of Jacob), as well as from the priestly tribe of Levi, who had links to ancient Samaria from the period of their entry into the land of Canaan (one thousand three hundred years ago after Moses had led us out of Egypt). The split between the Samaritans and us, their brothers, the children of Judah (the Jewish people), had begun during the time of Eli, the priest (over twelve hundred years ago), and culminated during the kingdom of Israel and kingdom of Judah (about nine hundred years ago) when the Samaritans (then kingdom of Israel) refused to accept Jerusalem as the elect and remained on Mount Gerizim.

The Samaritans said Mount Gerizim was the original holy place of Israel from the time Joshua conquered Israel (almost fourteen hundred years ago). The major issue between Jews and Samaritans had always been the location of the chosen place to worship God: Jerusalem according to the Jewish faith or Mount Gerizim according to the Samaritan version. There was also a story going back over seven hundred years when the Assyrians conquered this area and hauled most of the Israelites into captivity. New inhabitants were brought in from the east, forming a new population, a mixture of local Israelites with imported Assyrians, impure Jews, the Samaritans.

So it was today; with all that sorted history, the Jews didn't speak to, or have anything to do with, the Samaritans. And we were passing through their territory. We couldn't convince Jesus to take any other route. Jewish people weren't allowed to speak to or interact with the Samaritans, and we suspected that Jesus was passing through for this very purpose: to teach us and the wider community something more. Jesus was always pushing the envelope of our understanding of how life was supposed to be, of how we were to act and even understand right and wrong.

The route we took through Samaria was a mountainous path, and we wound our way to the east through the valleys to avoid having to climb the many steep hills. We took a route that led east and then north when we came alongside the Jordan River. It was hardly a straight path; however, it saved a lot of time and hardship. On the route, we passed through a small Samaritan town called Sychar.

We started walking early in the day, and everyone was getting tired. By the time we reached Sychar, it was midafternoon already, and we had been walking continuously for over eight hours with just a couple of brief rest stops. We approached Jacob's well in Sychar, the famous well from our great forefather Jacob. The well was very deep, over forty meters, and it never ran dry, not even during the long summers and times of droughts.

Stopping at the well, Jesus wanted to rest, and we decided to go into the village to find food. Andrew and the others went together to find food. Jesus remained at the well, wanting to rest and pray. I stayed behind with Jesus as well and lay under a date tree near the well to rest.

A short while later, a woman approached the well. Jesus was sitting with His back resting against the side of the well wall. The woman approached from the other side of the well and didn't see Jesus resting there. How He knew someone was approaching, no less a woman, was beyond me. When she got to the well, Jesus, still sitting on the ground with his back to the well, called out, "Will you give me a drink?" Startled, the woman came around the well and stopped short of the Teacher, just staring at him for a moment, seemingly unsure whether He was actually talking to her.

But, seeing no other woman around, she responded, "You are a Jew and I am a Samaritan woman. How can you ask me for a drink?" Her voice was a bit shaky and unsteady, since Jews never associated with the Samaritans due to their long history of disagreement. It was a very sad state of affairs that we had built these walls around ourselves and our neighbors, walls of prejudice and conflict spanning generations based on nuances of where and how to worship our same God, the God of Abraham. How could any of us know for sure whether we were pure Jewish or a mix, since we have been conquered so many times before?

Jesus simply replied to her, "If you knew the gift of God and who it is that asks you for a drink, you would have asked him and he would have given you living water." The woman was clearly confused by Jesus's response, as was I, and that this conversation was even taking place between the Master and this Samaritan. And a woman no less! In addition to her being a Samaritan, it was very improper for a man to speak to an unaccompanied woman.

They continued back and forth in discussion as the woman inquired more about this living water Jesus had talked about. Jesus at one point told her about her life, that she had five husbands and that she wasn't married to the man she was with now. Amazed by how Jesus could know these things about her, being a stranger, she set her water jug down and left, running to the village.

By this point the other disciples had returned and saw the last part of the exchange between the woman and Jesus, wondering as I was why Jesus had even been talking to her. They asked me this question, and I had no answer except that somehow Jesus knew everything about this stranger and that He had been talking to her about living water, worship, and the fact that the Christ to come was Jesus. It would be some time, as in all the events we witnessed with our Lord and Savior, before the truths would start to make sense. The message was that the call to our Lord and Savior was meant for all, not just for us Jews. Andrew and the others beside us gave us the food they had brought from town. We hadn't eaten since early that morning, and I was starving. But Jesus didn't eat. He said, "I have food to eat that you know nothing about." What food? No one had seen Jesus eat since the morning. "My food" said Jesus, "is to do the will of him who sent me and to finish his work." He went on to explain what His plan for us was. It was to spread His good news and draw all to believe in Him, Jesus, the Christ.

The woman returned with many others from the village since she had told them about this stranger who knew all about her life and said He was the Christ, the Messiah they have been waiting for all these generations. The villagers urged Jesus to stay with them and speak with them. And in the fashion of Jesus, showing love and compassion for all, regardless of being a Jew, Samaritan, Roman, or other, He accepted their offer; and we all stayed in Sychar for two more days. We ate well, and Jesus spoke to the village in small groups at night in the house where we stayed; and during the day the whole village came out to the main square, where Jesus preached to all.

After two days, we packed up to leave. They begged us to stay longer; Jesus explained that there were other villagers who needed to hear the good news. The leader of the town came to see us off and announced to everyone that at first; they believed just because of what the woman from the well had told them about what Jesus spoke to her about her life. They had heard and now truly believed that Jesus was the Savior of the world. The village rejoiced in their blessing of having seen and heard the Messiah in their lifetime. We left with high spirits from our time with the Samaritans, and it forever changed the way we viewed them. We saw the Samaritans in the eyes of Jesus, not as second-class citizens; they were the same as us, people who needed to hear the good news.

We continued through Samaria into Galilee. As we passed some of the local villages, the residents welcomed us as news of what Jesus had done in Jerusalem filtered into the communities. This included how Jesus had rebuked the learned men, the Pharisees and Sadducees, the healing Jesus had performed, and His bold teachings of love and mercy. The Galilean people were always skeptical, asking Jesus to perform miracles so they could see His power for themselves. Jesus lamented that a prophet had no honor in his own country.

As we continued through Galilee, we stopped in Cana, the place where Jesus had turned water into wine; this was the first miracle we'd seen Jesus perform. Walking through the village, we stopped in one of the open squares to rest since we had been on our feet all morning. Being with Jesus was a bit grueling. He was always on the move from village to village, never stopping for too long. We understood completely why Jesus never wanted to stay in any one place too long. The longer we stayed in any one place, the larger crowd Jesus drew, and the situation became a bit too chaotic. The Pharisees then tried to stir the crowds against us, and then even more chaos erupted.

Sitting in the square, we ate some dried figs and drank cool water. Andrew (my brother), James and John (the sons of Zebedee), Phillip and Nathaniel, the Teacher, Jesus, and I chatted away about nothing really. It was one of those few times when we had nowhere to go and just relaxed a bit. We had been away from Galilee for some time now. There was the cool breeze from the water, the misty mornings, the smells of fresh fish, and that freedom and connection to the sea that only someone who has spent a lifetime on a boat can understand. I felt a longing to be back at my old life but also hoped our time with this newly formed band of brothers and our Teacher wouldn't end.

We heard a commotion in the distance; there was a large chariot guarded on all sides by Roman soldiers on horseback. Kicking up a large dust storm in its path, it looked like a small storm headed our way. Stopping for a minute, the lead soldier dismounted and called for one of the locals. He then went about, talking to whoever was in sight; he was looking for something. Then one of the locals pointed in our direction. He wasn't looking for something but for someone. The soldier remounted, and the procession headed our way.

*Can't they leave us alone for even a minute?*

Stopping a good distance away from us, the soldiers dismounted. Unusual. Normally soldiers rode right up to whomever they were seeking, kicking up dust and debris everywhere and not caring about their lowly subjects, who were left coughing in their dust storms. From the chariot, an elderly man was helped down. Covered in fine robes and gold, he approached us. He wore clothes signifying a Roman official. As the golden, gilded man approached, he waved his soldiers away and walked the last few steps alone. Now this was getting very interesting. He headed straight for Jesus and stopped just an arm's length from the Teacher. He called out softly, "Are you the Jesus of Nazareth who heals the sick?"

By then a small crowd had approached from behind, staying a respectful distance but within ear shot. I say *respectful* since getting any closer would have drawn some serious pain from the Roman soldiers, who gave their superior the room he wanted. That didn't mean anyone could get close to him except the ones whom he wanted to speak to. The Roman official bent down, almost in a kneeling position, head hung low with blood-red eyes and such large bags under his eyes that it looked like he hadn't slept for a week.

Trembling, he stammered, "I have heard of your miraculous healing power. My son has been sick for weeks and has turned for the worse. Everyone is telling me to let him go, for death is near. Save him, Jesus, for he is my only son. From whom you get your power, I don't know. The ways of your people are foreign to me. They say you teach a new way, a way of love and forgiveness. Teacher, forgive me of my trespasses and heal my son, and I will believe."

Jesus looked at the Roman official, and then, looking around and seeing the gathered crowd, he announced, "Unless you people see signs and wonders you will never believe.". The royal official wailed in a guttural voice, raspy and low, his voice hoarse from bouts of emotions. Trembling, he pleaded, "Teacher, come to my house in Capernaum before he dies." Jesus looked on this man, the soldier of soldiers who commanded legions, a man who gave orders, cracking the whip on the Jewish people and taking from them more than what was owed to Caesar. But there was only compassion in Jesus's face.

Jesus approached the royal official, placed His hand on his shoulder, looked into his eyes, and said, "Go. Your son will live." Upon hearing this, the royal official noticeably brightened; his sagging shoulders lifted. And I can't say for sure, but if I hadn't seen it for myself, I wouldn't have believed it; it appeared as if his reddened eyes cleared, and those big sags under his eyes disappeared. He bowed respectfully and barked at his soldiers to depart back to Capernaum with full speed. The crowd seemed disappointed that Jesus hadn't performed some type of miracle right then and there before their eyes. This fact seemed only to make Jesus even more irritated with His own people, who wouldn't believe in Him unless they witnessed a miracle with their own eyes.

# 7
# Transitions

*Come, follow me, and I will send you out to fish for people.*
—JESUS, THE CHRIST (MATTHEW 4:19)

We stayed the rest of the day in Cana and departed the next morning to travel back to Capernaum. We had been away for some months now, and it was time to get back to earning wages on the fishing boats. Jesus headed in the other direction, back to His hometown of Nazareth.

When we arrived in Capernaum a day later, the temperature was cooling as winter was nearing. Stretching before us, the Sea of Galilee was surrounded by mountains. When I looked south, it seemed as if the sea stretched forever, with a light fog hanging low on the water. We were surrounded on three sides with the south open as the Sea of Galilee stretched to the south, ending where the Jordan River had started. It was midmorning, and all the boats were close to shore, anchored for the day. The fishermen and village women were on the shore, mending nets and cleaning baskets. The fish had already been cleaned and sold off. We couldn't tell whether they'd had a good catch the night before. Some fires near the shore brought that familiar smell of fish cooking on an open fire. Our stomachs signaled the receipt of those fine smells and loudly noted to us that it had been some time since we'd last eaten.

"Brothers," I shouted, "breakfast awaits us. Let's pick up the pace." There was no grumbling or hesitation. We all picked up our step and started singing. Getting closer, we saw some Roman soldiers approaching from the distance. They saw us and picked up their approach speed.

*Uh-oh.* We didn't have Jesus to back us up. This wasn't good. We stopped and looked at each other. What do we do? Nothing, since the soldiers were now running toward us, their hands waving up and down. As they drew near, we could see they were the same soldiers who'd come to us in Cana. Had the royal official's son died, and now we were to pay the price for failure? Where was our Master? The lead Roman soldier approached us, out of breath.

"We saw you as you made your way down the mountain." The soldier gestured to us to follow him. He turned and started to walk away with haste. We had no choice but to also follow at a quick step. It was obvious where we were headed. In the distance was a large house surrounded by a beautiful garden near the sea; it was set on a small hill overlooking Capernaum town. We were headed straight for it. This couldn't be good.

About a quarter mile away, the large house door opened, and one of the soldiers escorting us ran ahead to the house to announce our coming. Getting nearer, I started to sweat, even with a cold breeze in the air. The crowd around the house grew larger and larger. Closer and closer, we drew to the house. Unconsciously we started to slow our walk. Our band of brothers weren't the same merry and bold band without our fearless leader, Jesus. Then the royal official himself stepped through the doorway.

We were less than fifty feet away now, and we stopped. Everyone stopped talking. Dead silence. The royal official walked slowly up to us with a neutral expression. He stopped just a few arms' lengths from us, looking at us for what I thought was eternity; the moment lasted only a few moments.

"Where is Jesus of Nazareth?" he asked in a soft tone, which seemed out of place coming from a man dressed to the hilt. It looked like an outfit for a ceremony Caesar would attend. "My soldiers told me they saw you approaching from the mountain, so we dressed up to welcome Jesus."

At that moment a young boy burst from the house, running full speed toward the royal official. Taking his last few steps, the boy gave a loud, gleeful shout and leaped in the air; the official was just able to catch him in midflight.

Setting him down, he turned to us, announcing, "My son, Maximus. Several days ago, he was near death with no hope. Your teacher, Jesus, spoke to me and said that Maximus was healed. Upon my arrival back to Capernaum, my servants ran out to announce that my son had been fully recovered at the exact moment Jesus had pronounced him well. Glory be to God! Our whole family and I now believe in your Jesus, that He is a prophet and miracle worker. Come, friends, and dine with us tonight, for tonight we celebrate life. We celebrate in honor of your God."

So it was that we ate, drank, and sang that night with the Roman official and his family.

The next day came soon, waking me in my bed. Sounds of roosters crowing and smells of fish frying came from somewhere nearby. There were distant shouts of fishermen yelling about someone not anchoring the boat, and it was drifting out. More yelling, then laughter. Yes, it was good to be home, although perhaps I had drunk a bit too much last night with the wine being so good (and free). My head was paying the price today. And where had those body aches come from? *Old age, Shi'mon. It's old age.*

There was still summer left and much to do in the warm weather. The fish were plentiful, and my brother Andrew and I quickly got back into the daily routine of the business of fishing, as did our fishing partners, the sons of Zebedee, James and John. During the Sabbath the six of us—Andrew, Philip, Nathaniel, James, John, and I—had lunch and talked about the week's happenings and what we'd heard about what Jesus was doing in Nazareth. Communication from outside Capernaum was always a few days old and many times weeks old. One could never be certain when events really occurred or even whether they were true. Unless you spoke with the person who witnessed the events, things tended to get exaggerated way out of proportion. One person came up to us and shouted, "Here are the men who saved the royal official's son last month!" It took us an hour to explain to the crowd that gathered that Jesus, our Teacher, had healed the royal official's son, not us.

"Then why," the man bellowed, "did he invite you all in for dinner and exclaim his thankfulness to you?"

Embarrassed to say, I replied, "We are the disciples of Jesus, and the official was just being gracious since he was thankful that our Master had healed his son." Mental note to self: *Be careful of taking in too much thanks for the work done by our Teacher. People can get the wrong idea, and we can easily get a big head.*

Alone again with our small group, John spoke up. "Ever since we've returned without Jesus, life here in Capernaum is not the same. The people are the same, our work as fishermen is the same, and the weather is the same, but I don't feel the same. This last journey with Jesus, with all the miracles we've seen and His great teachings of love and forgiveness, has left me feeling an emptiness without our Teacher and a constant longing to be with Him and you all, spreading Jesus's good news. Life here, while good, doesn't hold the same for me anymore."

John was speaking what we all felt. Nodding in silence, we all looked at each other. What was to become of us now? We were all disciples of John the Baptist, and now we were disciples of Jesus. What did it mean to be disciples of Jesus? His words and actions were far more powerful and deep than John the Baptist's. In fact, John the Baptist himself had proclaimed that Jesus was the Messiah. Is it possible to leave all we have here to follow Jesus?

A few weeks passed, and we got back into our routine of being fishermen, working long days and nights. As always, the fishing was done at night, followed by selling the fish in the mornings along with mending nets; fixing and repairing the old boats, which needed constant maintenance; getting a bite to eat; resupplying the boat, and finding a period of rest before it all began again the following evening. All in all, it was a good life with the only worries being the weather and what the night would bring for the catch.

It was a bright, cloudless morning as we made our way back to shore. The fishing that evening was good, and we netted three baskets of the best catch musht (tilapia) and looked forward to a good sale on shore. As we approached the cove, there was something different, not the usual raucous sounds. The boats from the evening were there, and some fires were burning with smells of recently cooked fish. It was the lack of any sound at all. A stillness everywhere. No people! Where was everyone?

A bit of concern grew over Andrew and me along with the rest of our small crew. Had there been an accident? We hurriedly got off the boat once it was anchored in shallow waters. When we scanned the area, it looked as if everything were normal with the fires, boats, and netting; yet everyone dropped what he was doing and just left. Looking out into town, we then saw it. Saw them.

The villagers were all crowded in the center of the town square. We too left everything and went to see what was happening. As we grew closer, we expected to hear the commotion. There was still the silence. Then we heard a voice, not loud but very clear, as if the voice were next to us. It was Jesus! He had come to Capernaum and was in the middle of the town square, speaking. We tried to get through the crowd but couldn't get through; everyone was packed in shoulder to shoulder, so we listened from the outside.

Jesus said, "The time has come. The kingdom of God has come near. Repent and believe the good news!" He then continued to speak for hours on the good news of forgiveness and redemption. So captivated was the town that no one left. Afterward, the crowd around Jesus was still so big that we couldn't get through. We went back to the cove and went about the remainder of the morning, unloading our fish, selling them, and paying the wretched taxes to our supposed Jewish brothers, the tax collectors. Thieves, all of them, took more than what was owed to line their pockets. With the backing of the Roman army standing by close to them, who could argue? Look at what had happened to Barabbas. Of course, he did go way beyond protesting and had confronted the Roman soldiers.

The morning was gone, and we were just finishing up for the day. On the boat Andrew and I had just finished cleaning everything. Andrew, always tinkering with something, had made a net larger than the normal-sized throw nets we used. The normal cast net was circular and about six meters in diameter, with weights on the perimeter to allow the net to sink and capture the fish inside. Six meters was a big net, and it took a lot of skill to throw the net away from the boat, unraveling the full circular net before it hit the water. Andrew had made a net that was eight meters in diameter, saying we could catch much more fish with a larger net. A larger net! We could barely handle the current net, and he wanted to go bigger?

"Andrew, there is no way you are going to get that sized net open before it hits the water," I said.

Andrew came back with, "Shi'mon, we must always look to getting better at what we do. Watch and learn, big brother. Watch and learn."

I watched as Andrew struggled for the next half hour with no success. "I am watching, Andrew, and I am learning." I learned that eight meters is a big net. "Woooo haaaa. Keep it up!" I bellowed to my struggling brother. "I haven't had this much fun in a long time!"

Just then we heard a voice call from shore. "Come, follow me, and I will send you out to fish for people".

It was Jesus! I jumped from the boat and swam to shore. Andrew followed soon after he'd tied up the boat. It was finally time. Truthfully, we had made the decision before; it just hadn't yet sunk into us that we would give up our jobs to follow Jesus as His full-time disciples. Jesus always in His way knew what we needed. There was a bit of time among us after our last long journey with Him to fully understand what the Teacher was all about. He was the Messiah, the Savior. And we were His chosen disciples. With us both on shore now, Jesus approached us, and we gave Him a huge hug. We were the first true disciples of the Teacher, and I was no longer Shi'mon. The name had been cast off, and from now on to myself and everyone I was Peter.

We walked together farther down the cove and saw James and John, the sons of Zebedee, on their boat with their father, tending the nets. Jesus again called to them as He had called to us. James and John looked at each other, and then they looked at Andrew and me. We waved and smiled, and they knew. James and John had been in our discussions about what we were to do with our lives. Were we to continue living only as fishermen, or was there more to life? The answer was now before us, calling us to action.

The two brothers left their nets, climbed off the boat, and swam to shore. The elder Zebedee, their father, called out to his two sons, "Sons, where are you going? We haven't yet finished with the nets. There is much work to do." Zebedee, the elder, was a stern man, self-made in his life, coming from nothing; he'd built up a fleet of several boats. Even Andrew and I had worked for him. A devout Jew, Zebedee, the elder, had worked his whole life to create a future for his family and his sons. I knew he knew of Jesus and some of His teachings. He agreed with Jesus that the Pharisees, our supposed teachers of the law, were getting out of hand and asking too much from our people. They were asking for too many sacrifices. The Sabbath had become almost unbearable due to the number of laws and rules one had to abide. All the while our Jewish holy men took and gave us back only words.

Zebedee, the elder, was an infinitely practical man given to hard work yet knowing compassion for the common man and his struggles in life. Like everyone else, he struggled as well; and now that everything was looking up, he was finally getting ahead. They had a nice house; food and comfort came regularly. Life was good or at least better. Now where were his sons going?

Andrew and Shi'mon, who worked his other boat for him, were onshore as well! They were supposed to be on the boat, fixing the nets, as were his sons. Reaching the shore, James Z. and Zebedee John met Andrew, Jesus, and me. Zebedee, the elder, called out again to his sons. James and John turned to their father on the boat and called back. "Father, you know where we go and who we go with. It is time."

Zebedee, the elder, looked past his sons to Jesus standing there next to them. He knew where his sons were going and who they were going with. He had spent his life telling his sons right from wrong, teaching them compassion for others while also teaching them the trade. If he had been his son's age, would he have done the same? Jesus smiled at Zebedee, the elder. A warm and kind smile.

A sadness enveloped Zebedee's heart with mixed emotions. He was proud due to the fact that the Teacher Jesus would select his sons to be His disciples but sad knowing that the road ahead for his sons would be a hard one, since the teachings of Jesus were antagonistic against the Pharisees. He was frustrated with his sons. There was work to be done, but he could hire others. The profits would be less, but the work would still get done.

He whispered softly, "God be with you, my sons." To his astonishment and the surprise of everyone (except Jesus, of course), all on shore heard his whisper.

We placed our hands on our hearts, then extended them to Zebedee as a farewell. We turned and continued walking into the unknown with anticipation in our hearts. We were now fishers of men, whatever that meant.

# 8

# Too Many Rules

*What is impossible with man is possible with God.*
—JESUS, THE CHRIST (LUKE 18:27)

We followed Jesus throughout Galilee, His new band of full-time disciples. The mood was different now as we became more and more involved with the teachings of Jesus and learned from our Teacher as He preached the "good news," news of redemption and love, forgiveness through grace alone. We saw the people we'd met begin to understand His words, difficult as they were since they were different from all we had known before. They were different from the words taught by our Jewish leaders, the Pharisees and the Sadducees.

Jesus didn't tell us to abandon our Jewish teachings, laws, customs, and faith in the one true Lord. In fact, He spoke of and attended to all the rituals and ceremonies. What Jesus did preach was different and radical. Although we must respect the laws and traditions, He said, the true path to heaven, forgiveness of sin, and everlasting life cannot come from just listening or adhering to laws, from attending ceremonies or giving of tithes and offerings. No, the true path of eternity with God came from what we couldn't achieve through physical means. Only faith and love of our Lord would open the doors of heaven. The grace of God was what we needed. It was hard to explain the teachings of Jesus, for we, His own disciples, His closest companions, often argued among ourselves about what Jesus was telling us, what His teachings were about, and what and who Jesus was.

Capernaum. My hometown. Growing up in a seaside town meant spending one's whole life surrounded by friends and family; working for family and friends was a comfortable life. We didn't have much, yet we didn't need much in the way of physical things to be happy. It was the people we surrounded themselves with who made life rich and rewarding. I had had much, and I had lost much in my life while loving God and fighting with Him. He had given me a temper, anxiousness, and restlessness, which were a gift and curse during my life.

And now my friends and family looked at me differently. I looked at myself differently. Jesus taught a way that was so different from what we had ever known. This had caused many a friend and family to question our sanity while all along making new friends, and now I belonged to a new family as a disciple of Jesus. True, I had known most of my fellow disciples for most of my life since they were family and close friends, and every day our community grew larger with more and more following the way of Jesus. The hurtful part was losing close friends. They aren't openly mocking us. Instead they listened to the other teachers of the Law, the Torah, who said we were spreading a false truth, that we were leading our people away from our Jewish faith. So they turned away from us when we are in town, not coming over to talk and fellowship with us for fear of being branded a follower of Jesus. Yes, there was much to lose in the way of community respect developed over the years with the learned ones and being branded a troublemaker, one who was dividing the community. But there was much to gain, and I prayed that one day they too would see the good in Jesus.

Every seventh day, the Sabbath day, was a day of rest for the Jewish people. Since the time of Moses (some say it came even before then), we were to work six days a week; the seventh day was to be kept as a day of rest, reflection, and worship of our God. Moses even said, "This is what the Lord commanded: 'Tomorrow is to be a day of rest, a holy Sabbath to the Lord. So, bake what you want to bake … Save whatever is left and keep it until morning." Moses through our Lord gave us the Ten Commandments, the third commandment saying, "Remember the Sabbath day by keeping it holy. Six days you shall labor and do all your work, but the seventh day is a Sabbath to the Lord your God. On it you shall not do any work, neither you, nor your son or daughter, nor your manservant or maidservant, nor you animals, nor the alien within you gates."

It was clear to us that the Lord meant the Sabbath to be a day of rest and worship. The work was hard and long, days and nights of backbreaking work. A day of rest was a godsend, for life couldn't always be about work. Food, shelter, and water were all important and necessary for life; these days it seemed like everyone was going beyond the necessities, working harder and longer hours not just for the necessities but for more, as if more were better and needed for happiness and good standing in the community. Our Teacher saw through this man-made push for more.

The Pharisees themselves seemed almost to instigate and promote this need for more. It seemed like every year there were more and more rules to follow on the Sabbath. Now there were two whole tractates of the Mishnah, the Shabbat and the eruvin, devoted to the Sabbath and what was required. At last count there were thirty-nine! Thirty-nine prohibited actions on the Sabbath ranging from baking to making a knot with rope and even to just lighting a fire. Who could keep up with the rules and still have a normal, restful Sabbath? These thirty-nine prohibited actions were hundreds when elaborated on.

We worshipped on the Sabbath by bringing burnt offerings and studying the Law. Of course, most couldn't read and write, so studying of the Law for most meant listening to the Pharisees teachings in the temple square. Sabbath began at sundown on Friday and ended at sundown on Saturday, so there was always a furious amount of work to be done on Friday mornings to ensure there was enough food for the Sabbath and that all work was finished before sundown that day. Jesus often rebuked the Pharisees in His Sunday teachings. We heard Him once say, "And you experts in the law, woe to you, because you load the people down with burdens they can hardly carry, and you your-selves will not lift one finger to help them." Those were provocative and dangerous words to the leaders who gained so much from our toils.

One Sunday we were listening to Jesus teaching in the synagogue. All were amazed at His teachings. He taught as one having authority, even more so than that of the Pharisees or Sadducees, and yet He wasn't even one of them. In the synagogue there was a man known to be possessed by a demon, an evil spirit; He shouted out at Jesus, crying out at the top of his lungs. The noise was so loud I had to cover my ears. "Ha, what do you want with us, Jesus of Nazareth? Have you come to destroy us? I know who you are—the Holy One of God!"

Jesus, irritated, raised His hands, outstretched to the ranting man. "Be quiet! Come out of him!" At once the man convulsed, the demon throwing him down to the ground; with a deafening shriek, the demon came out of the man, leaving his body. All the people in the synagogue stood awestruck at the scene. There was complete silence. A miracle had happened right before their eyes. Jesus had done it again! Then the murmuring started as a whisper to each other at first, gaining in strength to loud pronouncements. "What is this? A new teaching—and with authority! He even gives orders to impure spirits and they obey him."

A crowd began to follow us everywhere we went as word spread throughout Galilee of Jesus. Jesus continued to speak, keeping everyone wrapped with a great intensity. The faces of our fellow Galileans were those of anticipation and great joy at the teachings of Jesus; the faces of the Pharisees showed something else, a troubling look. I couldn't put my finger on it; it almost looked like they were nervous and afraid of Jesus. The morning drew on, and we left the synagogue. Andrew, James and John (sons of Zebedee), Jesus, and I headed to my house. When we arrived, we learned that my mother-in-law was in bed with a bad fever. I went to her room immediately and found her lying in bed asleep, breathing a very labored breath. Her expression was of discomfort from the illness and more than illness; there was a sadness in her expression. Standing there next to her, my mind receded back in time.

Sarah's mother had been with us for some years now. She'd moved in with us after her husband passed away. Many thought he'd died from a broken heart. A hopelessness had almost taken me as well. But Sarah's mother was strong willed and didn't cave in to the tremendous loss of her only child and then of her husband. She was a rock, and I knew Sarah had gotten her strong spirit from her mother; now she looked ill and frail, as when Sarah's father had been ill those many years ago, lost in thought to times when Sarah had still been with me. Tears began to roll down. It was such a long time ago, and yet it was just like yesterday.

A hand touched my shoulder, gentle yet firm. I turned, and Jesus was beside me. Tears were also in His eyes. With great emotion in his voice, He told me He had been greatly saddened that day when Sarah was taken up to the Father. It wasn't for us to understand why, only that there was a reason. Sarah was with the Father now and in peace. I had never spoken to Jesus about Sarah before. He could have heard about it since it was common knowledge in town about what had happened; it was the way Jesus had said it, as if He had been there that night. The pain in His voice had been so strong that it was as if He were feeling my feelings that night beside me. A comfort washed over me that moment. I cannot explain it. It was as if a weight of sorrow had lifted from my by one who understood what I had gone through, who was there with me to share my pain. In our sharing of the pain, He lifted it from my heart and took it into His.

He looked down on Sarah's mother and took her by the hand; her eyes opened. Slowly Jesus helped her to sit up. Her fever immediately left, and she stood up. Her strength returned to her right before my eyes. It was another miracle by Jesus, a miracle given to her not just out of compassion to heal the sick but out of much more. It was a miracle of healing given as a son would want to care for his mother and want to give a healing not only of the body but also of the mind and soul. It was a healing of the body to remove pain and sadness from the heart. Her expression was just that, a healed body and spirit. I had known Jesus for just over a year now, and I could hardly remember what life was like before the Teacher.

Just after sunset, the Sabbath was officially over, and we began to get many visitors, seeing and hearing about what had happened earlier in the day at the synagogue; everyone was bringing over their sick and demon possessed. It looked like the whole town was outside my house. It turned into a very long night. Jesus remained Jesus, ever giving of His full time and attention to the people, healing many who had various diseases, and He drove out many demons.

It was strange, though, about the demon-possessed people. Shrieking and writhing with terrible noises, they would leave the bodies; and always as they began to shout Jesus's name, Jesus rebuked the demons to be quiet, and they were immediately silenced as they left their hosts' bodies. What were the demons trying to say? Their cries were so loud, they hurt my ears. It was as if they were cries in fear of Jesus, shouting the name of Jesus as that first demon in the synagogue earlier in the day had shouted and then calling Jesus the Holy One of God. The Holy One of God. What had the demon been saying about Jesus? Was He more than a teacher? A prophet? Or something even more?

People kept on coming, and Jesus turned back no one. The night turned to early morning, and Jesus went out alone after everyone had left. It was a long night and morning. How the Master could have so much energy and compassion was incredible. We all tried to get Jesus to stop and rest; He wouldn't hear of it. Filled with love for the people, Jesus wouldn't stop healing the ill, lame, and demon possessed. Finally, the crowds lessened, and we convinced Jesus to send the few away to come back another day. Jesus walked off to pray, and a few hours later, He hadn't returned. We were worried since Jesus hadn't slept, eaten, or drunk any water all night and morning.

"Andrew, let's look for the Master," I said. "Bring a jug of water and some bread." The others joined us, and we fanned out in the village. The others looked around the shore area, and Andrew and I started inland. The hills around Capernaum sloped gently upward with great views of the Sea of Galilee. After about a half-hour walk up the sloping hill, we saw Jesus sitting under a large fig tree. The tree must have been at least six meters high; its branches and leaves spread out wide, giving a full covering of shade. We approached, and Jesus appeared to be asleep. We got close to Him, and Jesus opened His eyes.

I said, "Master, everyone is looking for You."

He replied, "Let us go somewhere else—to the nearby villages—so I can also preach there. That is why I have come." Jesus then ate some of the bread and drank water. We sat for a while more, just taking in the beauty of the scenery. There was nothing more beautiful than being on the hillside of Capernaum, looking over the Sea of Galilee. The town of fifteen hundred or so, with the large synagogue in the center of town near the water, spread out before us. Winding streets and houses clustered the area. Wisps of smoke wafted up from the center of clustered houses. A few puffy clouds overhead moved slowly across the sky like ships sailing across the sky and then the sea. Calm and bluish in color, with boats anchored near the shore, the water stretched out on all sides for huge distances held in place with mountains to the east and west, narrowing to the south. If I looked hard enough, I imagined the south side narrowing just a bit, with the Jordan River starting where the sea ended. Of course, one couldn't see that far; I didn't need to see it. I knew the sea so well. I have lived my whole life in this area with all my friends and family. So many good times and hard times. Life seemed so small when you could sit on a hill and see your whole life in front of you. Andrew was beside me, lost in his thoughts as well. We were simple-minded fishermen living a simple, small life in a small village on the backwaters of a small sea.

Jesus turned to us and stared into our eyes with a warm smile, and we talked for hours about our lives, our families. Jesus spoke of His life—of growing up as a carpenter's son, of being on the run as a refugee during His early childhood in Egypt, and of returning to live a normal, uneventful life in Nazareth. His life seemed not so different from ours. But He was no simple man, living no simple life with no simple dreams. He was inviting us to live a life beyond anything we had ever experienced before. Were we—was I—up to the task? I didn't know. Jesus thought so, and that was enough for us. This didn't remove my hesitancy and fear, but it wasn't a fear of Jesus or His teachings. It was a fear that, through all my loud and abrasive acts, I would fail Him one day. The fear was taking over my mind and body. In Jesus's eyes, I was Peter, the rock. I hoped the rock wouldn't crack when struck.

# 9

(Start of Second Year with Jesus, Fall-Winter, AD 29)
# Spreading the Word

*As you go, proclaim this message: "The kingdom of
heaven has come near." Heal the sick, raise the dead,
cleanse those who have leprosy, drive out demons.*
—JESUS, THE CHRIST (MATTHEW 10:7-8)

Winter was approaching, and the temperatures began to fall. Well,
cold was a relative term. To us who lived our lives in Galilee,
winter was a cold season. Average temperatures in January were bitter
(averaging 12 centigrade). That was frigid weather for Galileans. The
surrounding mountains and plains seemed to shelter the area from the
colder temperatures, but they also made the weather very unpredictable,
with violent storms dropping down on us at any time. We spent our
time walking from village to village around the area. Jesus spoke about
the good news of the kingdom of God. Repentance and forgiveness of
sins were free. One just needed to open his or her heart, ask God for
forgiveness, and forgiveness would be yours.

One day we were walking into one of the seaside towns, and as we
approached, already a crowd began to form. It was amazing how quickly
news traveled. Even I didn't know where Jesus's feet would take us; there
was always a waiting crowd in the towns we approached. After each
town, it seemed like more and more would gather in the next town.
People heard of the Teacher healing the sick and lame and preaching

that one didn't need all the rules (and costly sacrifices) the Pharisees demanded.

Just then we heard a scream, and the waiting crowd scattered like frightened sheep. At the center of the dispersed crowd stood a lone man. He was hunched over, his clothes worn and dirty. Tattered and frayed edges dragged on the ground; he moved ever so slowly, head down and fully covered. What was exposed of his face and hands was bandaged.

At first, I thought he had dirt on his hands and face. As we approached closer, I could see it wasn't dirt; it was dried blood. The dark-brown patches on his hands were sores. Where there should have been a nose, there was none. The smell hit us all at once. Like the smell of decaying flesh, the man stank of death itself. He was a leper. That was the most accursed of diseases. Once a leper, always a leper until one died a horrible, painful death. The disease was slow and gruesome to the body. You fell apart piece by piece until the last day. The body contorted; limbs twisted, disfigured, and fingers curled until the hands looked more like claws. All lepers lived by themselves in a leper colony far away from all villages. It was the most feared of all diseases; no wonder the crowd ran away from the leper man. But Jesus, not missing a beat, continued to walk closer to the gruesome figure. We all hung back behind Jesus, still walking forward with Him, just not quite at His side. We were more like ten or twenty steps behind.

Jesus stopped no more than a man's length from the leper. The crowd, including us, formed a circle around our teacher and the diseased man; it wasn't a close circle. The sickly man lifted his head slowly, gazed on the Master, and wailed a loud cry; the pain of his life poured out from his ragged voice. Guttural and deep, his wail made everyone turn his or her head for a second; tears from the women flowed since everyone knew someone in the family who was afflicted with this cursed disease. Could this man's sin be so great that he had been cursed with such an affliction? We knew, as did everyone, of good people, who had become cursed with the disease. Was it because this man sinned? Or was it a relative's sin that had befallen this man? Or was God an uncaring God that this man should suffer so? Who could know the mind of God?

The man dropped to the ground, his face not looking on the Master. He begged of Jesus, "Lord, if you are willing, you can make me clean."

Jesus reached and touched the man. "I am willing. Be clean!".

Instantly, the man's face became whole again. His clawed hands became soft, and his skin sores vanished. He was cured! Jesus told the man not to say anything about being cured, but everyone had seen this miracle, and the news of Jesus's healing powers spread even faster.

It became ever harder to travel into the towns as the crowd grew. A never-ending stream of misery, sickness, disease, and demon-possessed people awaited Jesus wherever we went. We were His crowd control and disciples, teaching others what words we had learned from Jesus and controlling the masses so they didn't get out of control. There were so much anxiousness and anticipation; people pushed and shoved just to get close to the Teacher. Jesus often had to remove Himself from the crowds for downtime to be alone. We watched and guarded Jesus from a distance, keeping others away to allow the Master some alone time. He always used that time alone in prayer. I often wondered what He asked God during those times. Some of those moments lasted a few moments, and at other times He knelt in prayer for much of the day.

As the winter season continued, we pressed on with our full-time mission with Jesus, going from town to town, preaching His good news to all who would listen. And as Jesus continued to heal, the crowd steadily grew. It came to a point that we could no longer easily enter the towns since the crowd became too large. The town officials were at first glad to see Jesus, since the crowd brought in some additional level of prosperity, for where there was a crowd, there was an opportunity to sell more goods and services. It was a good idea; however, the crowd soon grew too large for the small infrastructure of the towns. And the people who came to see Jesus were the sick, infirm, and demon possessed—not to mention that many had no money either. This put a great strain on what little the town had to begin with, including water and proper sanitary conditions.

Although the Sea of Galilee was fresh water, villagers close to shore normally boiled the water before drinking, and those in areas farther from sea got water from water wells. The towns already had some foul odors from the sewage; our normal practice was to dump our sewage into a small channel running down the middle of the streets. The sewage normally ending up in the sea, either directly or by being dumped into a stream. Either way, that was why we boiled the fresh water from the

Sea of Galilee or drank well water. When the large crowds coming to see Jesus inundated the towns, the foul-smell factor from the added sewage load stank up the place and put a strain on the fresh-water supplies.

It came to the point that the only way Jesus entered a town was under cover so the villagers wouldn't know He was coming. It was a stealthy move Jesus preferred not to do, but He understood the strain on the town when He was openly there. Most of His movements and sermons occurred outside the towns in the more remote locations far enough away from the towns so crowds were less or the nearby towns wouldn't feel the full brunt of the large crowd. The mild winter conditions also made it easy for a crowd to follow us outside the towns. It wasn't an ideal situation to be in, yet we were all thankful that the people were seeing what we saw in Jesus and wanted to follow our Master as we did.

Winter crept by, and spring was upon us. You wouldn't have known it by the temperature; there were a few telling changes. The region of Galilee was blessed to have fertile soil, running streams, and just enough rain to turn the area into a sea of wildflowers and blossoming trees. The hills became a blanket of green. Grapes, figs, olives, pomegranates, and oranges sprang to life in the subtropical climate. Galilee spread to the north and west of the Sea of Galilee, encompassing an area over 160 square kilometers with a population of over three hundred fifty thousand, including about one hundred thousand Jews. Greek was the language of the upper class and international business. The local Jews spoke mostly Aramaic, the language of the common man.

After traveling and preaching in many towns, we finally made it back to Capernaum. The inland areas were spectacular this time of the year with all the fruits and blooming plants, but there was nothing like coming home, especially to Capernaum by the sea. We sneaked into town under the cover of darkness and made our way to my house. It wasn't a large house; it was just big enough to comfortably fit our small band of brothers and the Teacher. Sarah's mom was delighted to have company over and made us some wonderful grilled fish dishes cooked on the open fire, directly on the charcoal with a little olive oil and a couple of spices, including oregano. It was a simple and very tasty way to cook fish.

My complex was a typical seaside home with an open-square courtyard with three attached house units encircling the courtyard, with one main large door serving as main entrance and exit to the courtyard. Each house unit had ground-floor rooms and rooms upstairs. The ground-level rooms had their own exterior door; most people preferred to use the main entrance. The house units adjoining the main door were larger since they curved around the corner. I owned one of the house units, which had been in our family for a few generations. In fact, my neighbors were my relatives, which made for a lot of fun while growing up with cousins next door; such was life in a small town. The walls were made of stone and brick with thatched roofing that required maintenance every few years. My roof was looking a bit old.

We relaxed for a day, lazing around the house and open courtyard, and then mustered our strength to go into town. Once word got out that Jesus was back in Capernaum, the crowd began to cluster around us as we walked the streets. The Pharisees and teachers also joined in the crowds, not chattering up as they normally did but accusing us of being demons and false prophets. They were hanging on, almost like watchers monitoring the crowds. Jesus took note of them and started back for the house. Entering the courtyard, He beckoned the people in. It was time for another session with the Teacher. Jesus sat on a stair on one side of the courtyard. Everywhere else people crowded around on the ground, some on the roofs; and many others who couldn't get in listened from outside. I don't know how they did it; somehow a lot of the Pharisees made it through the crowd and into the courtyard.

There were so many Pharisees that they must have come from all the neighboring towns. It was just like them to bully their way into the best spots. Jesus began teaching, preaching the good news of a kind and loving God. As Jesus was teaching, I saw four men carrying a man in a large blanket on the roof of my house. The man was in bad shape and obviously couldn't walk. What were they up to? There was no way to lower the man down over the side of the roof.

Oh no! Just as I was thinking about them, they did the unthinkable. They started to tear up my roof. The roof was in bad shape, and it didn't take them long to break a hole in it so they could lower the lame man down to the ground. The last couple of meters were hard; the men on the roof couldn't hold on, and the lame man crashed to the floor with a loud yelp.

I ran into my house as the four men who had been carrying the lame man climbed through the hole. I looked at the blanketed man lying on the ground, unmoving and still. I thought perhaps the fall had killed him. The four men gathered around the man and picked him up, each holding one edge of the blanket and pushing past me as if I weren't there. Their faces were solemn masks of determination; they weren't about to let anything get between themselves and Jesus. I knew that look since we had all had sick and dying family members, and we would do anything in the world if there was a chance to see them healed. I followed them out and watched as they laid the man in front of Jesus. The crowd didn't make a sound with everyone's attention fully focused on the lame man and Jesus.

The other four men knelt before Jesus with tears in their eyes; they bowed their heads and wouldn't look up. Jesus, greatly moved by their faith, placed his hand on each of the four men's heads one by one; then He went to the lame man. Jesus bent over the man and proclaimed, "Friend, your sins are forgiven."

The Pharisees erupted in outrage. "Did you hear that? Did you all hear that? This man claims to forgive sins now. That is blasphemy! Only God can forgive sins!"

The crowd began to get agitated. Everyone loved Jesus but also respected the Pharisees.

Jesus turned to the Pharisees. "Why are you thinking these things in your hearts? Which is easier—to say, 'Your sins are forgiven' or 'Get up and walk'? But that you may know that the Son of Man has authority on earth to forgive sins." So he said to the paralyzed man, "I tell you, get up, take your mat and go home." The lame man stood up slowly at first, a little wobbly; then he started to take steps on his own. The four men who had brought him in were also on their feet. A loud cheer came from them followed by everyone else (except the Pharisees); the noise was deafening with cheers and shouts. Jesus had healed the lame man right in front of everyone. There was no way for the Pharisees to deny this was a miracle.

After the healing of the lame man, there was no stopping the crowd and the noise, so we left the house, moving the crowd along with us into the street. Walking along, we came to the main square in Capernaum, where a lot of trading went on, including the wretched tax collectors. Vermin. How could our own people be in league with the Romans, exacting what little we had; and even then they took more than what was owed while sitting in their shaded canopies, with spotless clothes of white, their hands outstretched and wringing all who came to them of all they had. I would rather eat dinner with Pilate himself than with a tax collector, a traitor to his own people.

"Stay away from them if I were you," one of the Pharisees told us, pointing to the tax collectors, "lest their smelly filth might rub off on you." We all nodded in agreement. At least there were some things we and the Pharisees agreed on. Jesus then stopped in front of one of the tax collectors. Standing there, we were all confused. Why would Jesus consort with those snakes? Jesus looked at the man sitting before him with sad eyes.

The tax collector wouldn't look at the Master. He was visibly shaken by Jesus's presence, and he began to weep and shouted, "Lord, look not upon me for I am a sinner."

Jesus took his hand and said, "Follow me." Immediately the man got up and followed Jesus. That night we had dinner at the tax collector's house. All around us were other tax collectors, rough people, and other unsavory characters. It was a wild night for sure. We were all very nervous and were prepared for anything to happen. In my younger days, these types of nights ended with a fist fight and sometimes more than that; but there was something different about tonight's dinner. Those unsavory characters were seemingly on their best behavior, and all took turns huddling around the Master, asking Him questions, and telling Jesus about their sorrows and sins. Jesus, ever the listener and preacher, understood their pain, and in placing His hands on them, He lifted their spirits, almost as if He were healing their souls as He did while healing the sick and lame. Some of the Pharisees came to join the dinner as well, most likely just to catch Jesus or us in an act where they could discredit us.

"Why does your teacher eat with tax collectors and sinners?" one of them asked us.

Jesus heard the remark and said, "It is not the healthy who need a doctor, but the sick. I have not come to call the righteous, but sinners."

After that night Jesus added one more disciple to the group; the tax collector Matthew was now one of us. It took some getting used to to have Matthew around. We'd spent our whole lives hating tax collectors for what they'd taken from us, and now here was one of them as part of our group. Matthew was very open to admitting all his wrongs and asking for forgiveness. He was a quiet man with something in him, an inner strength; and as we learned more about him, we found Matthew to have a big heart to go with his even demeanor.

We continued moving back and forth among the villages of Galilee that spring, with Jesus teaching mostly on the Sabbath since that's when everyone had his or her day off, and Jesus's presence didn't disrupt the towns we were in. During the weekdays, depending on where we were, we worked odd jobs; and when we were near Capernaum, we spent some time on our boats to earn a bit of money for our basic needs. There was always a friend of a friend or someone who offered lodging and food most everywhere we went.

The crowd grew so large, with people coming now from everywhere: Judea, Jerusalem, Idumea, and the regions across the Jordan and around Tyre and Sidon. Everyone wanted to hear the words of Jesus, and even more came to be healed of their illnesses and afflictions. They said that to get healed, all one needed was faith that Jesus could heal and touch him or her. The large crowd pushed forward with the sick, trying to get a chance to touch the Master. Many times the situation got out of control, so Jesus preached near the shoreline, and we had a boat always at the ready. When the crowd got out of hand, Jesus boarded the boat and preached from the water. It was a good system borne out of a lot of trial and error on how to best serve the people while not getting ourselves crushed.

Jesus was always a bit conflicted about getting on the boats, since the sick and ill pleaded with the Teacher for a chance to touch Him and get healed. Jesus always told us that the needs of the people were so many. His heart always ached; He wanted to ease their suffering and give the people hope. By now there were many of us who followed Jesus around wherever He went, from town to town, listening to all His sermons, helping out with crowd control, and doing all the other things required for our travels. Some were full-time, and some were part-time. We got to know most of the full-timers and even many of those who followed Jesus around part-time. It was a lot of work for everyone, and the crowd grew larger and larger. All were seeking Jesus for healing. It came to the point that no matter how we were situated, there were too many to heal, and the crowd became unmanageable.

I remember the morning well when Jesus called all of us together and said He had spent the night in prayer. God had given Him direction to expand His ministry so more of our brothers and sisters may hear the good news and so we could heal more people. So Jesus chose Twelve to become His apostles to help share the good news, and He gave the Twelve authority to drive out evil spirits and heal disease and sickness. He called out names and asked them to join Him as His chosen leaders.

Jesus first called out my name, Peter, to come forward. At first, I hesitated to step forward. I still wasn't used to the name Peter instead of Shi'mon. I surely didn't want to walk forward only to have been told it was another Peter being called. Jesus looked at me directly and smiled His sly grin. *Okay, it's me.* So I came to the front, and Jesus placed His hand on my shoulder for reassurance. He then called out eleven more: my brother Andrew; James and John, the sons of Zebedee (also known as James Z. and John Z.); Phillip and Bartholomew; Thomas; Matthew (the tax collector); James, the son of Alphaeus (James A.), Thaddaeus; Simon, the Zealot; and Judas Iscariot. Jesus later nicknamed James Z. and John Z. Boanerges (which means the "sons of thunder") as a kind of tease from an event that had happened during one of our travels.

Then Jesus, with the Twelve of us in front of Him and all our other disciples, gathered around close to us and lifted His hands in the air. Everyone surrounding us placed his or her hand on our shoulders and on our heads. Jesus gave us a blessing to spread the good news and the gospel, giving us authority to heal the sick and drive out demons. We were to take with us nothing except the clothes we were wearing and to go among our Jewish brothers and sisters, preaching the word of God, the good news that the kingdom of heaven was near. So that was it. After about a year and a half from first meeting with Jesus, He was sending me out with the rest of His chosen apostles to expand His ministry of grace, forgiveness, and redemption.

Were we prepared for this day? Was I prepared for this day? Certainly not. Was one ever prepared enough? We would find out soon enough whether we were ready for the tasks Jesus had set out for us. We walked for a while, and Jesus led us down from the hill where we were to a more level field overlooking the Sea of Galilee. Wide and open, slightly sloping downward with just a few trees to obstruct the views beyond, it was a beautiful spot. Our town of Capernaum spread out below us, stretching to the Sea of Galilee; the sea, light blue in color, expanded wide and long, held together by land and rising mountains to the east and west. Out farther, straight south, the mountains to the east curved inwardly, wrapping to the southern shore and ending in a small opening, with the Jordan River. We took in the beautiful scenery.

A large crowd of other disciples of Jesus and people from all over—from Tyre, Sidon, Judea, and even Jerusalem—crowded into the flat plain area; all had come to hear Jesus and to touch Him for inspiration in hopes of being cured of their illness, disease, and suffering. Everyone who touched Jesus was cured. As always, the crowd became hard to handle. Today we had almost all the disciples, almost one hundred of us, to help with crowd control, so it was fairly organized. Jesus moved away from the crowd and stood on an outcropping, a small hill so all could see Him. It was time for Jesus to address everyone, and there was much anticipation in the air. Excitement was in all hearts, all except the Pharisees. I think it was dread for them every time Jesus spoke. Who could know what the Teacher would say? One thing for sure; it was never good for the Pharisees. We were nearest to Jesus with the crowd pressed up just behind us. There must have been thousands gathered; most were sitting. A patch of grass covered the area, which was still brown from the winter, but it was comfortable enough for sitting. There were areas where no one sat or stood in the wide-open field, where there were rocks outcropped or where animals had recently relieved themselves of their grazing.

Jesus focused His attention on us, His disciples, who were gathered close to Him; His words reached far beyond us, touching the hearts of everyone at all levels of the classes in our society, especially those who had challenges in their lives: the working class, the poor, the downtrodden, those left behind in the fringes of the community, the sick and elderly. Even the young were lifted in their spirits to live righteous lives. Jesus was calling out to His disciples and, even more than that, to all who were present that day.

Jesus spoke without shouting, yet even those far in the back said to me afterward that His voice had been so clear that it was as if He were right next to them, speaking. It was the most beautiful and difficult sermon the Teacher had spoken.

> Blessed are the poor in spirit,
> for theirs is the kingdom of heaven.
> Blessed are those who mourn,
> for they will be comforted.
> Blessed are the meek,
> for they will inherit the earth.
> Blessed are those who hunger and thirst for righteousness,
> for they will be filled.
> Blessed are the merciful,
> for they will be shown mercy.
> Blessed are the pure in heart,
> for they will see God.
> Blessed are the peacemakers,
> for they will be called children of God.
> Blessed are those who are persecuted because of righteousness,
> for theirs is the kingdom of heaven.
> Blessed are you when people insult you, persecute you and falsely say all kinds of evil against you because of me. Rejoice and be glad, because great is your reward in heaven, for in the same way they persecuted the prophets who were before you.

Jesus then looked right at us.

> You are the salt of the earth. But if the salt loses its saltiness, how can it be made salty again? It is no longer good for anything, except to be thrown out and trampled underfoot.

You are the light of the world. A town built on a hill cannot be hidden. Neither do people light a lamp and put it under a bowl. Instead they put it on its stand, and it gives light to everyone in the house. In the same way, let your light shine before others, that they may see your good deeds and glorify your Father in heaven.

The Teacher went on to preach to us about a great many other things, including treating those who didn't treat us well, forgiving our enemies, and even loving them. These were hard words to accept: to forgive those who had stolen from us, whipped and maimed us for no reason, placed us in bondage, and killed and abused our women. How could we forgive those who had done such abuses to us and continued to torment and mistreat us? And yet this was what Jesus was calling us to do.

# 10

## Momentum

*But seek first his kingdom and his righteousness,*
*and all these things will be given to you as well.*
—JESUS, THE CHRIST (MATTHEW 6:33)

We went out altogether at first with Jesus from town to town, preaching, healing, and being the witnesses to the miracles our Teacher performed. In Capernaum, Jesus healed a centurion's son by just saying the word without even the son being there. This was confirmed by the centurions' servants, who confirmed that the time of the son's healing had been the same time as Jesus's spoken words to the centurion. After Capernaum we went to a town called Nain. It was a full, hard day of walking. We rose early in the morning and walked continuously the whole day, stopping only briefly for a quick rest, a drink of water, and some figs. For most of the day, we walked along the Sea of Galilee, then along the Jordan River. At about eleven kilometers along the Jordan, a small river connected to the Jordan from the west. We followed the river to the west, slowly climbing up with low-set hills on either side. We could have gone in a more direct route over the undulating hills; however, the river afforded more shade and water to drink and cool off when it got too hot. At the end of the day, we walked over forty kilometers to reach Nain, a small, beautiful farming village sitting three kilometers south of Mount Tabor on Mount Moreh. From Nain, when we looked to the north, Mount Tabor stood out; it was an impressive mountain rising from the flat plains in the classical, conical shape of ancient volcanos.

Rising almost six hundred meters from the plains, there was a staircase that traversed to the top. There were more than 4,340 stairs. It was an impressive sight to behold.

We had many stories about Mount Tabor. The famous mount was mentioned for the first time in our Bible in Joshua 19:22 (thirteenth century BCE) as the border of three tribes: Zebulun, Issachar, and Naphtali. Its strategic location controlled the junction of the Galilee's north-south route with the east-west highway of the Jezreel Valley. Deborah, the Jewish prophetess, summoned Barak of the tribe of Naphtali and gave him God's command. She sent for Barak son of Abinoam from Kedesh in Naphtali and said to him, "The Lord, the God of Israel, commands you: 'Go, take with you ten thousand men of Naphtali and Zebulun and lead them up to Mount Tabor. Descending from the mountain, our Israelite ancestors attacked and vanquished Sisera and the Canaanites.

More recently, less than a hundred years ago, Alexander Maccabeus, the eldest son of Aristobulus II, king of Judaea, was taken prisoner, with his father and his brother Antigonus, by the Roman general Pompey. This took place during the capture of Jerusalem in 63 BCE; he escaped his captors as they were being transferred to Rome. He then appeared in Judea about five years later, raised an army of ten thousand infantry and fifteen hundred cavalry, and fortified Alexandrium (located near the Jordan River, east of Nain) and other strong posts. Alexander's uncle Hyrcanus (with whom Alexander's father, Aristobulus, had clashed) applied for aid to Gabinius, who brought a large army against Alexander, and sent Mark Antony with a body of troops in advance. In a battle fought near Jerusalem, Alexander was soundly defeated and took refuge in the fortress of Alexandrium. Through the mediation of his mother, he was permitted to depart on condition of surrendering all the fortresses still in his power. In the following year, during the expedition of Gabinius into Egypt, Alexander again incited the Jews to revolt and collected an army. He massacred all the Romans who fell in his way and besieged the rest, who had taken refuge on Mount Gerizim (two days' journey south of Mount Tabor). After rejecting the terms of peace, which Gabinius offered to him, he was defeated near Mount Tabor with the loss of ten thousand men.

There is lots of history in the Nain area. Nowadays, Mount Tabor is one of the mountain peaks on which beacons are lit to inform the northern villages of Jewish holy days and the beginnings of new months.

As we entered Nain, a large crowd followed us; the works of Jesus had spread far and wide in the land, and even here in Nain, people had heard of Jesus. We came upon a funeral procession with even more people, so many that the area was hard to pass. The funeral was for the only son of a prominent woman in town, who was also a widow. Many were weeping with the mother, for she was a good woman who was well liked by all. Also, by Jewish tradition, as the funeral procession passed, all who saw the procession had to join in out of respect.

Her only son stretched horizontally, face upward, on a bier held high by pallbearers. The bier (a flat stand) was made of simple wood with a cloth draped over it. Sorrowful wailing filled the air; dust rose around the procession like a light low fog rolling with the people as they slowly made their way to the burial. As we walked, we came on the mother of the dead son, her eyes red and her face puffy from crying. She looked up and gazed on us. The look of emptiness and sorrow in her eyes was unbearable, and I had to turn my eyes away.

Then I heard Jesus, who was standing next to me, whisper softly to the woman, "Don't cry." Jesus's face was seemingly contorted in agony and sadness to take in the suffering of this poor woman, who had lost her husband and now her only child. Jesus stepped in front of the woman and went to the bier, where her son lay. The pallbearers stopped and froze in their tracks, not knowing what to do. Instead of calling out to Jesus to step aside and not hold up the procession, the bearers of the son stood still as they saw the torment on Jesus's face and understood all too well that look of pain and sorrow. The wailing continued all around.

Then Jesus did something unexpected. He reached up to touch her son's head and said with authority, "Young man, I say to you, get up!" So loud was his voice that everyone in the crowd went instantly silent. Then for what seemed like an eternity, there were only a few moments when no one moved. No one even dared to breathe. The dust even seemingly vanished, and the blowing wind stopped. Not even the birds could be heard. Just pure silence.

Then a young man's voice could be heard—faint at first and then growing stronger. Where was it coming from? Then it happened! The young dead man, the only son of a grieving mother, sat up. He sat up! And we saw where the raspy voice had come from. The young man was talking. He was alive! Risen from the dead!

The young boy proceeded to climb down from the bier. The pallbearers froze in disbelief, and everyone stared with a mix of confusion and fear. The pallbearers dropped the bier and stepped back. The crowd also stepped back and gave room to this walking dead man. Everyone was afraid. Then Jesus moved forward, approached the son, and gave him a hug. The son's mother ran up with a wail of joy and hugged her son, then shouted at the top of her voice, "Thank You, Teacher!"

The crowd erupted, and wailing turned to shouts of joy. All began to yell, "A great prophet has appeared among us!"

"God has come to help His people!"

Scenes like this played over and over in the various towns, and the miracles and healings of Jesus continued to spread throughout Judea and the country.

From Nain we made our way from town to town in the Galilee area. In almost every village we entered, we stayed with a local resident believer in Jesus. Jesus was becoming known everywhere, with only very few towns that didn't have a resident who had become a believer in Jesus as a great Prophet. It was a blessing, but there were risks as well. There weren't as many local Pharisees here in the north Typically, the Pharisees looked on Jesus's teachings as a threat to their authority over the people. Our Teacher's radical preaching was of direct contact with the Father; these were teachings that adherence to rituals, temple sacrifices, rules, and prohibitions didn't make one holy or clean. These were teachings of simple goodness, love, sharing, and caring for the poor as the right way. All His teachings diminished the authority of those in power, the power of the Jewish leaders. Our learned men constantly tried to rebuke Jesus, to catch Him saying things outside Jewish Law and inciting the people against us.

We had to be cautious. I say "we," not meaning Jesus. He would speak to open the event and then go to whoever in the town had invited us to stay or to have dinner with them, even the Pharisees. We warned Jesus about the dangers; He never listened to us. In fact, it seemed like He preferred to be with the Pharisees, tax collectors, beggars, ill, crippled, and the more dangerous and seedy peoples. They were the ones drawn to Him more than the rest; one group wanted to rebuke and discredit Him, and the other sought healing and redemption from Him. This situation made for a very odd mix of people, who surrounded us wherever we went.

We came upon one town and were met with people who were our supporters, the ones who believed in Jesus and His teachings. There were even a few whom we had baptized in Aenon. I instantly let out a sigh of relief. This would be a good town for us. Some of the towns were openly hostile to us, whipping up frenzy against us by a local Pharisee leader or a prominent townsman who had something to lose by Jesus's teachings. Happily, this wouldn't be one of those towns. And then as we met the people and began talking to them, the crowd suddenly turned silent and parted for an approaching man.

Instantly my guard went up, and I felt a well of dread come over me. I looked to my right, and Jesus had that calm look of peace on His face, as He always did. The man approached and introduced himself as Simon, the local Pharisee and town elder. Strangely, Simon greeted Jesus and spoke to Him in a very respectful manner; his tone of voice had almost a hint of excitement at meeting Jesus. This was a big departure from the typical Pharisee we had come across, and he reminded me of another Pharisee we had met before in Jerusalem, Nicodemus. If anything, Simon was more curious of Jesus and His small band of followers. As we talked, Simon invited us to dine with him that evening at his house. I wanted to turn him down out of general suspicion of his true motives; Jesus would have nothing of it and readily accepted Simon's invite. So it was set that we would dine at one of the town's finer houses, the house of Simon, the Pharisee. At least we would have a good meal before things turned ugly.

Simon's more accepting behavior reminded me of some of the more snobbish sayings of the rabbi leaders in the south. "If any one wishes to be rich, let him go north; if he wants to be wise, let him come south." Such was the typical thought of the day; our southern elite tried to distinguish themselves as being supreme in Jewish traditions and teachings as opposed to the more uneducated, richer Galileans with our fishing, farming, and tending to animal herds but fewer rabbis to teach us and very little in the way of formal schooling. So perhaps Simon felt more akin to us than he did with his brethren to the south.

The air was cool and crisp in the early evening; there was a slight chill in the air with just a few clouds. Earlier in the day, there had been a small rain shower, not heavy; it was a sign that the drier summer months were almost upon us. The sea beckoned me to her, and I remembered the warm summer nights, the stars above, and the lights of the small towns on shore, tiny lights that looked like stars themselves. It was always a comforting memory. Perhaps I would be able to steal a night here and there to get back on my boat.

My thoughts quickly returned to the present as we approached Simon's house, and the smell of roasting lamb and fish carried on the gentle breeze. My mouth began to water. It had been a long few days of traveling with little to eat, and my empty stomach began to rumble. I sure hoped our rabbi had cooked a lot of food. When he invited Jesus and us to dinner, I don't think he understood that where Jesus went, so did a crowd of disciples, not just us but all who had come to believe in Jesus. And a lot of the converted were those people the rabbi would never talk to, much less allow in his house. Oh well, you couldn't invite Jesus without inviting His followers, since the Teacher wouldn't have it any other way. To invite Jesus was to invite those around Him as well.

As we entered the house, one woman followed closely behind us with a few of her friends. She was somewhat of a celebrity, known throughout Jerusalem as one who had gone north and settled in the area recently. Dressed in fine clothing, she stood out from the crowd; she tried very hard to stay out of the limelight and was very humble in her mannerisms. She was very different from the other affluent women in the area, who made it very clear they were important and that others should stay out of their way. I didn't know of her, but I soon did as the whispering gossip of the locals around me reached my ears.

The lady owned a very lucrative brothel in Jerusalem in the temple Court of the Gentiles. Recently she had heard Jesus speaking, accepted the teachings of our Master, convinced a lot of the women working for her to accept the words of Jesus, and closed her business. This made sense since I was wondering why she had her long hair down. Only the most disrespected, including the harlots, wore their hair down, forced by the Pharisees to show the world their sins. Even this woman, who had clearly seen her wrongs, repented, and converted her workers, couldn't escape the condemnation of the Pharisees. Was there no forgiveness in their hearts? Was there no forgiveness allowed by our people or our God?

One of the servants promptly guided us to an open room, where one wall was lined with couches and fine carpets on the floor. Next to the couches a long, low table set with food sat far enough from the couch-lined wall that one could fully stretch out and recline to eat in comfort. We got comfortable and reclined on the couches with our feet stretched out. Now this was a very nice setup; it was more of a Roman type of dining, different from our normal tradition of sitting cross- legged on the floor and eating next to a table. I guess it was to be expected since our host had more in common with the Romans and the elite than with the locals.

Curious also was the haste in which we were escorted to our table without any normal pleasantries of receiving an honored guest. Simon wasn't there to greet us; there were no warm, welcoming embraces, no slaves to wash the dust of the road from our sandaled feet, no sweet olive oil poured over our heads to soften our parched skin. This treatment was deliberate by our host. The question in our minds was, had he done this because he despised Jesus and had ill intentions for us, or had he done this out of caution lest someone report back to Rome of how Simon the Pharisee had turned into a follower of Jesus? Or at least a sympathizer of Jesus and His radical teachings?

As we reclined, the food was brought out to the table, and we began to eat. Our host Simon reclined next to Jesus and peppered Him with questions. All seemed to be having a good time, and Simon didn't seem to mind too much that the room slowly grew more crowded as Jesus's followers steadily entered the house and hovered near the dining table. The nicely dressed woman who had followed closely behind us as we entered the house earlier worked her way through the people and positioned herself directly in front of Jesus. She looked visibly distraught and yet so happy to be next to the Master. In her right hand, she held a beautiful flask; she opened it, and we all at once stopped talking as the scent from the lotion filled the air. Beautiful smells filled the air of scented plants, spikenard and saffron, sweet cane and cinnamon, incense-bearing trees, myrrh, and aloes. Just like the scents described in the Song of Songs, this was very expensive lotion.

The woman began to pour the lotion on the feet of Jesus, and Jesus, moved by her gesture, gave her a big smile and thanked her for her kindness. It was with these words and the smile from Jesus that the woman began to weep uncontrollably, her tears flowing on the feet of Jesus. They weren't tears of sadness; they were tears of profound joy and thankfulness. She looked around and for an instant was embarrassed; there were no wiping cloths around, so she used her long hair to wipe her tears off the feet of Jesus. Then she kissed His feet, not caring about what others may think of her. I was sitting to the right of Jesus, and to the left of Him was Simon, the Pharisee. I saw Simon from the corner of my eye, and he had a disgusted look on his face, one of contempt toward the woman. We all knew who she was. Simon obviously showed His disgust toward Jesus for allowing her to touch Him.

Jesus, knowing what was going on in Simon's mind, spoke up. "Simon, I have something to tell you."

"Tell me, Teacher," he said.

"Two people owed money to a certain moneylender. One owed him five hundred denarii and the other fifty. Neither of them had the money to pay him back, so he forgave the debts of both. Now which of them will love him more?"

Simon replied, "I suppose the one who had the bigger debt forgiven."

"You have judged correctly," Jesus said. Then He turned toward the woman and said to Simon, "Do you see this woman? I came into your house. You did not give me any water for my feet, but she wet my feet with her tears and wiped them with her hair. You did not give me a kiss, but this woman, from the time I entered, has not stopped kissing my feet. You did not put oil on my head, but she has poured perfume on my feet. Therefore, I tell you, her many sins have been forgiven-as her great love has shown. But whoever has been forgiven little loves little." Then Jesus said to her, "Your sins are forgiven."

If having the woman at the feet of Jesus seemed to astonish Simon, Jesus's words took his response to the next level. All around, the guests close to us who had heard Jesus began to whisper among themselves, "Who is this man Jesus that he thinks that he can forgive sins?"

Jesus, upon hearing the rumble, paid no attention to them, looked at the woman, and said, "Your faith has saved you; go in peace."

The murmuring guests and Simon himself, however, weren't outright mad at Jesus for telling the woman her sins were forgiven. They were more astounded by the authority of Jesus's words. How could you be mad at a person who was doing so much good for the poor and the sick? Everyone knew of Jesus as a great prophet, as one who had the power to heal illnesses and heal the cripple. He even had the power to bring back someone from the dead. His sayings of forgiveness and truth rang clear with everyone. Even this story Jesus had just spoken of, this parable of the wealthy moneylender, set deep in our hearts as pure truth.

We turned back to continue the dinner, and Jesus continued speaking with Simon and the guests. Later, as we stood up and made ready to leave, Jesus put His hand on Simon's shoulder to encourage him to look deep into himself, to be free from lingering doubts, to be free from the pride of life, of his title and station in life. Seek the truth and believe in Him, and he would be set free from all the bondage of this world.

This was the first time I had heard Jesus tell a parable, a story, to get a message across, and this wouldn't be the last. So many more teachings of Jesus were to come.

# II

# Son of Man

*The Son of Man is Lord of the Sabbath.*
—Jesus, the Christ (Matthew 12:3-8)

Springtime was almost over with summer approaching, and we continued our travels, the Twelve of us as well as others close to Jesus, including Mary (called Magdalene); Joanna, the wife of Chuza (the manager of Herod's household); and Susanna. It was a such a breath of fresh air and joy to us that Jesus included and invited all to be His disciples no matter what background we had come from. For some the dangers of following Jesus were evident, such as Joanna, whose husband worked directly for that wretched dictator Herod. And yet God's grace was upon Joanna, and her family was protected. Herod didn't know, or seemed to overlook, Joanna's closeness with us.

The danger of being a disciple to Jesus wasn't something I thought of often, but as followers of Jesus grew and His radical teachings took hold in the hearts of more and more people, the possibility of backlash from our Jewish leaders and Rome slowly crept into my thoughts. For the most part, in every town we entered, the people embraced us warmly as Jesus became well known as a prophet with healing powers. There was never a town that lacked the sick, ill, and disabled.

We traveled by walking and normally had no donkeys, so we had to carry everything. We didn't have much except the essentials, which included a change of clothes, a towel, a blanket, some rope, food, and water. The food was separately wrapped in cloth from the other items, and we used rope to create packs we could wear on our backs. Each of us also had a small satchel to carry small snacks (mostly figs and dates) and some heavier cloth to throw over our shoulders when it got cold. We also had a good supply of nuts to eat, mainly roasted walnuts, almonds, and pistachios. We carried water separately in goatskin containers with a sling used over our shoulders. We did have some money, and Judas had all of it since he was our designated treasurer. This was a questionable role since Judas seemed only too happy to carry that burden.

Walking from town to town took time, and sometimes we had to go a day or two without much to eat except our figs and dates. Burning energy while carrying everything we had and walking all the time made for some weary and hungry days. I remember that on one of those days, we got up early and were walking with no breakfast; we reached the outskirts of a town by early afternoon. In the distance the town's crowd was coming out to meet us. That meant another long day of a crowd surrounding us and Jesus talking and healing, which was a real blessing. However, when you are already hungry from a couple of days of walking and not having much to eat, it's hard to get excited. Blistered feet and aching legs were typical. Our clothes were a bit more smelly than usual due to constant walking without time to wash up properly. In fact, a bit of dread came over me as I saw the number of people in the distance.

As we walked, we came upon a wheat field. It was late spring, early summer, and normally by this time most of the wheat kernels would be fully ripe and dry, ready for harvesting and being made into bread. One couldn't eat dry kernels since they inedible, even raw at that point, so we moved quickly through the field. As we walked, however, we came across a big patch of wheat with its kernels still plump and soft, which we could pick out and eat raw. How was this possible? Jesus stood in the middle of the young wheat patch with a big grin. He knew we were all very hungry; and of course, He would be the same as us, not having much to eat in the past couple of days. Was this gift by His doing? We had seen many miracles. Could Jesus have turned a patch of wheat from being fully ripe and dry to being just budding where the kernels were plump and tasty?

We came closer to Jesus, and He told all of us to stop for a while and to pick and eat the young kernels. We all hesitated at first since this was the Sabbath day. In my mind I ran through the tractates of the Mishnah devoted to the Sabbath and the thirty-nine prohibited actions on the Sabbath, ranging from baking to making a knot with rope or even to just lighting a fire. My head started to hurt when I tried to remember all of them; I was pretty sure picking wheat kernels was considered work and therefore not allowed. It would have been one thing to just pick and eat the wheat by ourselves, but by standing in the middle of the wheat field, we were in plain sight of the villagers in the distance, and surely among them was a Pharisee or two.

During our youth, the Pharisees had pounded into our brains all thirty-nine rules of what not to do on the Sabbath; they had said these were commandments from our God and that there were consequences for breaking those rules. I can still hear our Pharisees quoting Exodus: "For six days work is to be done, but the seventh day is the day of Sabbath rest, holy to the Lord. Whoever does work on the Sabbath day is to be put to death." Now, in my mind I debated with myself about the definition of "work." Leviticus said that even lighting a fire on the Sabbath was prohibited. And there was the passage we had all heard every week from Leviticus about the time when we had been in the wilderness.

A man had been found gathering wood on the Sabbath day. He had been brought to Moses and Aaron for judgment. The Lord said to Moses "The man must die. The whole assembly must stone him outside the camp." Now of course time had moved on, and we as a people had grown very large and were practically enslaved by the Romans with their laws and taxes. There was so much to do in the week that doing absolutely nothing for one day was very difficult. So our "wise" leaders came up with a "sin offering" requirement rather than death. Of course, the sin offering was made to the Pharisees, and they grew richer while we remained poor and overworked. Nevertheless, we held to our traditions and tried not to do any work on the Sabbath, however difficult it was.

I heard someone say my name, Peter, which brought me back from my thoughts. It was John Z. "What should be we do?"

I responded, "Our teacher tells us it's okay to pick and eat on the Sabbath, and so we shall!" Now my boldness probably came more out of sheer hunger at that point than out of a philosophical agreement with Jesus's principles. So we all started to gather the wheat kernels and eat them—and having quite a good time of celebrating the food, I might add. Jesus also was picking and eating.

Sure enough, within a short time we heard a voice in the distance from a Pharisee. "Look! Your disciples are doing what is unlawful on the Sabbath." We all froze from our picking and grew nervous, looking at Jesus. Jesus remained perfectly calm as if what we were doing was normal. And of course it was, just not normal for picking wheat on the Sabbath.

Jesus turned to the Pharisees, who looked upon all of us with clear distain. They frowned with that look I remembered all too well of a parent displeased with his child, who had done something terribly wrong. The village people around the Pharisees were visibly nervous as well for a different reason. They were so happy while anticipating seeing the great prophet who healed and spoke of love and compassion. No one wanted anything to happen that would spoil his or her opportunity with the Teacher. And it was obvious Jesus had just performed a miracle since there was clearly no way at this time of year that there could be budding baby kernels of wheat. Clearly, we and the village people were nervous, since we were Jews. Disobeying our laws wasn't something we took lightly, no matter how difficult the rules.

Jesus turned and answered the Pharisees, "Haven't you read what David did when he and his companions were hungry? He entered the house of God, and he and his companions ate the consecrated bread— which was not lawful for them to do, but only for the priests. Or haven't you read in the Law that the priests on Sabbath duty in the temple desecrate the Sabbath and yet are innocent? I tell you that something greater than the temple is here. If you had known what these words mean, 'I desire mercy, not sacrifice,' you would not have condemned the innocent. For the Son of Man is Lord of the Sabbath."

Our Teacher's words were amazing. He had quoted our history like He was reading from a book or had spent His whole life in study like the greatest of the Sadducees or Pharisees. We held our breath, waiting from some response from the Pharisees; to everyone's surprise, nothing came back. They just stood there and looked at Jesus in bewilderment of this man. They turned to each other and mumbled something I couldn't hear, then turned and walked back toward the village.

The townspeople erupted in joy to see Jesus and ran to us. He had stood up to the Pharisees, and such words of truth had never been spoken before. Mercy, not sacrifice. Mercy, not sacrifice. These words penetrated our hearts as being so true. Jesus understood the hardships, trials, and sacrifices we made daily. What additional sacrifices in this harsh life did our God want us to make to adhere to ancient rituals? And who was the one who would decide who must adhere to these laws and who doesn't have to?

For me what affected me most was again those words Jesus had spoken at the end. "For the Son of Man is Lord of the Sabbath." Most didn't pay attention to that part since they were all so happy to see us and see that the Pharisees had turned away, allowing us to enter the town. Those words sank into my heart. Who was Jesus? What did He mean by the "Son of Man"? "Son of man" (bar-adam) was a common term in our texts, and it generally referred to all mankind and our frailties and weaknesses. I got to where Jesus had referred to all of us, but He had specifically said He was the "Son of Man" with such directness as if it were the truth, a fact not to be questioned, and that He was "Lord of the Sabbath." What did all that mean? His words spoken of Himself sank deeper and deeper into me.

We continued with the villagers and entered the town and synagogue. It was a fair-sized temple constructed in the typical octagon style. Villagers came to pray, sing, and listen to scripture from the rabbis. The Pharisees we'd seen in the wheat fields were all in the synagogue, still wearing those frowning, scowling faces we'd seen before. And they looked more disturbed at us for being in their private temple. Jesus liked the Sabbath to teach what the Sabbath was really for. He always said God had made the Sabbath for the people as a time of rest and recuperation; to the Pharisees, with all their rules, it had become that the people were made to serve the Sabbath.

As Jesus preached in the synagogue, I noticed a man sitting near us, straight backed, completely still, wide eyed, and attentive. While others normally fidgeted some, since the ground was hard, he remained unmoving. His clothes were disheveled and ragged, hair unkept, and his bare feet were hardened by years of walking barefoot. It wasn't an uncommon sight, yet there was something odd about him. It was his arms. One was hidden under his clothes. This was very strange. As

I looked around, several Pharisees also looked at the man with keen interest. This didn't look good. Was the man a plant by the Pharisees? What was he hiding under his clothes? He was close to the Master. Could he have a dagger? Cold sweat began to roll down my back, and I got up and eased myself closer to the man. He was far too close to the Master. If he leaped up now, there would be no time for me to stop him.

I edged myself next to the man. There was no way now that he would do any harm to Jesus. The Teacher looked at me as I sat down next to our mysterious man; a sly smile came across Jesus's face as if he knew why I had moved next to our mystery man. There was no concerned look on Jesus's face. He then abruptly stopped talking. Dead silence came for what seemed like an eternity. Jesus then pointed at our raggedly dressed man next to me and commanded, "Get up and stand in front of everyone." The man was hesitant but did as Jesus had asked. Did Jesus know this man was a hired thug? Was He about to call him out and accuse the Pharisees? I tipped my body and put my weight on the balls of my feet, ready to leap at our man with the hidden arm. If he even twitched, I would tackle him to the ground.

Jesus had another agenda in mind. He called out to the people while staring at the Pharisees, "I ask you, which is lawful on the Sabbath: to do good or to do evil, to save a life or to destroy it?" Had Jesus just called the man a hired murderer by the Pharisees? The unsteady man was very nervous, and sweat began to roll down his forehead. This was it!

I began to ready myself to tackle the would-be murderer. Jesus yelled, "Stretch out your hand!" The man was shaken by Jesus's command, and using his right arm, he lifted his left tattered robe and exposed his hidden left arm.

A gasp went through the whole crowd. There was no dagger in the man's left hand. Instead, where his arm was supposed to be, there was a shriveled and deformed stump. It was a ghastly sight. The skin on his stumpy arm looked made of leather with a thousand wrinkles; it was half the length of a normal arm with large bulges. Where his hand was supposed to be were five little, round ball-like spheres instead of fingers.

In shame the man fell to his knees, weeping, and he made a cry of anguish as only a man can whose entire life has been one of destitution and pain, a life of loneliness and an object of distain. Our society had no forgiveness for the deformed, since many thought it was a curse due to a great sin the man or his family had caused. He was someone to avoid.

We could see the longing in his eyes and something else. A glimmer of hope sparkled since it was common knowledge that Jesus had supernatural powers of healing. Just then one of the Pharisees approached us and asked Jesus, "Is it lawful to heal on the Sabbath?" Obviously, it was a question coming out of spite and a direct confrontation to see what our Master would say and to bring another charge against Jesus for breaking our Jewish laws.

Jesus looked at the disabled man and then directly at the Pharisee, and for the second time, He spoke in a parable. "If any of you has a sheep and it falls into a pit on the Sabbath, will you not take hold of it and lift it out? How much more valuable is a person than a sheep! Therefore, it is lawful to do good on the Sabbath." At this all heads in the synagogue nodded in approval of the words of Jesus. Well, all except for the Pharisees, of course.

And we could see the compassion in our Teacher's eyes as He looked on this poor soul. For a second time, Jesus commanded, "Stretch out your hand!" Slowly the man did as Jesus told him, doing his best. His right arm came up quickly, his stump hand still bent low; he struggled to stretch out his deformed arm toward the Teacher as He had commanded. And as the man stretched, his voice bellowed a heavy animallike sound, filled with pain and discomfort.

I had to refocus since I couldn't believe what I was seeing. I'm sure it wasn't a trick of my eyes since everyone else gasped as well. The man's left arm continued to stretch out, growing from a deformed stump to a normal whole arm. His tiny fingers elongating before our eyes! He was healed!

The man's face of discomfort turned to tears of gratitude and excitement, and he jumped up from his kneeled position and hugged Jesus. Sobs erupted, and tears of joy flowed from his eyes. He pulled back and extended both of his arms high in the air before us. They were two perfectly normal arms and hands.

The crowd went wild and rushed toward the man, putting their hands on him, yelling, and whooping. Everyone cheering Jesus, calling

Him "Prophet." They said He was Elijah. He was Moses. And He was even more. A wave of relief washed over me. I was mentally exhausted.

Jesus put His arm around my shoulder and thanked me for caring enough to put my life on the line, for He knew I had thought the man was a hired murderer. I am no hero, that's for sure; I did appreciate the acknowledgment from the Teacher. And I was a bit embarrassed that my old self had come out, always ready for a fight, always thinking about the darker side of people's motives instead of the good Jesus always did. Well, Jesus thought of the good side of everyone except when He dealt with the Pharisees and their scheming ways. Jesus had no tolerance for those who abused their status to the detriment of the poor and suffering. Would I have been so quick to think to pounce on the man if he had been a Roman soldier or a brute instead of a smaller-sized man who was much older than I? A lot of questions rolled around in my mind. I was just glad Jesus didn't question my bravery, as did I.

The Pharisees retreated to the far corner of the synagogue to get away from Jesus and the healed man. The crowd, overjoyed by the healing miracle, paid no attention to the Pharisees and were so thankful for Jesus—not only for the miracle but for His compassionate words. Yes, it was important to respect the Sabbath rules; that didn't mean following the rules so blindly and strictly that it left no room for doing good, doing what was right. Being the cynical man I was, growing up, and dealing with all sorts of people, I couldn't get over the quietness of the Pharisees off in the corner. They were a disturbing contrast to the joy of the villagers. Jesus, always knowing the thoughts of others and for some reason always being able to read my mind, a disturbing fact as my mind often wandered, nudged me and pointed me toward the door. It was obvious that Jesus, looking toward the Pharisees and then at me, then extending his hand and pointing to the door, could sense the thoughts in their hearts. They were up to no good, and it was time to leave.

The healings Jesus did wherever we went were truly miracles upon miracles, but like the scene in the synagogue, they also attracted negative attention from those who wanted to keep the status quo. Most of us lived every day with heavy burdens of labor and taxes. And as if life weren't hard enough, the ever-increasing rules and contributions we needed to give to our spiritual leaders were getting to be unmanageable. So it was these few at the top who despised Jesus for His words of compassion and tolerance since many weren't in keeping with the duties we had to fulfil to serve the few. The healings of Jesus made Him even more famous and brought ever-increasing crowds wherever we went, with increasing attention by those few on top.

We left the synagogue and made our way through town. We weren't planning on staying there overnight. The townspeople kept up with us, and Jesus wasn't in a hurry to leave, so we stopped often to enter homes, ushered in by the pleadings of those who had family members who were ill. Jesus healed them all. There was nothing our Teacher couldn't do. As Jesus healed the sick, we heard Him tell the recovered and the family not to tell anyone about Him but to be thankful to God the Father for the miracle that had blessed them, for His power (the power of healing from Jesus) came directly from the Father through Him to them. Believe, be thankful, be well, and be quiet. These were wise words, since Jesus truly had compassion for the ill and the deformed. He wanted to heal them to make them well and happy.

His healings brought out so much attention that people were losing sight of our Teacher's words and looking more to see signs and wonders. The skeptics wanted to see whether Jesus could really do what they had heard and were curious, wanting to see something spectacular like it was some type of show they could in turn brag about to others, that they had been there and had really seen the miracle. The Pharisees, not pleased with the miracles of Jesus, openly called him "Beelzebul." Jesus promptly retorted and put them in their place. Then the Pharisees asked Jesus to perform a miracle. Again, Jesus exploded on them and called them "a wicked and adulterous generation." After that short speech, the Pharisees' demeanor turned even more sour—to the delight of many, I might add; of course, none would openly show this emotion since no one wanted to incur their wrath. I saw upturned smiles of the many who believed in Jesus. The Teacher, as He often did, said a great many things, which I didn't understand at that time until many years later. In this response to the Pharisees, Jesus also said, "For as Jonah was three days and three nights in the belly of a huge fish, so the Son of Man will be three days and three nights in the heart of the earth." What in the world did that mean? Surely, Jesus wasn't talking about being swallowed by a giant fish. These were more questions that only time and future events would make clear.

As we continued walking, the crowd grew ever larger. As word of Jesus being in the village spread, others came from surrounding towns. It came to a point that there were so many people, there was no way everyone could see Jesus. The Teacher, ever understanding and knowing how to handle all situations, moved us to the edge of the Sea of Galilee, where the fishing boats were docked for the day. It was early afternoon by then, so there were just a few workers tending their nets or doing small repairs on the boats. Most of all the action happened in the mornings when the boats returned from their nightly fishing.

Jesus called out to a fisherman who was still in his boat to come in closer so Jesus could get on it. It was such a brilliant idea. The boat owner anchored close to shore, where everyone could get a view. Normally, boats were docked in a flatter shore cove area to protect the boats from the weather and provide a larger expanse area to clean the nets and the fish. The trees around the area had been cut down to open the area for all the dock activities that accompanied the fishing boats. We were lucky to have front row seats at the edge of the water.

As Jesus began to speak, the crowd grew deafly silent. It was as if even the birds stopped their chirping to listen to Him. Jesus spoke softly, but we could hear Him just as if He were next to us. And to my amazement, even those in the far back didn't yell out for Jesus to speak louder. Later, curious, I asked those who were far away from the shore whether they could hear Jesus, and they said they had heard every word as if Jesus were right next to them. Thousands of people gathered around the shore, all hearing the word of Jesus. This was another miracle I kept close to my heart. Who was this Prophet, this Teacher, this Man of miracles?

And in His new way, Jesus spoke to the crowds only in parables. Everyone was rapt with attention, and we listened for hours. Of the many parables, a few stood out as being so right and basic that everyone who heard these words subconscious nodded and murmured softly in agreement. Many had confusion on their faces at the same time. The words spoke into our hearts and lives as farmers and fishermen, simple people trying to make a living and do what was right. The confusion came for many of us because we knew in our hearts there was a deeper meaning to Jesus's parables and that the deeper meaning remained just beyond our reach. One such parable was the parable of the sower. It went something like this:

> A farmer went out to sow his seed. As he was scattering the seed, some fell along the path, and the birds came and ate it up. Some fell on rocky places, where it did not have much soil. It sprang up quickly, because the soil was shallow. But when the sun came up, the plants were scorched, and they withered because they had no root. Other seed fell among thorns, which grew up and choked the plants. Still other seed fell on good soil, where it produced a crop—a hundred, sixty or thirty times what was sown. Whoever has ears, let them hear.

By the time Jesus finished His teachings, it was too late to journey to the next town, and the owner of the boat Jesus had preached from was only too happy to invite Jesus and us to stay the night at his house. We were thankful for the offer and were overjoyed when Jesus accepted. Spending one more night in the open with no food wasn't something I looked forward to. That evening we dined with the boat owner and his family. Respectfully, after dinner they retreated to other rooms to allow us some alone time with Jesus. It was there that we asked Him why He spoke to the people only in parables. The Teacher replied that the parables were the secrets to the kingdom of heaven. To understand the parables was to understand heaven, and only a few would understand what Isaiah had written, and to those who understood and lived the parables, there would be given more, and they would live abundant life. For those who heard but didn't understand or take the time to understand, all would be lost. Now for me that was a problem, for I was clearly in the lost category, since I didn't understand the parables; and in talking to the others, I saw that neither did they. Then Jesus said thankfully that He would explain the parables to us so we could understand, and He proceeded to do so. About the parable of the sower, He said this:

> When anyone hears the message about the kingdom and does not understand it, the evil one comes and snatches

away what was sown in their heart. This is the seed sown along the path. The seed falling on rocky ground refers to someone who hears the word and at once receives it with joy. But since they have no root, they last only a short time. When trouble or persecution comes because of the word, they quickly fall away. The seed falling among the thorns refers to someone who hears the word, but the worries of this life and the deceitfulness of wealth choke the word, making it unfruitful. But the seed falling on good soil refers to someone who hears the word and understands it. This is the one who produces a crop, yielding a hundred, sixty or thirty times what was sown.

After Jesus explained the story, it was if we were in a dark room but someone had lit a candle, allowing us to see. It was so clear and simple, yet without explanation the meaning would have escaped us. We took down to memory the parables and explanations from our teacher.

# 12

## Even the Dead Live!

*Talitha koum!*
—Jesus, the Christ (Mark 5:41)

The next day the crowd was still there, knowing Jesus had stayed the night, and our Teacher continued to heal the ill and speak truths to the people, encouraging them; also, at the same time, He was dumbfounding them with His parables. The morning turned to early afternoon and then late afternoon. Instead of staying the night, Jesus told us to make our way to the other side of the sea. Getting a boat at any time in the area was easy, since we'd been fishermen our whole lives; there wasn't a seaside village I didn't know or someone to ask who would let us borrow a boat. However, this day it was a bit challenging, and by the time we found the boat and loaded our belongings, it was already early evening.

In the distance I saw dark-gray clouds forming over the mountain ridges heading our way. With some anxiety, we all got on the boat and started to make our way across the Sea of Galilee. As we made off, the crowd on the shore was there with shouts of praise to Jesus. I turned to see the boat owner among the crowd. His face, however, wasn't full of joy and gratitude. Instead of a look of joy, a frown was on his face, a mask of concern; and I knew what He was thinking. Living your life on the water, you knew the times and seasons as well as the best times to catch various types of fish. And you also knew the signs in the sky when there most likely would be storms. My mind wandered as I turned from the frowning man and gazed over the sea. The Sea of Galilee was my home. I had spent my whole life on the waters, as had my father and his father before him.

With such a long history, the sea went by many names: Sea of Kinnereth, Lake of Gennesaret, Sea of Tiberias; I preferred, as did many fishermen, to simply call it "the Lake." Thirteen kilometers wide and more than twenty kilometers long, it was surrounded on all side by the high hills rising over six hundred meters from the shoreline; it was a spectacular view. Off in the northeast, towering above them all, was the Decapolis hill rising steadily over nine hundred meters above the shoreline and even higher in the distance. It was hard to tell sometimes where the mountaintop ended and the sky began. There were thousands of years of history surrounding us at all times, looking down on us from the high hills. Green and full of life in the spring, the hills were now turning a shade of brown since the warmer and dryer summer months were upon us. From those same magnificent hills that silently looked on us often came violent winds, blustery clouds, and torrential rains. And the waters, being shallow, sixty meters at the deepest parts, felt like we were on a very wide frying pan with just enough water to cover the bottom of the pan. And our boat was like a tiny stick floating on that pan. Any small splash easily rocked the stick and bounced it up and down. Many fishermen had been lost to those violent waves, which the storms kicked up so easily and quickly. Thinking too much of my own personal loss on this lake (this lake that gave life to us also so easily took it away) always filled me with some anxiety. I felt Jesus's hand on my shoulder, a reassuring grip, as if to say, *I know, Brother, take heart, for I am with you.*

We set the sail and began our journey across the lake and our Teacher; weary from a long day of preaching and healing, we slipped into a corner of the boat and quickly fell asleep. It wasn't long before those clouds from the hills crept up to the shoreline, then headed like a fury toward our little boat. With the dark, black clouds came the winds, and we could feel the boat beginning to rock side to side. Slowly at first, the winds whipped up the waters, and the waves became ever larger. The twilight that had once shined some orange rays of light quickly disappeared, and rays of rain took its place, beating down on us. Darkness enveloped us like someone had thrown a thick blanket over the skies. There were the light, the few stars in the twilight, and the hills in the distance. They all vanished, replaced by the deafening drumbeat of rain and howling winds. We quickly took down the sails and tied down what we could. The wind and rain grew stronger, turning the sea into a froth of white. We couldn't see anything in front of us, so black was the sky. And with each passing moment, my heart beat faster and faster in tune with the rising storm. As I looked around, brave faces looked back at me; we were men of the sea, and we all had been in many storms. We would handle this one too. But the storm kept growing stronger, and the waves now overtopped the side of our boat. The sea began to swamp the boat, and our feet, once dry, were now submerged in the cold waters, sloshing around our tiny wooden container.

Brave men and women turned to Jesus as did I, and to our surprise the Teacher was in the stern (back) of the boat, sleeping on a large cushion propped up from the bottom of the boat on a wooden ledge. He was seemly oblivious to the raging terror around Him, as if nothing could faze the Master. John Z, Matthew, a few others, and I made our way to Jesus, bouncing around the boat like flopping fish on a boat deck. We yelled to Jesus to wake Him up and ask Him to save us from drowning. Jesus slowly came out of His slumber as I reached Him and grabbed His shoulder. Of course, my shoulder grab wasn't the same as the gentle touch Jesus had given me earlier in the day when we first got on the boat. My grab was more like the vice grip of desperation of a drowning man reaching to grasp a piece of floating wood on a choppy sea.

Jesus looked at us and gave us that *What now?* look, which parents give their children when they come crying to them too often. Our Teacher stood up on the rocky boat, outstretched His hands, and turned His head toward the howling winds and rain.

He yelled, "Quiet! Be still!" with an authoritative tone a schoolmaster would give to unruly students who were making too much noise in a class. And then the strangest thing I had ever seen happened. Immediately the howling winds stopped, the rain ceased, and the black night became twilight as the clouds retreated. The last vestiges of what was day peeked through. The boat sat as still as if we were docked in the harbor on a clam day. Jesus turned His gaze from the horizon to us, His stern look retreated to a look of almost sadness to us, and He said, "Why are you so afraid? Do you still have no faith?" So penetrating was His gaze that we all had to look away in embarrassment.

He was right, of course, as always. We have seen so many miracles happen right before our eyes, and yet when the first bit of trouble hit us, we trembled and called out to our Teacher to save us, not believing harm wouldn't come on us. Our embarrassment turned to fear as the magnitude of what Jesus had done sank in our minds. Healing the sick was one thing; now even the winds, waves, and rains obeyed His every word. Who was this man? Was Jesus greater than Moses, who had parted the Red Sea? In my heart I asked myself, *Was Jesus even a man, or was He an angel like Gabriel or even greater?*

With the lake calm and easy low winds blowing from the west, we asked Jesus where we should be headed. Jesus turned and said, "Keep to the east for the Gadara area." We were all a bit relieved by the directions from Jesus. The Gadara area had several towns, and the residents there were mainly Gentiles and Jewish people who over the centuries had become more Roman than Jewish, even to the point of making idols and eating unclean animals. They weren't in any sense Jewish anymore, and we considered them as Romans. At first, I wondered why Jesus was setting out for this heathen area, and then I got to thinking that at least it would be a nice break for all of us. We had been traveling from town to town for some time now. Everywhere we went there was an ever-growing crowd of people. Quite frankly it was getting very tiresome, and all of us were feeling burned out. I am sure that none felt this more than Jesus, who was constantly teaching and healing wherever we went. So perhaps this break was also for Him too.

By morning we reached the eastern shore and ended up in Gergesa, a small town in the Gadera area. It was beautiful. The steep hills angled down all the way to the shoreline. Directly in front of us, I began to see tiny clusters of dots moving around as we drew closer to shore. The grassy, steep hillside was perfect for grazing animals, and the animals seemed to appreciate the area as much as we did; they lazily moved very slowly, focused on the food at their feet. My stomach began to grumble. The long night of surviving the storm with little sleep turned the grazing lambs into roasting lambs on a spit over the fire. My mouth began to water, and my stomach started growling. I signaled to the others to get out the oars so we could get to shore quicker. As we got closer, those tasty animal dots grew bigger and bigger; then it hit me. There was something different about those animals. They weren't white and slender like lambs. They were squat and fat. Then the noise came.

Oink! Oink! Oink!

Oh no! They weren't lambs; they were pigs. In an instant my watering lips went dry. Unclean animals. We were in Gentile territory. Maybe this location Jesus had decided on wasn't ideal. Ugh, another day of vegetables?

I cursed under my breath, perhaps a little too loudly as I looked around; Jesus was staring at me. There was no way He could have heard me from across the boat. He raised His hand toward me and said, "Peter, Peter, I know what you are thinking. Don't let your stomach rule you! Vegetables are good for your health."

The whole boat erupted in laughter, as did I. *Ouch*. Slapped on the wrist again by Jesus.

The steep hills in front of us ran all the way to the shore, and we couldn't dock there, As we got closer, we turned the boat to the north toward the village where the slopes were gentler; and there were places where we could dock close to shore. As we got off the boat, we hesitated for a second, waiting for an onrush of people. All we heard were the gentle breeze and some hammering in the background from one of the local craft shops. The near silence was a beautiful respite. Yes, this would be a nice place for several days, heathens or not, the people here were respectful and minded their own business.

It was a scene very similar to the village where I had grown up. There were other boats next to us. A few had some fishermen making repairs, and on shore some were mending nets. There were more sounds of people selling wares, the smells of cooking, and the pounding of hammers. The place was familiar and comforting. The only odd sounds were from those disgusting pigs. Just to the south of the village near us, there was a large flock of pigs grazing and oinking. A few Pig keepers surrounded the pigs to keep them herded and protect them from the other wilder animals that didn't see them as unclean. A disturbing sound and sight; I did hear they were very good tasting. I wonder what Jesus would have said if we had tried some pig.

My thoughts of roasted pig were disturbed by the loudest shriek I had ever heard. Then there was more commotion. The people on shore began to run in our direction with panic on their faces. They ran past us, and behind them close behind was the hugest man I had ever seen, standing higher than a Roman horse on two legs and as wide as two full-grown men. He was a giant. A crazy, screaming, naked giant!

We were so scared that we were frozen in our tracks. It would have made no difference whether we tried to run since that crazy man was already too close to us, and he was running faster than a chariot. Jesus stepped in front of us just as the giant was upon us. I yelled for Jesus to get out of the way, and John and I jumped in front of the Teacher, if only to soften the blow that would surely come on Him, now on us. Just then the screaming man fell to his knees in front of us.

Jesus stepped forward in front of us to face the man. Silence. No one even dared to take a breath; even the pigs stopped their oinking. All the village noises ceased as everyone was captivated by the scene of this giant, naked man bowing to Jesus. Jesus, instead of being filled with fear, looked on this man with the same sympathy we'd seen when Jesus healed the sick and the lame. The naked man, obviously demon possessed, lived in the wilderness. His hair was wild and long with a full beard. His wrists and feet had clamps on them, with broken chains dangling from each clamp. Nothing could hold this brute. Scars ran across his whole body.

Jesus moved forward and placed His hand on the man's head, saying a soft prayer. The giant, now softly sobbing with tears rolling down his face, looked up at Jesus and yelled, "What do you want with me, Jesus, Son of the most high God? I beg you don't torture me!" "Do not torture me?" How could Jesus possibly torture this giant of a man? Jesus asked the man's name. The giant responded, "Legion, for I am many demons. Do not send me into the abyss, mighty one. Have pity on us! Send us into the pig's master!" Jesus then raised His hands into the air, looked up, and gave the command. "Come out of him!"

The weeping giant lifted his head; his arms began to flail around, fists balled up, and he gave a wild, animal-like cry. "AAAARRRGGGHHHH! We are free at last!" The giant's contorted, tortured face relaxed, and he slumped to the ground. No one dared to make a sound during this incredible scene, and as if it couldn't get any more unreal, in the distance a group of pigs began to squeal uncontrollably. They were oinking and kicking, and then the pigs started to run into each other like they were crazy, like they were demon possessed.

Jesus did it! He had moved the demons from the giant to the pigs, and now the pigs were going crazy. The pig keepers frantically tried to corral the pigs, but there was nothing they could do. Then all at once the pigs started rushing down the steep hill toward the lake. Then they went into the lake! All the while the pigs made so much noise, a crazy wild sound. Then there was silence. All the pigs had drowned in the water!

Jesus called to us to bring clothes to the giant, and the man gratefully took the clothes and dressed himself. A moment later the villagers, hearing all the commotion, came to us; those who had been near the scene when it happened described to them what had happened. At first there was general disbelief; but when they saw the demon-possessed giant sitting calmly at the feet of Jesus, talking to us like any other normal man, they believed and grew frightened. The dead pigs floating in the waters were too much for them. Who was this man who could control demons? Afraid, they told us to leave their village at once. The now-gentle giant pleaded with Jesus to take him with us; so happy was he to be finally healed of the demons. Jesus told the man to go home and praise God for his healing. He promptly got up and ran, yelling shrieks of joy where before there had been only sounds of agony and torment.

Obviously, our downtime to relax and rejuvenate away from the crowds was quickly over, and we set our boat out back west to the shores from whence we had come. As we sailed, Jesus told us to turn north to Capernaum. Several of us at once gave a loud cheer. "Yes!" It would be good to get back home to Capernaum, even if it was just for a short time. Capernaum was a beautiful town on the north edges of the Sea of Galilee, blessed with a nice, wide, flat plain area on the shoreline with soft, gentle rising hills to the north. With a population of about fifteen hundred spread over sixty dunams (six hectares), we weren't the largest town in Galilee; we were fair sized and had all manner of trade, crafts, farming, and of course, fishing boats. It was a lively town, small and compact, and one could feel the energy of people hustling, working here and there. Capernaum was truly the most beautiful town in Galilee. Of course, I might have been biased because my home was there and my family had been in Capernaum for several generations. I thought the only person who was a little weary of Capernaum was Matthew. It was his home too; however, as one of the local tax collectors, Matthew's fame there wasn't a good one. Thanks to Jesus, even the most hardened of souls had to admit that since becoming a disciple of Jesus, Matthew wasn't the same person. One could say that one of the greatest of Jesus's miracles wasn't miraculously healing someone or even raising someone from the dead; it was our Teacher's ability to save someone's heart, mend a broken spirit, and soften the most hardened souls to the simple truths Jesus taught: love and compassion, not rules and rituals. And at the very center of my lovely town was a large synagogue, a place familiar to us all since several of us had grown up here, and most of our other disciples often came to Capernaum to visit relatives, work, or come to Sabbath prayers. Even Jesus often came to teach there, and we knew the synagogue leader, Jairus, very well. In most towns the local Jewish leaders were weary of us and generally against the teachings of Jesus. Here we were more like family. Many of us had grown up in this synagogue: me, my cousin Andrew, John, James, and of course, Matthew.

Jairus, to his credit, always treated Jesus well, secretly of course, lest he be seen as a collaborator, a Jesus lover, or even worse, labeled as a disciple of Jesus. That wouldn't do well for his position. As synagogue leader, Jairus ran the operations of the synagogue, maintenance, schedule of all events, and the Sabbath services, which typically consisted of a recitation of the Shema (confession of faith in the one God), prayers, scripture readings from the Law and the Prophets, a sermon, and a benediction. It was a very respectable position, and everyone held Jairus in high regard. If he got on the bad side of the town elders or the Pharisees, his position would be ended very quickly.

As we approached Capernaum, I made out a wave of shifting movement on the shore of the lake. Moving ever so slowly, it was hard to make it out. It was a dark band of dots that moved slightly from side to side with specks of various colors. No, not dots! There were hundreds of people crammed on the shoreline of the water, waiting for Jesus. The boat drew us closer and closer, and the dots turned to little sticks and then to faces clothed in our normal clothing. In our everyday lives, men and women alike wore what we call tunics. A tunic is a simple, one-piece robe, with an opening for our heads and arms. People wore both an inner tunic and an outer tunic, each with a similar shape. The inner tunic was normally shorter, to knee length, and made of thinner cloth, linen, cotton, or softer wool. The outer tunic, also called a mantle or robe, was sturdier and longer. Used as a protective covering, it was made of a square or oblong strip of heavier cloth with an opening for the head. Sometimes it had sleeves. Normally both the inner and outer tunics had a belt to keep the flowing material easy to wear. You could easily tell the difference between men and women since the men's tunics were simple, and the women wore more elaborate, longer tunics normally made of various materials, colors, and patterns.

Gazing into the crowds, I saw young boys and girls chasing each other and playing tag. The sight brought back memories from my youth when life had been simpler. Normally their mothers and fathers would scold them to settle down; today everyone had his or her attention drawn to a single boat slowly making its way toward the shore. Willing helpers jumped into the water, took our rope line, and pulled us closer to shore. The boat got as close to shore as we could without bottoming out the boat; the water was about waist deep. I jumped out first with Nathanial, James, and John right behind me. Once in the water, I motioned to the others to hold our arms out to Jesus, who was just getting over the boat's edge, to help carry Him to shore, lest our Teacher get soaking wet. Jesus would have none of it, and He waved us away, preferring to jump into the water as we had. Thankfully, we were close to shore, and we waded in with warm welcomes from many of those overly excited who were in the water with us.

There was an honest sincerity about the smiles that welcomed us, which was a little different from other towns, where the people who greeted us had a mixture of hope and thrill to see a famous person and a touch of fear due to the power they had heard Jesus possessed. Add to that a touch of anxiety and wariness of the ever-watchful eyes of Jewish elders, who looked on Jesus as a teacher bringing radical ideas normally made for uncomfortable times, not today. There were the faces of townspeople welcoming their brothers and sisters, whom they had known their whole lives, and a man, a Teacher, they had grown to love as one of their own, as one us, a "Capernaumian." Okay, maybe there was no such thing as a Capernaumian, but it had a nice sound to it. I was from Capernaum; therefore I was a Capernaumian.

As we walked out of the waters, the sporadic crowd welcoming us at the lake turned to a denser mass of people. All of them wanted to touch Jesus. Just then the crowd parted in front of us, and the raucous crowd settled down. The pushing and shoving of people wanting to get close to the Teacher gave way to make a path for an oncoming visitor. There appeared to be deep respect among the people who parted a path for our oncoming visitor, so I thought it was a Pharisee.

The wiry man who approached wore only a simple off-white tunic with no special adornments or fine-colored cloth typical of one of our Pharisee spiritual leaders. Normally you could see Pharisees from far away because their fine clothing stood out from a common man's attire. Their clothing was made of the finest white or even purple, embroidered with curiously wrought silk upper girdles. It was around this upper garment that additional clothing was worn, which the Pharisees enlarged. Their headdresses consisted of a pointed cap or a kind of turban made of exquisite material, which was intricately wound; the ends often hung gracefully behind the man. Altogether, almost eighteen garments were used to complete the elegant ensemble.

Unusually, this simply dressed man had the same respect of the people, and as he drew near, we knew why. It was Jairus, the synagogue leader. His normally easy walk and smiling face were replaced by a very hurried stride, and he wore a mask of worry and concern. As he approached, the parting crowd also changed their excited looks to see Jesus to the same masks of concern. Within just steps of Jesus, Jairus threw himself at our Teacher's feet. When he slowly looked up, his eyes, puffy and red with large, dark rings, were signs of someone who hadn't slept in days. His voice, cracking and low at first, turned loud. He wasn't worried about what others may think or that people would see him as a convert of Jesus's teachings or even a disciple. Jarius said, "My little daughter is dying. Please come and put your hands on her so that she will be healed and live." Jairus's daughter was only twelve years old, and everyone in town knew her and was deeply anguished by her illness. We knew her well too and were all concerned. Why had this calamity come upon such a good man? Jesus's face was also clearly distraught due to the agony of His friend.

Bending down, Jesus grasped Jairus's shoulders and lifted him up, giving him a word of encouragement and asking him to lead the way back to his house. Quickly, Jairus spun around and walked back in the same direction he had come. Jesus followed directly behind him. The parted crowds now came ever closer and pressed us on all sides as we made our way up the narrowing streets. Everyone wanted to touch Jesus and also hoped to get some blessing. Family members brought the crippled, blind, ill, and injured, trying to push them forward to be able to touch or just be in the shadow of Jesus, hoping for healing. Jesus remained focused on his friend Jairus and kept moving forward, not acknowledging the crowd. Hands were everywhere. People called out to the Teacher and to us. The street was narrow, and people pressed us from all sides.

Just then Jesus froze and turned around, so fast everyone took a step back. The people pressing Jesus giving Him some space, partly in shock and fear of what Jesus would do. Jesus looked at the crowd and said, "Who touched my clothes?" This question obviously didn't make any sense since everyone had been touching us and Jesus.

John and I, who were standing next to Jesus, replied, "You see people crowding against you and yet you can ask, 'Who touched me?'" For a second, we thought our Teacher was just angry because of all the people pressing against Him and literally grabbing onto Him, almost crushing us.

I was a bit irritated too and was about to tell everyone what was on my mind. "Back off, everyone! Give us some space! See, you are making even our great Teacher angry!"

Jesus just stood rock still with both hands on His hips. His face was a neutral mask, neither angry nor happy. He was like a teacher who had called out to His students to answer a question and was awaiting a reply. No one dared to make a sound, and heads started to bob around, people looking at each other in curiosity to see who could have possibly offended the Teacher.

Then just in front of Jesus, a woman came forward, walking unsteadily and trembling fearfully. Her clothes were tattered with some dried red stains. Tears streamed down her face as I looked upon her unsteady walk. Her tears weren't ones of fear; they almost looked like tears of joy. A very odd mixture of both fear and joy. She stepped in front of our Teacher, dropped to her knees, and continued to weep on His sandals. She looked up and said, "Master, I have been terribly ill for the last twelve years with uncontrollable bleeding. I have been suffering so long that I lost all hope. I heard of Your healing powers and gathered all the strength I had left remaining in my broken body to journey here to see You today. Just to be in Your presence and touch Your cloak, I knew I would be healed. Look now upon me. I beg Your forgiveness, Master, for touching Your cloak. Look upon me for You have healed me. Have mercy on me, Jesus, and do not take away what You have given me."

The crowd, hearing all this, remained completely silent. Jesus looked down on the weeping woman, and His face turned from the neutral teacher look, melting away. A tear formed in His eye, and with choked compassion in His voice, He softly said, "Daughter, your faith has healed you. Go in peace and be freed from your suffering." He then bent down and grasped the woman's shoulders. He lifted her up and gave her a big hug. Both were weeping for joy.

The crowd turned from silence to a cheerful shout for joy. It was such a loud and instant thunder that it shook me to the core. Many began to weep for joy with the woman and Jesus for her miraculous healing, They called out Jesus's name. "Jesus, thank You! Jesus, thank You! Praise be God for bringing a great Prophet and Healer to us!"

The praising continued, and Jesus settled the crowd down. He again began to make His way up the path, with Jairus leading the way. The crowd once again pressed in on us. Though Jairus was thankful for the woman's healing, the mask of concern never left his face, for his own daughter was dying. The healed woman stayed pinned to Jesus's side, not wanting to leave her Master. Her eyes were still red from tears. There were tears of joy, and the look on her face of complete peace was something I will never forget. I was almost envious of her complete peace and faith in Jesus. I have witnessed all our Teacher's miracles; that is much different from being gravely ill, suffering for years, and then being healed. It's the understanding and feeling of a personal miracle occurring to oneself that is indescribable or nontransferable. Will I also one day be blessed with a miracle from Jesus that will save my life? So that I also may proclaim His greatness, not from just seeing His miracles but also from telling my personal experience of Jesus in my life?

A commotion just up ahead broke my mind's wandering. A few men pushed forward through the packed crowd, and people reluctantly gave way to them. No one wanted to give his or her position away since everyone wanted to be close to Jesus, and the men weren't high in social standing. They made their way through and came to stop in front of Jairus. They were relatives of Jairus. Putting their hands on Jairus's shoulders, they whispered something to him.

Immediately Jairus's face, his mask of concern, changed. His whole body slumped, his head turned down, and his knees gave away. He dropped to the ground, his hands covering his face. Jairus began to weep softly as the men's hands remained on his shoulders to comfort him. One of the men from the house told us, "Jairus's daughter has died." Looking down at Jairus, the man said respectfully, "Why bother the Teacher anymore?" We were next to Jarus and heard and saw everything.

Jesus was deeply distraught while seeing the agony of his friend. Jairus looked up at Jesus, his face now appearing to have aged twenty years in an instant. When he slowly stood up, even his stance now, shaky and hunched over, was that of a man of much older years. Jesus drew close to Jairus and with a soft, confident voice said, "Don't be afraid. Just believe." Their eyes locked.

Jairus slowly stood straighter, his red eyes turning from sorrow to something else. His eyes began to radiate a determination, his lips flatlined like a trained soldier just given an order from his commander. Jesus, never turning His eyes away from Jairus, declared to the crowd to depart. He turned and waved His hands for everyone to go away, even to us, so He might be alone with Jairus. Reluctantly the crowd parted and started to disperse. The once-jubilant crowd, shouting and praising Jesus for the miracle of healing the woman and for the hope and excitement of Jesus's healing powers extending to the daughter of Jairus and to themselves, instantly vanished. Their look was replaced with sorrow and even disappointment that Jesus hadn't been in time to save her. As we all turned to leave, letting Jesus have some alone time with Jairus, He called out and asked that James, James's brother John, and I would remain with them. The other disciples looked a bit confused. Why would the Teacher select only us to stay? No matter; it wasn't time to be hurt with petty squabbles over favoritism due to such a tragedy befalling a respected friend. So they too left with the crowd, most of whom went back to their homes or their jobs; some continued to the house of Jairus to console his relatives. Our band of disciples went on to the house of Jairus.

And then just like that, silence was once again upon us. We were alone with Jairus. Waiting a little more, Jesus spoke something softly to Jairus and motioned him to continue to his house. Jairus turned and started walking, leading us on. His walk and stance weren't those of a defeated man; he had a stride of determination and purpose like when Jesus had first told Jairus to believe. My thoughts went back to that poor widow's son Jesus had raised from the dead just a few months ago in Nain. Would our Teacher once again do an incredible miracle? My palms became sweaty with anticipation and nervousness. I looked at James and John, locking onto their eyes. I knew they were thinking the same thing; their eyes were filled not with sadness anymore but with an expression of wonder. Would Jesus do it again?

We grew excited and fell into line behind Jesus and Jairus as they walked toward the house. As we grew near, just becoming visible in the distance was a small crowd standing outside the house, and we could hear them wailing. As we approached, Jesus called out to the people, "Why all this commotion and wailing? The child is not dead but asleep."

The crowd abruptly stopped and turned to the one calling out to them. Confusion covered their faces. Didn't this man know what had happened here? Some of them appeared to be even offended, since the words were disrespectful. A man's daughter was dead. He was making light of the situation? Some even laughed at the remark and scornfully retorted that the child was dead. Have some respect for the family. They turned to Jairus with an expression as if to say that even if Jesus was supposed to be great a prophet, He had just disrespected Jairus's daughter's death. Why wasn't Jairus also mad at Jesus?

Jairus stood rock solid and silent by Jesus's side, never moving or flinching at their stares or the strange words of Jesus. Jesus then called out for everyone to leave them alone and to depart. The crowd looked at Jairus, and his face said it all. *Do as the Teacher says.* Everyone departed, and we were alone, standing outside the house of Jairus.

The door opened, and Jairus's wife came out, going straight to

Jairus and falling into his outstretched arms in visible agony. She wept uncontrollably. Jairus let her cry and then whispered something softly into her ear. Jairus's wife, like Jairus, had deep respect for Jesus and His teachings. Her sobs lessened and then stopped. Her expression changed from despair and grief to hope. Her lips tightened, and her eyes began to shine and be in sync with Jairus's determined look.

They turned to Jesus, and our Teacher told them to take us to where the child was. Jairus's wife motioned them to go into the house, for the daughter had just died earlier in the day, and she was still lying in her bedroom. Normally, according to our traditions, as soon as a person was dead, his or her eyes were to be closed while being kissed with love. Then the body was washed and anointed with perfume. Nard was the most usual perfume used; myrrh and aloes were also used.

After washing, the body was elaborately wrapped in a shroud, and the face was covered with a special cloth, called a "sudarium." The hands and feet were tied with strips of cloth. The burial was performed the same day, as was the custom; more to the point was that the body rapidly began to decay and smell in our hot climate, making haste an imperative.

We came into the bedroom and saw the child lying peacefully, her hands folded, and her eyes closed. Jairus's wife mentioned that the ceremonial washing and anointing hadn't been done yet since she was waiting for Jairus to come and kiss their daughter, as was the custom. We all approached and surrounded her. Jairus and his wife's brave, determined faces were now cracking a bit, their eyes clearly showing deep sorrow. Their once-firm lips now quavered. Jairus bit his tongue to stave away his lips from trembling.

Jesus then took the child's hand and said to her in a commanding voice, "Talitha koum!" which means, "Little girl, I say to you, get up!" Time stood still for what seemed like an eternity. We all held our breaths; there wasn't a sound in the room. Only complete silence. The air was still, as if all were frozen in time. Waiting. Waiting. Our eyes opened wide and fixed on the child.

Then it happened! The little girl's eyes opened. She sat up, rotated her body, and jumped to the floor to stand up. Confusion filled her face, and she stretched as if she had been in a deep sleep and had just awakened. Jairus and his wife went to her and gave her a big hug. Silence turned to weeping for joy. Jesus had done it again! He had raised another person from the dead. Truly our Teacher was a great prophet, a miracle man, anointed by God Himself. Jesus then told Jairus and His wife not to tell anyone of this great miracle and to give the little girl something to eat. The parents were so grateful to Jesus that they would have done anything He asked.

James, John, and I looked to Jesus with amazement at His power but also with a questioning look. Surely a miracle like this wouldn't stay hidden, for all the community knew the little girl had died, and everyone would come to learn that Jesus had raised her from the dead. This was just one of the many things our Teacher said I would never understand. I could see Jesus's point. He was already so widely known and famous for His healings. There wasn't a place we could go to anymore in peace. A crowd followed us everywhere; towns would hear of Jesus's coming, and thousands would crush us when we arrived. And then there were the Pharisees and other Jewish leaders who plotted against us, always pushing a crowd against us, trying to incite people that Jesus and His band of disciples were heretics and should be punished and stoned. They even spread rumors that now they wanted us dead! We all knew this miracle wouldn't remain hidden, and, looking to Jesus, we knew He knew this as well.

# 13

(Start of Third Year with Jesus, Fall-Winter, AD 30)

# Receiving Power

*The harvest is plentiful, but the workers are few. Ask the Lord of the harvest, therefore, to send out workers into his harvest field.*
—JESUS, THE CHRIST (MATTHEW 9:37-38)

Jesus performed many more miraculous healings that summer and into the fall, continuing from town to town. Healing blind men to a cripple in the town of Bethesda, Jesus continued and infuriated our Jewish leaders more and more. The Teacher never stopped His preaching and healing, even on the Sabbath. As word grew of the healings, we couldn't go anywhere without literally thousands of people following us, shouting the name of Jesus and pushing and shoving each other just to touch a piece of our Teacher's clothes. I could sense that the attention, nonstop preaching, and healings were beginning to take a toll on Jesus.

The weather started to turn colder with winter approaching, and there were even some mornings of frost on the trees and plants. And yet there was no lessening of the crowd. Jesus gathered us together after one of the long days with the multitude. We were still out in the open on a gentle, rocky hillside. Sunlight still bathed the tips of the mountains surrounding the Sea of Galilee. There were no clouds and very little wind. Even the air around us seemed to warm up a bit, making staying a bit longer outside a pleasure. One couldn't ask for a better way to end a long day than perfect temperatures, surrounded by our best friends, and of course being with our great teacher, Jesus. Although Jesus was young, He was so much more than a teacher, a prophet; He was like a father to all of us. We could all feel His deep care and love for us, and we, of course, could never get enough of being around Him. So much wisdom and love He poured out on everyone, and His compassion for the poor, sick, and elderly was so refreshing in a time when everyone cared only about themselves and were beaten down by the punishing rules and taxes of the Romans—not to mention the self-inflected burdens from our own high priests. Between the Romans and Pharisees, there were so many rules and taxes; none could keep up with them all.

Jesus my mind back. He motioned us to gather close, and we closed in on Jesus and all sat down all in from of Him. Jesus too then sat down, facing all of us, and looked into each of our eyes. A penetrating look mixed with great joy in His eyes seemed to twinkle in the refection from the sun. He said to us, "The harvest is plentiful, but the workers are few. Ask the Lord of the harvest, therefore, to send out workers into his harvest field." I was the first to speak up and reply; as usual I spoke without really thinking too much, always saying what was on my mind that instant.

"Yes, Jesus the harvest is plentiful, and there is a lot of food."

Jesus just sat there, looking at us and me with that look of a teacher to his students who don't understand anything the teacher is saying. He gave me the eye twitch, which meant for me to be quiet. And then after a moment of silence, the Teacher then spoke up again and explained that our Father in heaven knew there were so many to teach and heal. It was too much even for Him to keep up with the growing numbers. Jesus motioned us in closer, His twelve disciples, and said He would give us the same authority to drive out impure spirits and heal every disease and sickness. He was giving us the power! Jesus continued, "Do not go among the Gentiles or enter any town of the Samaritans. Go rather to the lost sheep of Israel. As you go, proclaim this message: 'The kingdom of heaven has come near.' Heal the sick, raise the dead, cleanse those who have leprosy, drive out demons. Freely you have received; freely give." He continued, "Take nothing for the journey—no staff, no bag, no bread, no money, no extra shirt. Whatever house you enter, stay there until you leave that town. If people do not welcome you, leave their town and shake the dust off your feet as a testimony against them."

Jesus then stood up and motioned us to stand up as well, calling us forward two by two: my brother Andrew (the first one of us to meet Jesus) and me (with my new name, Peter); the sons of Zebedee, James and John; Phillip and Bartholomew; Thomas and Matthew; James, the son of Alphaeus, and Thaddaeus; and Simon the Zealot and Judas Iscariot. We paired up and formed a line, each pair coming in front of Jesus, and as we approached, Jesus raised His hands. We kneeled. Jesus placed His hands on our heads and said a prayer each time. After the last pair, Simon and Judas, we retired for the night at the house we were staying in and prepared ourselves for the next day; it was the day we would go out, preach, and heal as we had watched Jesus do so many times.

That evening was a solemn evening. We dined all together as usual, sitting around a long table, the mood more reserved. There was less loud talking and joking around. We were all lost in our thoughts over what was to come. We had been together for some time now, and tomorrow we would go our separate ways, in pairs, to do what we had watched our Teacher do. There were mixed feelings of excitement to preach and heal, a bit of sadness from disbanding the team, and a bit of fear. Jesus said that, as we had seen, the authorities would be after us—the Romans, the Pharisees, and the local Jewish leaders. We had to be careful but not hesitant to preach the good news our Teacher had been preaching and to place hands on the ill and the lame to heal them. It was strange at dinner as I looked around. Everyone sat in his or her assigned pairs. Thinking about it, it made sense to me. We would be traveling with our assigned brother while facing uncertain times. Naturally there was much to talk to our partner about. For me it was the same anyway, since I always sat at dinner next to my brother Andrew. Jesus, sensing our thoughts, retired early from dinner to allow us time by ourselves. Jesus often spent a long time after dinner alone, walking or sitting in a garden while praying. He always said it was through prayer to our Father in heaven that we derived all our strength, and He always encouraged us to have that same alone time with God.

After dinner Andrew and I stepped outside to stretch our legs. Sitting down after a long day of standing felt good, but after a long dinner, my legs felt stiff. As we talked, we realized it was almost two years to the date when we had first met Jesus. Andrew had met Him first when he was a disciple of John the Baptist. Shortly afterward, Andrew had come to me excitedly, saying He had met the Messiah. It seemed like such a long time ago. So many things had happened since then, and we had seen so much—from just living day to day and getting by as fishermen with only sadness, bitterness, and despair over the loss of Sarah to a whole new life. I would have never dreamed of giving up fishing, the only thing I knew how to do, to follow and become a disciple of a great prophet, our Messiah. We also realized it was almost one year to the date since Andrew and I had been out on our boat, mending our nets and making repairs, when Jesus called to us to become full-time disciples and leave fishing the waters to become "fishers of men." That phrase didn't hit home to me today, the day when we stopped watching Jesus throw His net and make new disciples. Now He called us to throw our nets out and become "fishers of men."

And now what was next in store for us? From watching Jesus preach and heal, now we too should become teachers and healers, all in a span of two years since the first time we'd met Jesus. It felt a bit overwhelming, and I could see the same thoughts in Andrew's eyes as well as in the eyes of the other ten disciples at dinner tonight.

Sleep didn't come easily that night, and in the morning we all gathered for a light breakfast of bread and some dates, figs, and olives. There was little talk, and we again sat paired together as we had for last night's supper. Each of us was sad that the group was disbanding, even if it was only temporarily, but we were excited to be an active part of our Teacher's ministry. We knew we would see each other in many of the villages where we preached, since there were only so many towns in the region. At last count someone had remarked that there were about 240 villages in the Galilee area. With six pairs of us running around, we were bound to run into each other at some point. And of course, we could also bump into Jesus and the rest of His disciples from time to time. Comforting thoughts.

So we went out two by two into the various villages and towns. There was really no plan of where we were going, how long we would stay in each place, or even whether we would still go together in groups of pairs or our separate ways. At first, as we departed and started walking, James and John came with us just as they had done a year ago when we'd cast our fishing nets for the last time and became full-time disciples of Jesus. It was exciting! After a long morning of walking, we came upon a small village of not more than one hundred people. Even with that small-sized village, there was someone who recognized us since we were in and out of most villages at one time or another. They welcomed us warmly, and we walked to the center of town and began to speak to them about Jesus and His good news of forgiveness and grace by speaking directly to God our Father. We preached that everyone should follow the rules of the Law and that there must be compassion. If someone needed help on the Sabbath, then it was right to help him or her out, even if that meant some work. Some were clearly nervous about our preaching since this was clearly against our Jewish tradition and laws, but the people understood and knew in their hearts that this was right. One of the locals who had an extra room invited us to spend the night with them, and we dined with his family. After dinner they graciously left us alone, and Andrew, John, James, and I were able to talk in private.

It had been a tiring day, having to walk and then speak for long periods about Jesus and His teachings. How did Jesus ever do this every day, all day long? We had just finished part of an afternoon of preaching, and we were completely drained. We had a new appreciation for just how difficult it was, and then we spoke about the other part. We didn't actually come out and try to heal anyone. It was just as Jesus had said, and we did it. We brought nothing with us, preached His teachings, and then we were blessed to have a good meal and a roof over our heads to sleep comfortably. All we needed we were given without having to bring anything with us.

The people in the town who knew about us still listened to us, even without the Teacher around. Some seemed disappointed that they couldn't hear directly from Jesus; they did respect what we had to say and generally were approving—that is, everyone except the Pharisees and the town Jewish leaders. Thankfully they didn't pay much attention to us since Jesus wasn't there. The Jewish leaders didn't pay much attention to us in part because the people had come when they saw us, thinking Jesus was with us, and had brought some of the sick and ill.

That day we didn't do any healing Jesus had said for us to do. It wasn't out of disrespect or unbelief in Jesus. The problem was us, our own hesitancy. Were we capable of performing miracles and healing people just as the Teacher did? We spoke of what Jesus had said about healing the sick, the lame, and the demon possessed. The message was all about true faith in God's presence, love, and power to heal. Jesus had placed His hands on us and told us we had the same power of God He had. We needed only faith to unlock it.

We spent some time in prayer to God for His wisdom, guidance, and strength; then we formulated a plan. Today Andrew and I spoke to the villagers; tomorrow James and John would speak about Jesus and His teachings. Andrew and I would listen and be in prayer. After James and John finished speaking, Andrew and I called out to anyone who was ill, and then we placed our hands on them, and just like Jesus did, we healed him or her in the name of God.

Rest didn't come easily that night since thoughts of the coming day filled my mind. Could we really do what Jesus had asked of us? Did we have the same power as Jesus to heal the sick and the lame? The thoughts continued; eventually I was able to sleep. As unrestful as it was, I was thankful to see the dawn light arise. It was morning, and as I got up from the bed, I heard my other brothers also getting up, and we gathered for a light breakfast. Our hosts were so grateful to have us as their guests, telling us that some time ago Jesus had come to the village and healed the host's son, who'd had a high fever for many days. We ate light that morning, just bread since we were too nervous to eat a larger meal.

After breakfast the four of us gathered together and prayed to God for wisdom, discernment, a glad heart, and a humble spirit. We prayed that as we went out to preach the good news of Jesus, we would do so out of true love, wanting to share without any pretense of any of the words and actions being from us. All praise and thankfulness went to God, and we were only vessels, conduits of Jesus's teachings about our God.

It was a bright and sunny morning with a crisp, soft breeze. A few puffy, pure, white, oval-shaped clouds hovered over the lake. There were exactly four clouds clustered together; I looked up and remarked that this was another sign from God that He was blessing the four of us today. And as I said that, the others looked up, and I could have sworn I saw a flash of light twinkle in the middle of the clouds. It definitely put us in a charged-up mood full of hope for what could be coming that day.

As we walked toward the square, about twenty or so people met us in the town center. Like a typical Galilean town, the streets were narrow with houses fronting right up to the edges of the roads. In the center of the town was an open area with some shops and the community water well. This particular town was nearer to the shore, and from the town center I could see the sun glistening off the shimmery waters and our four clouds still hovering above as if they were quietly watching over us. This town was a bit atypical since most towns were more elevated and in areas where it was more difficult for bandits or others to access. However, this was a fishing village, and the people needed to be close to the sea.

Like we planned, James and John spoke for about an hour, retelling some of the parables we had learned from Jesus. The people were happy to hear us. In the back a couple of the local leaders stood silent and stony faced the entire time, not entirely with an angry look probably because the crowd was a bit small; and Jesus wasn't with us. What harm could four unlearned fishermen do? Many of the villagers heard us yesterday and didn't return this morning.

As James and John spoke, I noticed a young boy in the crowd who had red eyes and a damp cloth over his head. He was leaning on his father with unsteady legs. The sun was shining and the day warming, but he was still shivering as if it were about to snow. He was in pain, and the crowd gave them a good amount of space since no one wanted to be close to the boy who was obviously diseased. Many people had passed away recently; with the changing weather came sudden and grave sickness, especially from the young boys who tended to stay out too late, not dressing for the cold or sudden rains.

I whispered to Andrew and pointed toward the boy. Just as John and James finished the last parable, Andrew and I walked to the boy and his father. The crowd, seeing us, gathered around us. Both Andrew and I placed our hands on the boy's head. His father, weeping, told us this was his only son and that he had caught the fever over a week ago, and it was getting worse. Unsteadily at first, his father helped his son to kneel, our hands never leaving the child's head. I then said a prayer and thanked Jesus, our Teacher, for His wisdom and guidance. Then I said, "In the name of Jesus I call out to our Father God in heaven to heal this young child of his illness. Be healed my son and have faith that it is our

God in heaven that has restored your health." The crowd was completely silent, all looking intently. Did the disciples of Jesus have the power to heal? Nothing appeared to be happening; the child was still shaking with fever. My hands and Andrew's never left the boy's head, and we continued in prayer.

Slowly the boy stopped his shaking, his pale, pasty face started to turn a shade of pink, and his sweating lessened. Most of all it was his eyes. They turned from bright-red bloodshot eyes back to a light blue. Unsteadily at first, the young boy rose, his arms locked on with his father's arm. Then he let go, gave a joyous squeal, and started to dance around his father as if he'd never been sick. The crowd erupted in shouts of joy. The crowd of ten multiplied tenfold in an instant as the news spread like wildfire that the disciples of Jesus had the power of healing. James and John came to us, and the four of us began to lay hands on the lame and sick lining up before us, always giving all praise and honor to Jesus and the God of our fathers. Our hands, the conduit of God through faith, healed all who came before us. Sometimes the healing was easy, and it took only moments to heal, and at other times we learned that the four of us had to join hands and pray as one to heal. Praying sometimes all morning, all together, we sweated and shook, calling out God's name, calling on our Teacher Jesus, calling for the crowds themselves to get down on their hands and knees, and shout out to God. And they did. Hundreds of people were on their knees, their hands on others' shoulders, encircling us with the sick in the center. Four unschooled fishermen were clothed in simple garments, with no possessions, formal education in the Jewish texts, or training in medicine, yet here we were, conduits of the almighty God, healing the sick, lame, and demon possessed through faith and faith alone.

At the end of the day, we were exhausted. My throat hurt from shouting prayers all day, and I had a bit of a headache. I looked at James, John, and Andrew, and their faces told me they were feeling the same exhaustion. And yet in our weariness we locked arms once more, not to heal anyone but to give thanks to Jesus for the day. We closed our eyes and prayed for a few moments. A cool wind came upon us and seemed to flush out our weariness, and our headaches lessened. Opening our eyes, we saw before us a blanket with a pitcher of water, bread, and a few cooked fish. The villagers had respectfully laid out the food and departed, leaving us with some time to rest and eat. We ate in silence, happy to sit, drink, and eat. It was John who spoke up first and said, "Hey, Peter, your head looks a little bigger. Do you want me to lay hands on you to bring you back down to earth with us mere mortals? Lord, save Peter so that his head doesn't grow too fat and explode with pride!"

That gave us all a big laugh. God, forgive me! At the end of the day, before the crowd left, some of the people were slapping me on the shoulder, thanking me, and for an instant I "forgot" to tell them it was all from Jesus and God. John, James, and Andrew were right next to me; and they all gave me that "look." Of course, I then shouted to the departing that it was through Jesus and God that the healing had taken place and not from us. It was a bit late, an afterthought, and the guys weren't about to let me get away that easily from my brief mental lapse.

Through the winter months, we continued, the four of us; at times we broke apart for a few days. James and John, and Andrew and I went to neighboring villages to share the good news and to heal. At times we came into a village to be pleasantly surprised and to see some of our other twelve brothers. It was like a mini reunion, and we filled our souls with shared stories of God's power. I asked whether anyone had bumped into Jesus in the villages, and curiously they all said no. It was as if Jesus knew where we all were and was leaving us to continue His mission works so we could grow in faith.

As we met more and more people, preaching the words of Jesus and healing, I felt my faith in Jesus grow more and more. Who was this great Teacher, this Prophet who preached forgiveness and hope, and spoke as if He knew God Himself? We all had faith in God, but Jesus was different. He talked as if He really did speak with God and God spoke to Him. It was a real father-son relationship. And who could deny the power of Jesus to heal? And even more amazing was that He had given this healing ability to us, His twelve apostles. Who had that kind of power? Thoughts such as these rolled around in my head more often than not; I kept these thoughts to myself. I was sure the others were having the same questions.

Winter turned to spring, and we were still on the road, carrying nothing with us except a change of clothes and some small personal items; all fit into a small sack. One evening as we sat to dine with our current host, a young man with a small parchment message arrived at the house. I read the message aloud to Andrew, John, and James; and we all at once yelled a loud "Hallelujah!" Our host came running from the other room with great concern on this face, thinking terrible news had arrived; as soon as he entered the room, he saw our faces and relaxed at once. There was no distress or fear on our faces. Quite the opposite. We were overjoyed! We immediately went to our host and told him the good news. After months of being on the road, Jesus had sent for all of us to gather and continue our mission together again as one group. The team was getting back together again with the Teacher. And where was this reunion to happen? Of course, Jesus couldn't have picked a better place. It was to be in my hometown of Capernaum at my house.

We were so excited. It was hard to sleep that night. Jesus wanted all of us to make way as soon as the message was received, so we planned to leave the next morning. It would take a couple of days to get there from our current place. Our host was also very excited and wanted to come with us on our journey back so he could meet Jesus. He said he had heard Jesus speak once but couldn't get near Him since the crowd was too large. We were more than happy to have our host, who had given so much to us freely, that opportunity we too longed to have: to be near Jesus, our great Teacher and Prophet. Our host lit up with the biggest smile I have ever seen, and he rushed quickly to tell his wife and children about the good news. Until that moment I knew of the impact Jesus had had on my life and the lives of my fellow apostles; we saw our host tell his family and then watched them weep uncontrollably with joy at the mere prospect of being able to meet Jesus. Their response hit me hard, and James, John, Andrew, and I also began crying tears of joy and awe at this purest scene. Finally, I was beginning to understand the impact Jesus was having on people, one of hope, love, forgiveness, and grace instead of rules and punishment. These were the teachings of our God, who loved and cared for us without the need for sacrifice.

# 14
## Faith

*All of my mind and body was focused on his command to come over to him on the black waters. And then it happened. Nothing! My feet didn't sink. I was standing on the water the same as Jesus!*
—SHI'MON BAR JONAH (PETER)

Spring was a beautiful time of the year, especially in the Galilee area. Flowers were beginning to bloom, and all the area was a blanket of green from the winter rains. The temperature was also warming up. The weather was still cool in the mornings, but it quickly warmed up as the sunshine blanketed the skies. And as if the heavens knew we were on a journey, the days of walking to Capernaum were bright and sunny, with only a few clouds with a gentle breeze. We couldn't have asked for better conditions, and so our little band made our way through a few smaller villages, the hosts' family happily keeping up with us. Our pace was a little faster than normal, and Andrew mentioned to me several times to slow down since our new family was having a hard time keeping up with us, even though they had brought along a couple of donkeys to carry their supplies, and the young children took turns riding them to keep up the pace. "Okay, okay, Andrew. We do need to slow down some. We will get there soon enough." We all felt the excitement of the gathering.

With the good weather and thankfully a host in every village to give us a place to stay and dinner, we made it to Capernaum in three days. I asked our former host family to stay with us at my home in Capernaum; they respectfully said they had relatives there and would stay with them.

Perhaps that was for the best. My house was big since it would be filled with all twelve of us and Jesus. I say "big"; my house was just slightly larger than other houses, with four small rooms clustered together and doors that faced an open inner courtyard. The courtyard was open with no roof and generally served as a place where meals were cooked and in times of good weather where we would have our meals. The rooms were made of stone walls with wooden beams supporting a slightly pitched roof. The roof was weatherproof and sturdy enough that sometimes during the hot summer nights we went up and slept there. Rainwater flowed off the roof and collected into cisterns we kept for drinking and cooking water. Two rooms were adjoined side by side and faced each other separated by the courtyard. The courtyard was then enclosed by walls on each side, with each wall having a large double door. A good-sized house and too big just for me. My mind flickered back to what might have been if Sarah had still been there with me. My momentary thoughts were interrupted by my host calling out to me. We arrived at his relative's house.

As we passed through Capernaum, we first stopped at the host's relative's house. At his entrance doorway, we said our thanks again for his hospitality and his faith in our Teacher. Striding on, we made our way toward the sea and my house. "A fisherman's house is always near the water," or so that is what my father always said, and that is what I did many years ago in acquiring a house by the sea. And now I am still a fisherman, but as Jesus said, we were now "fishers of men." I always liked that about Jesus. He always knew how to explain things to us in ways we could understand and relate to.

By the time we got to the house, it was late afternoon, and my belly was rumbling. Not wanting to waste more time, we rose early that morning and didn't stop walking except for a few short rests (and restroom breaks). No large breakfast or any lunch; we ate dried dates for energy as we walked. My eyes spied smoke wafting from the inner courtyard, and as it almost lazily drifted on a gentle breeze toward us, my nose perked up, and my belly began to grumble. It was the best smell one could ever encounter, the smell of fish cooking on the open flame. In the background, a softer scent of the ocean was there, a bit of a salty, seaweed smell that signaled open waters nearby. Our walk turned into a trot.

James and John raced ahead, obviously smelling the fish as I did, and they banged on the door. No answer. James and John banged again and yelled, "Friends, it's James, John, Andrew, and Peter. Let us in." We heard a small latch click, and our hearts grew big with anticipation—and not only of the fish; there was much anticipation to see our fellow friends and Jesus. It had been so many months since we were last together. But the door didn't open. Instead it was the small latched window in the door. The voice on the other side softly said, "James, John, and Andrew, we know. But who is this Peter fellow?"

*Argh.* I jumped forward. "Is that you, Bartholomew? It is I, Shi'mon, the owner of this house! Let us in!"

Silence for a second, and then a booming reply came: "What is the password, Shi'mon, the Rockman?"

"Password? Password? What is he talking about?"

Just then a small cooked fish appeared in the door hole. "Bet you want some of this, eh?" Laughter erupted from inside, and the door opened. There, standing at attention, were our other fellow eight apostles (Phillip; Bartholomew; Thomas; Matthew, the tax collector; James, the son of Alphaeus (James A.); Thaddaeus; Simon the Zealot; and Judas Iscariot). They lined up on either side, making a corridor. Mary was with them, and at the very end in the center was Jesus. Everyone bowed, and Jesus said, "Welcome, Shi'mon, Peter, the Rock, owner of this fine house, and our fellow friends."

We all spit out a big laugh. Jesus, if you didn't know, liked to have fun since that was His ever-positive personality. Sometimes I do think His fun came at my expense. Jesus walked up to us and gave us warm hugs. His smile said it all. Together again at last! We all embraced. And Matthew and John even shed some tears of joy. It was so good to see everyone again. It was great to be all together. I had forgotten all the laugher and joy that came from being part of a bigger group.

I had especially missed Mary's big smiles and laughter; she always filled anyplace she went with her energy, kindness, and positive personality. Most women were reserved, and we all mused that Mary must have grown up with a lot of brothers since she was always at ease with us, treating us all like we were family. Mary had been with us for some time now after Jesus healed her of a grave illness torturing her mind and body. Mary was a common name for Jewish women, so we called her based on the city where she'd come from, Magadan (which means "tower"), a small fishing village on the western shore of the Sea of Galilee bordering the town of Dalmanutha. It wasn't at all far from my hometown of Capernaum, just a half-day walk.

One thing for sure: at first, she didn't like to be called Mary Magadan. I thought it was because she resented something about Magadan; we came to learn later that she didn't like the name because it wasn't pretty. One of our group (I forgot who it was, most likely Andrew or John), called her Mary Magdalene once, and the name stuck. Mary liked it since it had meaning, "her prophet," and yet a very nice sound to it. There and then our Mary Magdalene was born. She had always been there with us since we traveled from town to town, and she and several other women helped us with finances.

We never directly asked; it seemed that Mary had come from a wealthy background and had no trouble helping out. I learned later, as we were all talking, that when Jesus had split us up into pairs to go out and preach Jesus's teachings, Mary had gone with Thomas and Matthew. The arrangement made sense since Mary helped with our finances, and Matthew had a strong background with numbers (at least he was great in taking others' money). That was a fun jab at Matthew; we often teased him some about his unsavory past. Matthew always took the jabs well since we had come to love him, and he could feel the genuine love and respect we had for him for radically changing his ways. And we kind of grew to like the reformed bad boy image of our group, which showed grace was open to all, not just to the righteous.

That night was one I will always remember. The weather was perfect, not too cold, with no breeze. We sat outside on a long table and had such a spread of food as if we were at a large wedding party. There was of course the open-fire wood-cooked fish for the main course; we also had beans, lentils, grain bread with honey from bees, and thickened juices from grapes. Other tasty items set before us were frog legs, snails, live oysters, and some locusts as well. My favorite way to eat locusts was to cook it rapidly in salt water; that gave them a shrimplike taste and color. The other way was to sun-dry them, then grind them down to a powder, which tasted rather bitter. Mixing it with flour made a bitter biscuit. I put some fish into the biscuit, and the combination of slight bitterness with the white fish was heavenly. There were also plates of roasted walnuts, almonds, and pistachios we had to munch on while we drank wine.

We talked late into the night, and I didn't think it was possible, but we nearly finished all the food. There were so many stories to tell Jesus about our works over the last few months of preaching and healings. Jesus took it all in like a proud teacher of His students, never interrupting us to give us more advice or tips. He simply wanted to hear our stories and learn how the people reacted.

I slept well that night. Being on the road for so many months had been very exciting, and we'd learned so much—not only about getting comfortable preaching to large crowds but also about having faith in our Teacher's power. He'd given us authority to heal, and by faith and prayer people had been healed. We had to have faith that we would always be taken care of as we walked with nothing except what we could carry with us. We had to have that constant faith every day. Not knowing what tomorrow would bring or where we would be, or whether we would have a place to stay or enough to eat, did make us anxious from time to time, and there were a lot of restless nights while thinking about it all. However, here in my house, surrounded by friends and of course with Jesus, I fell asleep and had such a rest I hadn't enjoyed in months.

"Shi'mon, Shi'mon." I heard my name, softly at first; then the voice grew loud. A hand gripped my shoulder, and I slowly opened my eyes to my brother Andrew. "Shi'mon, it's nearly midmorning, and we have things to do, Brother."

I got up slowly, wiping away the fuzziness from a deep rest and washing my face with water to remove the last vestiges of sleep. We all gathered in the courtyard, and Jesus began to teach us more parables, always emphasizing the need to show compassion and grace to everyone, since our Father in heaven wanted our minds, spirits, and love for Him. And He wanted us to equally care for others. Sacrifices, rituals, and rules came at a distant second to love, forgiveness, and grace. These were at the core of Jesus's teachings, and we never got tired of hearing about them. Just then a banging on the front door disturbed Jesus midsentence. He waved to me to see who was there.

There was something different. Jesus's face changed from His teaching mode. The enthusiastic half smile He wore whenever He taught changed to one of concern and almost sadness. I quickly moved to the door, first asking who it was, since one never knew who could be there. We were quickly gaining as many enemies as followers. The familiar voices on the other side of the door lifted my heart, since they were from dear friends of ours, fellow followers of John the Baptist.

Unlocking the door, I opened it with a huge smile. Andrew was by my side, as were James and John, with the same excitement when seeing our brothers; our smiles evaporated instantly when we saw their solemn faces. Excitement turned instantly to dread as they slowly shuffled in and embraced us with faces of pain. There were seven of them, and, shuffling their heavy feet to the center of the courtyard where Jesus and the rest of our group were, they told the story of how our dearest brother John the Baptist had died, beheaded by command of Herod himself.

It had been common knowledge that John was in prison at the order of Herod, because of Herodias, his brother Philip's wife, whom he had married. John had told Herod, "It is not lawful for you to have your brother's wife." So Herodias held a grudge against John and constantly complained to Herod, finally making him arrest John and put him in prison. Herod never executed John, not even at the request of Herodias, since Herod feared John and protected him, knowing him to be a righteous and holy man.

The disciples of John told us the story of Herod's birthday. He had given a banquet for his high officials, military commanders, and the leading men of Galilee. When the daughter of Herodias came in and danced, she pleased Herod and his dinner guests. The king said to the girl, "Ask me for anything you want, and I'll give it to you." He promised her with an oath, "Whatever you ask I will give you, up to half my kingdom."

She said to her mother, "What shall I ask for?"

"The head of John the Baptist," her mother answered.

At once the girl hurried to the king with the request. "I want you to give me right now the head of John the Baptist on a platter." Herod was greatly distressed, however, because of his oaths and his dinner guests; he didn't want to refuse her. So he immediately sent an executioner with orders to bring John's head. The man went, beheaded John in the prison, and brought back his head on a platter. He presented it to the girl, and she gave it to her mother. The body of John was given back to the disciples at Herod's order, and they buried him in a tomb.

We were shocked and saddened, but this news wasn't completely unexpected. We knew Herod would have a hard time getting John released since his wife was so opposed to John; no one, however, thought he would be killed. Such is the way of human nature; evil will find a way into weak men's hearts, and yet the shock of it hit us hard. John was no longer with us. He had been the beginning of our movement, the initial cry calling on us to repent, to clear our hearts and minds, and to make way for the coming of the one who would save us all. There wasn't a person in the courtyard, including Jesus, whom John hadn't baptized. We all laid hands on each other's shoulders as Jesus said a prayer for John that he may finally be at rest with God, our Father, in heaven. His years of preaching, teaching, and suffering were now over; his work was finished, and finally he had eternal peace. We all knew John, but none were more distraught than Jesus. He stepped away and told us He wanted some time alone while walking out of the courtyard and along the shoreline.

Returning just a little later, Jesus said He needed to get away for a few days from the town and people to be able to reflect and pray better. We went to the boat and made ready to sail, thinking that by traveling by boat, no one would know where we were headed. Whenever we walked from village to village, there was always a large following. Heading just east, we could sail to isolated areas quickly. Unfortunately, today the winds weren't quite in our favor, and it took much longer than I thought it would. A few complained that we could have walked faster. Yeah, yeah. No one is ever happy.

After some time, Jesus pointed out a nice shoreline. It was near Bethsaida, and it was a good place to stop, since there were no villages near the shoreline. It was late afternoon by the time we arrived. The depth of the water was a nice, gradual slope, and we could get very close to shore to drop anchor. The shoreline itself gradually sloped upward and crested; beyond that the terrain sloped down so we couldn't see what was beyond, but I knew the area well, and it was a large plane of grasslands that eventually sloped up again, climbing to the mountains beyond.

The sun was still out with just a few clouds; the wind was gentle.

It was a perfect, quiet place for Jesus, since He wanted to be away from everything. Matthew, Judas, and Simon were first off the boat, with Mary not far behind, making their way to the top of the shoreline slope to see what was on the other side. Or so that is what they said. Actually, I don't think it was curiosity that got them off the boat so quickly. None of them spent a lot of time on boats since they weren't in the fishing business, and in spite of my boat, as big as it was and as calm a day as today was, there was still a lot to get used to with the constant rocking of the boat. We often teased Simon "the zealot" when he got a bit too loud and pushy on his radical views of change. He would say, "We need to get up off our butts and do it."

I would then reply, "Let's do it, Simon! We will prepare the boat and leave at once."

Simon usually came back and said in a softer tone, "Hold on there. I was thinking, *How about taking the shoreline route so we can meet more people?*" Yeah, right, the shoreline route! It always gave us a bit of laughter.

"Come quickly!" I heard Simon shouting and waving his arms at us from the top of the shoreline crest. Was there something wrong? We all hurried off the boats and made the climb up to the top, and it was the most amazing thing I've seen. There before us must have been at least five thousand people! They must have been following our boat from the shoreline. We were going slowly enough—that's for sure. So much for Jesus's quiet time.

As I looked at Jesus, His face wasn't one of dismay at not having time to reflect and pray. He looked energized, and we all felt it too. The people were with us! This was no small gathering in a village of a few hundred curious people. There were now thousands before us wanting to hear the words of our Teacher and to heal the sick and lame. Jesus was instantly charged up, and He went to the crowd and immediately went into teaching and healing. This went on for the better part of the day, and it was getting late.

Mary mentioned to Jesus that the people needed to leave to get back to the villages since it was a long walk, and no one had eaten all day. Jesus faced Mary and the rest of us and said, "They do not need to go away. You give them something to eat." I looked around to see whether Jesus was talking to someone behind us, since He knew we hadn't brought much with us. I answered Jesus, "We have here only five loaves of bread and two fish." The Teacher replied, "Bring them here to me." Judas ran back to the boat and returned with two baskets; one had the fish, and the other had bread. Jesus took the two baskets and told everyone to sit down. There was complete silence since all five thousand people sat down and looked intently at the Teacher. He took the five loaves of bread, broke them up in the basket, and held up the basket of bread in both arms. Lifting it up, He gave thanks to our Father in heaven for the bread brought before us. Putting the basket down, He lifted the basket of fish and gave the same thanks. Turning to us, Jesus told us to start taking the bread and fish out of the baskets and give them to the people. Well, this was going to be fast. Five loaves of bread and two fish would take one of us only a moment to give it away.

Mary put her hands in the basket of broken loaves and passed it on to the person next to her. The basket then went back down, and the process repeated. John did the same with the basket of two fish. And to my, and everyone else's, amazement, they keep bringing out pieces of bread and fish. This kept going on and on. Judas and a few others raced back to the boat and brought back more empty baskets, placing fish and loaves of bread in them from the other miracle baskets. Jesus said a prayer over the baskets and gave them to us—and it was the same! We put our hands in the baskets and gave out the fish and bread, and the baskets never went empty. We did this until all five thousand had received some bread and fish, and we still had bread and fish left in the baskets. Truly Jesus could perform unlimited miracles. He healed the ill and lame; now He could even call to God to miraculously create food to feed thousands. Deep down inside me, I began to realize in my heart that with Jesus nothing was impossible. He seemed to have direct communication with God, and God gave to Jesus power and authority.

Sunlight was getting dimmer now as early evening started to set in. Jesus told the crowd to go back home to their villages, and turning to us, He told us to get on the boat and meet Him back in Capernaum. Our land-loving crew asked Jesus whether they could walk with Him, obviously trying not to get back on the boat, especially looking up at the darkening sky. This wasn't just due to the end of the day coming; there were dark, heavy clouds breaking over the mountains to the east, and the wind started to change from a light breeze to something stronger and more foreboding. Jesus put them off and said to stay together. Andrew, John, James, and I, who were the most seasoned fishermen, started to ready the boat for bad weather. Everyone else on board looked at us with some apprehension and looked to Jesus, who was now walking away in the distance.

Thomas and Judas spoke up. "Shi'mon, I don't think it's wise for us to be on the sea tonight. The weather is turning bad. We could all be killed out here." I was about to say something when Mary spoke up.

"Jesus told us to get on the boat and meet us in Capernaum. You've seen the power of our Teacher. He wouldn't tell us to do something that would bring us harm. We must trust in His power." There were a few grumbles from Thomas and Judas, but Mary put them in their place. I couldn't have said it better myself. Mary turned to Andrew and gave us that look that said, "Don't mess it up, guys. We're counting on you." No pressure, just everyone's lives our hands.

As we set sail, it soon became apparent that the storm clouds we'd seen in the fading light in the mountains were now moving much faster than we had thought, fully engulfing us in their black inkiness. The winds picked up and changed from a strong breeze to a whirlwind. Lashing rain hit us; it was so powerful that we had to take down the sail lest it tear off the mast, and then we would be truly unable to get back to shore.

The boat started to move wildly from side to side as the waves seemly hit us from all directions. Larger and larger waves were coming into our boat; blackness all around was broken only by a few lamps we had tied to the mast. I lost track of how long we were out on the water, our concentration and fear solely focused on keeping the boat afloat. At one point I began to rethink Mary's words from before. "We must believe in Jesus's power; we will be okay." Surely Jesus wouldn't forsake us. The intense storm brought me back to that horrible time so many years ago when I'd lost my life, my Sarah. So much loss. So much pain. I didn't ever think there would be a tomorrow after that terrible period of loneliness and sadness. Now we had Jesus. I had Jesus in my life, and my fellow brothers and sisters surrounded me with love. We had a mission, Jesus's mission of hope, love, and grace. My thoughts were interrupted by shouts from Bartholomew and Thaddeus. "Look there is something out there on the water!"

I cursed myself for letting my thoughts drift off. *Get with it, Shi'mon. You are on the sea and in a storm! One false decision or moment of indecision could spell disaster.*

Thomas shouted, "It's a ghost! We are all going to die!"

"No!" Mary yelled. "It's not a ghost!"

"It's Jesus!"

It was so hard to see. The wind and rain were blowing so hard. Our boat rocked back and forth. Waves crashed over the sides, and our dim lights barely reached beyond the tip of the boat to illuminate the dark waters beyond. Lightning flashed, illuminating the sky every other moment, temporarily giving light to the darkness but also blinding us with its intensity. It was clear that something, someone was out there. We were still far from shore, so how this could be?

Then Thomas yelled, "Praise God! It is Jesus! He has come to save us!" I looked harder through the whipping rain. It was Jesus, and He wasn't on a boat. He was walking on the water!

Lightning kept flashing, and thunder roared so loudly my ears hurt. In the flashes of lightning, I could see His face. About a few boat lengths away, He stood there with an absolutely calm look. And then He lifted His right hand and extended it toward us. Toward *me*! It was then that I heard His words as clear as day. I will never forget them for the rest of my life. It was almost as if time itself had stopped. I no longer heard or felt the wind, the rain, the crashing waves, or the thunder. All was calm; there was no noise, except for the words of Jesus. Looking directly at me, the Teacher said, "Come." And as if I were in a dream, I moved forward on the boat.

I could hear Mary and the others yelling at me. "Shi'mon, what are you doing?" I got to the front of the boat and eased my body over the side, touching one foot on the raging waters and then the other. The others were so shocked by my actions; they were all frozen in place.

My gaze never left the sight of Jesus. All my mind and body were focused on His command to come over to Him on the black, rolling waters.

And then it happened. My feet didn't sink. I was standing on the water the same way as Jesus! Fixed on His gaze, I stepped forward, breaching the gap between me and our Teacher, our Prophet. It was Andrew's voice that shattered my concentration.

"Shi'mon! Peter!"

I stopped for an instant and looked back. The boat was a dim light in the background now. A flash of lightning illuminated the sky, and I saw how far away I was from the boat and the frightened faces staring back at me in shock of the miracle before them. I was walking on water.

And just for a moment, my total concentration on Jesus was broken, and I thought of the impossibility of what I was doing. I hesitated for a moment. Then all went black. Enveloped in the angry sea, my whole body was numbed by the cold waters. I was under the water and drowning! My chest felt like it was about to explode, and my uncontrollable gasping for air just brought in more water into my already-burning lungs. My last thought before I went unconscious was, "Jesus, save me!"

I felt a warmth over my whole body and then a burning sensation in my eyes. The light was so bright. Was I dead? Was I in some horrible nightmare? My throat hurt, and my mouth felt like I had just eaten a handful of salt. Gasping for breath and coughing uncontrollably, I bolted my head up. Everything was hazy, and then as I wiped my eyes and gained some control of my senses of the surroundings, I found myself lying on the shore. The aroma of burning wood and cooking fish was a smell close to heaven. After a few more moments to get my thoughts back, I looked around, and concerned but relieved faces were looking back at me. I was alive! Jesus placed His hand on my shoulder. "Peter, you of little faith. Why did you doubt?"

Giving me that look of a disappointed teacher, He then gave me a warm smile. It was truly a great morning, and a breakfast of fish and bread was one of the best I had ever had. And that cool drink of water down my raw throat—I will never forget it. Andrew, Matthew, James, Mary, and the others were all talking about it as we ate. It was no dream. We were on the boat in a huge storm, and Jesus was walking on the water. And I also walked on the water for a few moments. My mind was reeling from the thought. *What does this mean? How powerful is Jesus? Does His power have no limits so that, having absolute faith in Him, we can do whatever He says we can do?*

There were so many questions in my mind; the power of Jesus was undeniable, and His words were those of pure truth. We continued from there with Jesus; all of us were together again, learning again about more parables, more teachings, and being witness to more and more miracle healings. All the while Jesus's teachings were directly an affront to our Jewish leaders, slamming them for their hypocrisy of traditions. As Jews we had so many rules. Even before we ate, there were rules on how we were to wash our hands, including the washing of cups, pitchers, kettles; and the list went on and on.

On one occasion, some Jewish leaders caught us for eating without washing our hands. Jesus's response to them was a tirade of how the Jewish leaders chose to hold or break our traditions when it suited them; however, we, as the people, did not have those same allowances. Jesus said, "For Moses said honor your mother and father, … but you [the Pharisees] say that if anyone declares what might have been used to help their father or mother is instead given to God then you [the Pharisees] no longer let them do anything for their mother or father." He went on to say in our defense, "Nothing outside a person can defile them by going into them. Rather, it is what comes out of a person that defiles them." So many great teachings by Jesus were so simple, simple enough once Jesus explained them to us.

We often asked the Teacher at night when we were eating dinner alone way from the crowds to explain the parables to us. Often Jesus gave us an exasperated moan and called us names. I think He liked to use words such as *dull*; He did so lovingly though, I would say, as a parent to his or her child, who just didn't ever quite get what the parents was trying to teach him or her. Oh well. You had to have a bit of a thick skin around Jesus since He didn't tolerate fools, and we were often a bunch of them. We did remind Jesus that He had picked us, so we were *His* fools. That always gave Him a smile and a big laugh from all of us.

The summer passed with all of us together walking from town to town; Jesus preached His good news. More and more people followed us; interestingly enough, the crowd was a mix of Jews and Gentiles. Although Jesus specifically taught to save our people (the Jews), His teachings were so full of wisdom, compassion, and grace that the Gentiles were there, wherever we were, in the hundreds.

We traveled around the Galilee area only as we heard news from our fellow followers in Judea that our Jewish leaders in Jerusalem wanted to arrest Jesus as well as His most devout disciples. We were gaining so many followers that our leaders felt even more threatened by Jesus and His radical teachings of grace and forgiveness over rules. The summer was passing quickly, and the Feast of the Tabernacles, the Sukkot, was fast approaching. One of our big three temple pilgrimage holidays (Shelosh Regalim), it was celebrated on the fifteenth day of the seventh month (Tishrei) and required all Jewish peoples to gather at the temple in Jerusalem for festivities and ritual worship with the temple priests (Kohanim). We gathered to remember God's provision in the wilderness and to look forward to that promised messianic age when all nations would flow to this city to worship the Lord.

I especially loved the Sukkot, since it was a celebration for everyone, Jews and Gentiles. On this holiday the Gentile nations were also invited to come to Jerusalem to worship the Lord at this "appointed time." The Lord had told Moses to gather all men, women, and children along with the foreigners in their land so they could learn to fear the Lord. When Solomon later dedicated the temple at Sukkot, he asked the Lord to hear the prayers of any foreigners who would come there to pray. It was a time for everyone.

Jerusalem filled with people from all over the region. The sights, sounds, and smells of all kinds of foods were amazing. It was a time to remember our ancestors during the Exodus, traveling for forty years like nomads, living in temporary houses made from whatever they could find, and being totally dependent on our Lord God to provide for all their needs. The name of the festival, Sukkot, or the booth/tabernacle, commemorated the temporary structure our ancestors lived in. During the festival the whole city of Jerusalem was filled with these small, temporary booths. Many of them were adorned with colorful fruit, ribbons, and pictures. We were supposed to live in the makeshift huts for the eight days of the festival, but they were so small that very few actually did it. Some families ate their meals in the "sukkot" and even slept there at night.

It was a time to remember our past and to look forward to the future. It was a time to look forward to the day of the coming of the Messiah.

Zechariah had foretold of a time when all nations would ascend to Jerusalem each year to "worship the King, the Lord of hosts, and to keep the Feast of Tabernacles."

It was a dangerous time for us to go to Jerusalem with the chief priests looking for us. Would we go? If we didn't, what did that say about our Teacher, Jesus? If we didn't go, did that mean He wasn't our promised Messiah? For surely the Feast of the Tabernacles was made especially for the one who would deliver us from our misery and suffering and lead us into a new Jewish kingdom.

My thoughts were interrupted by some men pushing forward through the crowd, approaching us, approaching Jesus. As they drew near, my racing heart calmed. For a second, I thought it was the Jewish guards from Jerusalem coming to arrest us. The approaching men were the brothers of Jesus: James, Joses (we also called him Joseph sometimes), Jude (we also called him Judas), and Simon. Jesus and his brothers got along fairly well. They weren't followers of Jesus like we were, but they were witnesses of many of Jesus's miracle healings and believed He had special powers. Somehow their beliefs in Jesus didn't run as deep, and they weren't "followers of Jesus."

Jesus and His brothers embraced with warm hugs and spoke for some time about how they were doing as well as His sisters and His mother, Mary. Jesus was always asking especially about His mother. It hadn't been an easy life for her after Jesus's father, Joseph, died those many years ago. Mary had remained strong, and all the brothers rallied to support the family. Jesus always saw the sadness in His mother's eyes. The days and nights were long without Joseph by her side. I wonder sometimes whether Jesus questioned why God would take away His father so early in His life and make life so hard on His mother. Mary was always so positive, a beacon of hope and love. Why would God bring such tragedy to her life? As for me, I hadn't lived such a good life and could understand why God had punished me by taking Sarah way from me. But Mary? She'd lived a perfect life of humbleness, sacrifice, and love. I also wondered sometimes whether Jesus's brothers, who had seen the miracles of Jesus, somehow held them against Jesus. With all His powers of healing, why had Jesus not healed His father? They never directly asked Jesus this question; for myself I would have asked Him.

I was close to Jesus and His brothers as they spoke. The brothers were on their way to the festival and came to town to ask Jesus to join them. The festival of the Tabernacles was one of the pilgrim feasts when Jewish males were commanded to go to Jerusalem. It was also the time when we brought tithes and offerings to the temple.

I heard one of Jesus's brothers say to Him, "Leave Galilee and go to Judea, so that your disciples there may see the works You do. No one who wants to become a public figure acts in secret. Since You are doing these things, show Yourself to the world." It was a strange remark from them since they have seen Jesus in action and the miracles He performed. Such was that of family for they had lived together their whole lives, and although they believed their brother could perform healings, they couldn't bring themselves to fully believe in Jesus as a prophet. Jesus responded to His brothers, "My time is not yet here; for you any time will do. The world cannot hate you, but it hates me because I testify that its works are evil. You go to the festival. I am not going up to this festival, because my time has not yet fully come."

Hearing the words of Jesus, I was both happy and sad at the same time. It was a relief that we weren't going to Jerusalem, since we had all heard that our Jewish leaders would be looking for us and would probably put us all in jail or worse. Yet I did so enjoy the festival with all its excitement; part of me was looking forward to it. Jesus and His brothers talked more, and we all had lunch together. After lunch they departed, heading to Jerusalem, since the festival would start in a few days, and the journey was long. Many were also leaving for Jerusalem, and after a day or two, there were only a few Jewish people remaining in the towns of Galilee.

We all went about our business as usual; Jesus gave sermons every day in a town center, and we helped with the crowd and taught in smaller groups when Jesus wasn't speaking. It was the first day of the festival, and my thoughts all day were there in Jerusalem with all the others. So much excitement was in the air, with thousands upon thousands of people coming together to remember and celebrate God's deliverance and His provision. The scene of thousands of temporary shelters was spectacular. Ritual sacrifices were everywhere, with people bringing their offerings to the temple. The sounds of singing and smells of food permeated everything.

I didn't even notice Jesus next to me. He had come up so quietly and just stood there by my side. "Jesus, how long have You been here?"

He gave me a sly smile and put His hand on my shoulder. "Shi'mon, I know what you are thinking and feeling. I feel the same way. God, our Father, tugs at our hearts to go to Him at the temple to give thanks for His deliverance for us all those many years ago." I waited for Jesus to also say we looked forward to the coming of the Messiah as by Zechariah foretold. He didn't say anything.

Jesus just stood there next to me, looking into the distance. Then He turned to me, looked me in the eyes, and placed both hands on my shoulders. "Shi'mon, we leave for Jerusalem today. Go and gather the others and make ready to depart." I ran at once back to the place where we were staying and broke the news to the others. Like me, they were both overjoyed to go to the festival and at the same time concerned about the safety of Jesus and us. The priests would be looking for us. Leaving that day, we would miss only the first couple of days of the festival.

Apprehension and joy at the same time were an unusual mix of feelings, but we were all used to them being around Jesus for the last three years. Wherever we went, it was a new day; and each day was a blessing. It was Jesus who told us that today was a gift from God, so we should cherish and make the most of it, for our Father in heaven had never promised tomorrow. Gathering what we needed for a week on the road, we set off early in the afternoon and made a long day of it, walking until late that evening.

As ever we found a small town along the way, and there was always someone who had heard of Jesus to readily invite us to spend the evening with them. Dinner was light since there were many of us, fourteen in all, including Jesus, His appointed Twelve, and the ever-faithful Mary. Mary was our sister, and even more she was an apostle just as much as the Twelve Jesus had called, and we all treated her as one of the chosen few. Jesus felt the same was too. I initially wondered why Jesus didn't call Mary one of the twelve apostles, since she was just as worthy and even worthier than us to be the chosen few. I initially thought it was because she was a woman, and in our day and culture, it was a man's world. It would be only years in the future when we truly learned what it meant to be an apostle. It was a life of hunger, cold, torture, and horrible deaths. It was then, at the last moments of my life, that I realized Jesus was just sparing Mary from what we had gone through.

# 15

## (Start of Fourth Year with Jesus, Fall-Winter, AD 31)
# Revelations

*You are the Messiah, the Son of the living God.*
— SHI'MON BAR JONAH (MATTHEW 16:16)

Blessed are you, Simon son of Jonah, for this was not revealed to you by flesh and blood, but by my Father in heaven. And I tell you that you are Peter, and on this rock I will build my church, and the gates of Hades will not overcome it. I will give you the keys of the kingdom of heaven; whatever you bind on earth will be bound in heaven, and whatever you loose on earth will be loosed in heaven.
—JESUS, THE CHRIST (MATTHEW 16:17-19)

We were family, and it felt so good to be back together again. No matter what tomorrow might bring, we would face it together. Our host felt a bit ashamed that all he and his family could provide us were some local vegetables and bread. No matter. After a long day of walking, it just felt good to be able to stretch out and lie down. The vegetables and bread never tasted so good. We thanked our host warmly, and he could see it in our eyes and smiles that he had provided well for us. His slight hesitancy toward the Teacher and us was replaced with a sparkle in His eyes of satisfaction that He had provided well for us. Amazingly, our host didn't ask Jesus for anything. Normally, when staying over, our host asked for a special healing for one of the family members or to teach some wisdom; our host was content just to have us there with him and his family. There was something familiar about his wife, and I couldn't put my finger on it, as if we had seen her somewhere before. It was only sometime later, upon telling the story of the kind host to some people in another town, that they told us his story.

His wife had had a severe problem with bleeding for many years, and it had drained all her energy. They had tried every type of healing and even went as far south as Egypt; no one could heal her. His wife was a great woman of strong faith, and she prayed every night to God to heal her. Never getting angry and frustrated that God hadn't heard her prayers, she rebuked her husband when sometimes he shouted at God in anger. Why wouldn't He hear her prayers? They were both followers of John the Baptist, and John had baptized their whole family, including their children, in the river.

One day while listening to John, they heard John speak of the Prophet, the Messiah to come; and she began to seek out this Prophet John spoke about. It took many months; at long last he passed through their town. The crowd was all around the Prophet, and she couldn't get close to Him; she believed so much that she pushed her way through, forcing people away, so she might just touch His clothes. And she did and felt the power of God enter her body, instantly healing her.

Upon hearing that story, I remembered that time. It was amazing that people had surrounded us, hands from all over touching Jesus, but only the woman who had just touched the edge of Jesus's clothes had been healed. The matter was all about faith. Did I have that kind of faith? I felt a bit weak at the thought of her; as I looked to myself, I didn't yet find that faith within me. Maybe I did for an instant when I walked on the water; however, it wasn't the deep-lasting faith of the healed woman.

We made good time to Jerusalem and made it there midway through the festival. As we entered the city, some of the followers of Jesus had told us that many people were asking about the Teacher and whether He would be coming to the festival. There was a split camp among the Jews in Jerusalem. Many, even though they wouldn't profess themselves as followers of Jesus, believed He was a prophet. Some even said He was the Messiah. Many believed He was a blasphemer and a fake. Some even said He was demon possessed. But none could deny He performed miracles, and all who heard His word were amazed by His teachings. Speaking with authority and full understanding of our history and our scriptures, none could deny Jesus's words, and they rang so true on a basic level. Although the people disagreed with Jesus (and there were many loyal to our Jewish leaders), none tried to harm us physically, not even the temple guards, who were always close by.

It was a good time of the year, and the weather was pleasant during the day, and the evenings were warm. We made camp just outside the city walls among the thousands of pilgrims who came from all over the region. I remember that night well, since it was a special night. We celebrated Jesus's birthday. He didn't want to make a big fuss of it, and we kept it simple. John, Mary, and I were the main cooks that night, and we made Jesus's favorite dishes. The main course was our best fish from the Sea of Galilee, the musht (tilapia); we had bought some big ones from the market. We served the fish with olives, roasted onions, cucumbers, lentils, and bread; and for dessert we had fresh figs. We even had one of my favorites, roast locust. Of course, we washed it all down with red wine. With this feast of food and drink, we all ate well. It made for a great evening, and Jesus gave us chefs the ultimate compliment after dinner by giving us the loudest and longest burp I had ever heard. It was a big laugh, and we appreciated it as a complement to the chefs.

There were so many things I loved about the Feast of the Tabernacles aside from the foods, the sights, and the bonding of having so many Jews and Gentiles together. There were also special rituals performed daily during the Feast of the Tabernacles for us to remember and be thankful for God's provisions in our lives: past, present, and future.

One of my favorites was the water ritual. During the festival, every morning began with a water-drawing ritual, which was a great time of rejoicing over God's provision of water for the crops and for the Holy Spirit, who would provide personal refreshment. One of the temple priests took a golden pitcher and led a musical procession to the pool of Siloam, where he plunged the pitcher into the waters while reciting from our scripture, Isaiah. "With joy you shall draw water from the wells of salvation."

The pool of Siloam, fed from the Gihon Spring, was especially sacred for us since it was the only source of fresh water in Jerusalem. It was precious water. The pool of Siloam was also recorded among the writings of the oral Law as the Messiah's pool. Even the word *Siloam* meant "apostle" or "missionary."

The priest returned to the temple with the golden pitcher of water and began to pour it out over the altar while reciting from Psalm 118:25. "Lord save us! Lord grant us success!" The pouring of the water symbolized the pouring out of the Holy Spirit and was followed by a great silence, which descended on the sanctuary as everyone reflected on the Holy Spirit, the true refreshment for our thirsty souls. The water ritual took place every day; on the seventh day, it took on an intensity filled with excitement and anticipation of the actual presence of the Holy Spirit.

In our Jewish traditions and scripture, the Holy Spirit was a divine power capable of transforming people and the world. In our language "Spirit" came from the word *ruah*, which in its primary sense meant "breath," "air," or "wind." The Holy Spirit was everywhere around us, and we needed Him to live, and His power was far greater. The thought brought me back to the time when the head Pharisee priest, Nicodemus, had visited us while we were eating dinner. What was it Jesus had told Nicodemus? "The wind blows wherever it pleases. You hear its sound, but you cannot tell where it comes from or where it is going. So it is with everyone born of the Spirit" Jesus had talked about being born again in the Spirit with difficult words that rolled around in my head. Jesus's words were very simple yet so difficult to comprehend.

My other favorite ceremony during the festival was the lights ceremony called the "illumination of the Temple." Each day late in the day, when the sun was beginning to set, four huge menorahs, approximately forty-five ell high (23meters high), illuminated the Court of the Women in the temple with golden oil-filled lamps, and Israel's most holy men would dance and sing before the lamps with burning torches in their hands. The light from these massive menorahs was so bright that it seemingly penetrated every courtyard in Jerusalem. The shining menorahs and the torch dancing lasted all night until dawn. The menorahs reminded us of the pillar of fire that had guided us in our wilderness journey. They also reminded us of God's promise to send the light to a sin-darkened world, the light of the coming Messiah, who would renew Israel's glory, releasing us from bondage and restoring us to joy.

The water, the lights ceremony, and other activities continued each day, leading up to the last day of the festival. The eighth and last day of the Feast of Tabernacles was called the "Last Good Day." It was always a Sabbath day, designed for rest and reflection on all that had been celebrated during the previous seven days of the festival. It was on this day that Jesus preached His most powerful of teachings and truly brought His words to life. The Teacher stood boldly in the temple courtyard in front of the crowds with the temple police near and said, "Let anyone who is thirsty come to me and drink. Whoever believes in me, as Scripture has said, rivers of living water will flow from within them." The temple priests looked on Jesus, their mouths wide open at the words of Jesus. Jesus said He was the embodiment of the water ceremony, the foretold Messiah, the living water we sought to quench our thirst. All the people around us were in silence as well. Many of their faces bore the same look as the temple priests, with faces of skepticism in response to the words of this preacher man from Galilee. There were just as many faces of hope and utter joy at the words of Jesus, for many had seen His miracles and heard His teachings of compassion and simple faith.

Before the aggravated temple priests could whip up the crowd against Jesus, there was a loud commotion in the back. A blind man yelled at the top of his lungs, "Jesus! Jesus! Have mercy on me!" Some in the crowd tried to calm the man down, but he pushed on, guided by another who looked to be his brother. They approached Jesus, and the man fell before our Teacher, sobbing and crying. "I have been blind since birth, Master, and long to have sight. I have heard of Your great teachings but never had the chance to get close to You. Have mercy on me and heal me! I believe You are the living water!"

Jesus bent down, touched the man's head, and began to pray softly. He then reached to the ground and gathered some dust and clay. He held up the clay, cupped in both of His hands, and said a thank-you to God for His greatness and love. Spitting on the clay to soften it and make it sticky, Jesus placed it over the man's eyes. He then directed the man to go to the pool of Siloam to wash it off. The crowd and the temple priests followed the man to the pool of Siloam and watched as he washed his mud-caked eyes. I followed behind the man with John, Mary, and a few others from our group. Jesus was also with us a little farther behind, talking to the crowd as we made our way to the pool. I also saw a few of the temple guards in the crowds, no doubt at the direction of the high priests to keep an eye on us.

Upon washing his eyes, the man bent over on the ground but didn't open his eyes. The man who had come with him and guided him to Jesus asked him to open his eyes; the man wouldn't. "Brother, Jesus has placed His hand on you as you wanted for so long. Why will you not open your eyes now?"

The blind man's reply was soft and short. "As I was washing my eyes, I heard a voice that said, 'Wait and see.' So I am waiting." As he waited, the crowd following him gathered into what looked like thousands, all wanting to see what would happen. Jesus then caught up with us and approached the blind man.

Jesus gently placed His right hand on the man's bowed head and lifted His left hand to the sky. "I am the light of the world. Whoever follows me will never walk in darkness, but will have the light of life." He then lowered His left hand to the man's arm and guided him to stand up, then asked him to open his eyes. At first the man hesitated; opening his eyes, he blinked many times while at first describing blurred shapes. Then his voice became excited and loud as the shapes took form and clarity. Since he'd never seen before, he didn't know how to describe colors; he did describe the shapes of the people's bodies, clothes, and faces. The crowd erupted in cheers along with the man. Darkness was lifted, and the man walked forever more in the light of the world. The light of Jesus! Jesus was not only the manifestation of the living water but also the promised Light in the darkened world.

Many shouted that Jesus was the Prophet. Many said He was the Messiah. There were still many who didn't believe. How could the Messiah come from Galilee? The Messiah was to be a descendant of David and come from Bethlehem, the town where David lived, for many didn't know the true background of the Teacher. The temple guards, confused, left without harassing us.

The festival ending, and we went back up north. The fall season was turning to winter, and we spent most of the time in the Galilee area, the south part of the Sea of Galilee at the Jordan River, where John used to baptize in his early days. This was now the end of the third year since I had first met Jesus. The Teacher had changed my name to Cephas (Peter, which meant "rock") that day. Have I lived up to Jesus's expectations as His "rock?" I mused sometimes that I was a hard rock of granite, and other times I was more like a soft rock made of mud. We had all seen so many wondrous miracles from Jesus's power over these last three years. His power was undeniable, and He was even able to give us some of His same healing powers to help others, including His words of simple faith without all the rituals and sacrifices. *Just believe in God. Believe in Him.* All this constantly ran through my head as we went from town to town. Jesus preached and healed, with more and more people coming to follow Him as a prophet and great teacher.

We continued moving around, and by late winter, we had made our way to the region of Caesarea Philippi, located at the southwestern base of Mount Hermon. It was a leisurely two to three days' journey to the north from Capernaum. One evening there, as we all sat around an open fire at night to keep warm, Jesus asked, "Who do people say the Son of Man is?" John answered, along with some of the others, "Some say John the Baptist brought back to life. Others say Elijah. And still others, Jeremiah or one of the prophets." But Jesus didn't want to know what the *people* thought of Him. He wanted to know what His own disciples thought He was.

He asked us directly, "But what about you? Who do you say I am?" Jesus looked around intently at each of us. No one spoke. His eyes then rested on mine. In an instant I remembered the three years we had spent together and being witness to Jesus's miracles, His teachings, His giving us of His powers to heal, the time when Jesus had called to me, and that brief moment of total faith when I'd actually walked on the water just like the Teacher. All the images flashed before me, and I knew to the bone who Jesus really was. Without hesitation, looking directly at Jesus, I said, "You are the Messiah, the Son of the living God." I will never forget the words Jesus spoke in reply.

"Blessed are you, Simon son of Jonah, for this was not revealed to you by flesh and blood, but by my Father in heaven. And I tell you that you are Peter, and on this rock I will build my church, and the gates of Hades will not overcome it. I will give you the keys of the kingdom of heaven; whatever you bind on earth will be bound in heaven, and whatever you loose on earth will be loosed in heaven."

This was a huge statement by Jesus, and I felt overwhelmed. I loved the Teacher with all my heart and wanted to be all He had asked of me. It was great to be called His "rock," but until that moment, I hadn't appreciated or understood the full meaning of what that meant. As the oldest of the twelve disciples with my loud mouth, I was naturally the unspoken leader of the group; this had never been said openly until now. Was I up to the task?

Jesus continued talking to us, saying it wasn't time yet for anyone else to know who He really was. Our Teacher, our Messiah, told us about many things that were going to happen in the near future—namely, that our Jewish leaders would torture and kill Him. Strangely, He said that upon His death, He would be raised on the third day. At that moment, my mind wasn't on that last part, about Him being raised from the dead. Jesus had just told me that I was His rock, and now He had said He would be tortured and killed.

My blood began to boil as I thought about those evil temple priests. They hated Jesus out of jealousy and fear that they would lose their authority, their power, with all the fine and easy living they had become accustomed to. I looked to the Messiah and shouted, "Never, Lord! This shall never happen to You!" I was Jesus's rock, and the rock would never let any harm come to Jesus. Instead of thanking me for protecting Him, Jesus pushed me aside and with deep anger said, "Get behind me, Satan! You are a stumbling block to me; you do not have in mind the concerns of God, but merely human concerns."

Jesus then explained to all of us that to follow Him, we must deny the physical world to gain eternal life. That was what He was telling us of the future, God's plan. The Teacher's words hit us all very hard. We knew there were many against us; however, the idea of torture and death had never really surfaced as a real possibility. Where was our faith in the midst of danger and harm? Jesus's mighty rock had turned once more into mud. Would I ever learn?

Over the next few days, I tried to get over my verbal beating by

Jesus. I knew as far as Jesus was concerned, He still thought of me as His rock and the elder of our band of disciples. Jesus often rebuked us, and I think I received more of this since words just slipped out of me before I had time to think them through. This was my gift and curse. We all talked often during those precious days, and Jesus continued to talk to us about a future that held more hardships for all of us. Changing the world wasn't for the faint of heart.

We stayed around the base of Mount Hermon that week. The weather was good with plenty to eat and fresh springs for water, and there were many in the area who hadn't heard Jesus's teachings.

It was the sixth day since what we called the revealing of who Jesus really was to us. The morning was bright with just a few clouds overhead, and the temperature was so warm enough that we didn't need extra clothing. Jesus came to me and the two brothers, James and John; and told us to pack some light necessities for a journey of one to two days up Mount Hermon. The other disciples were to remain and continue preaching and healing in the area villages. Jesus always had a plan.

Even though we started early that morning, it took us all day to reach less than one quarter of the way up the mountain. Mount Hermon was actually a series of mountains with three peaks, each about the same height (of about 5,500 ell high, over 2,800 meters). As we journeyed up the mountain, Jesus said we weren't going to the top, since it was still far too cold. Snow covered the mountain summits for most of the year, and in the late winter there was far more snow and ice still there.

We reached a nice, flat plateau area and made a small camp, while Jesus went off to pray. The plateau was very small, so the Teacher didn't walk far from our makeshift camp. We were close enough so we could hear Him praying. The sun was getting low in the horizon, and the sky began to turn a beautiful orange red. It was my favorite time of the day to watch the colors in the sky since they changed so fast, normally from orange to fiery red and then to a dark purple draping the sky, turning day into night.

As I gazed at the sunset, something wasn't right; the fiery red changed to a bright-white, piercing light. The white blaze grew so intense I had to squint and place my hands in front of my eyes so I wouldn't be blinded. The light was so bright it actually warmed me. It had to be the strangest fire ever. As we strained our eyes, I realized it wasn't a fire. The white light was Jesus! His face shone as brightly as the sun, and His clothes became as an intense white light as well. Then like a mirage in the distance, other forms around the white light, which was Jesus, started to take shape. Willowy wisps of smoke-like strands began to grow and take the form of two men standing on either side of Jesus. They spoke, and Jesus called out their names, Moses and Elijah!

John, James, and I were in utter shock of what was before us. What should we do? They were so close; we could make out every detail of their faces. I was overcome by the moment. We should do something for these great men of God. I spoke hesitantly, "Lord, it is good for us to be here. If you wish, I will put up three shelters, one for you, one for Moses, and one for Elijah." That was the best I could stammer. As soon as I said this, I regretted it, since it was foolish and small in the greatness of the moment. Sometimes in moments of true awe, it's better to soak them in and say nothing, but my mouth wouldn't allow the great moment to pass without a word from me to interrupt the beauty of the scene. As I finished my stammered sentence, a bright cloud descended on us. And in the cloud, we heard a very deep voice. It was so loud we had to cover our ears. "This is my Son, whom I love; with him I am well pleased. Listen to him!"

This was too much for us to bear. James, John, and I fell at once to the ground, our faces pressed to the cold earth. The bright-white light from Jesus and the cloud seemed to penetrate through my eyelids, burning my eyes. Terror was all I felt, a smallness compared to the vast power of God. Then just as quickly as the light came, it disappeared, and darkness fell on us. The burning white light was gone and left us only with the black ink of night, our small campfire providing a flicker of illumination.

Complete silence. Then we heard the familiar voice of Jesus bidding us not to be afraid and to get up to our feet. As we walked down the mountain, my heart was again filled with such fullness that I thought it would burst. Jesus was our Messiah, and even more than that, He was truly the Son of God. Jesus told us not to tell anyone what we had seen, so we committed all that we saw to memory. I would replay that scene in my mind for the rest of my life, never forgetting the privilege and honor Jesus had given to us to be witnesses of such greatness.

At the base of the mountain, we approached the town we were staying in, and at the center of the town, there was a crowd of people with the rest of the disciples. Mary, Andrew, and Judas were kneeling with their hands laid over a young boy. The boy's face was contorted, and he was in a visible state of anguish, his body twisted in an odd shape. He wasn't moving at that moment; one could hardly believe that he could hold that position for very long. It was very unnatural and must be very uncomfortable.

An older man approached us and knelt before the feet of Jesus. "Lord, have mercy on my son," he said. "He has seizures and is suffering greatly. He often falls into the fire or into the water. I brought him to your disciples, but they could not heal him."

Jesus put his hands on the man's shoulder and lifted him to his feet. With a tired look on His face, Jesus replied, "You unbelieving and perverse generation. How long shall I stay with you? How long shall I put up with you? Bring the boy here to me." Andrew, Mary, and Judas's faces went from intense concentration of trying to heal the boy to ones of awkward shame at being rebuked by Jesus in front of the crowd. They immediately backed off to allow the father to take the boy in his arms and bring him to Jesus.

I felt a bit sorry for them although inside I felt a sense of relief that it hadn't been me Jesus had scolded. I had had my fair share of Jesus's frowning face and scolding in public. The Teacher rebuked the demon, and it came out of the boy, who was healed at that moment. Jesus's power was amazing. There seemed to be nothing He couldn't do.

As we finished with the crowd and headed back to the house where we were staying, curiosity got the better of our brothers and sister who were laying hands on the boy. They had healed others. Why couldn't they heal the boy? Jesus's answer was a one-liner. Faith. It was all about faith. Jesus said if we had enough faith, just as small as a mustard seed, we could say to the great mountain before us to move from here to there, and it would move.

My mind wandered back to that moment on the stormy sea when Jesus had called out to me. My focus had been so intense, my mind so clear and open, that I actually walked on water. The slightest hesitation, the slightest doubt, and my supernatural power was gone. The issue was about complete and unwavering faith, faith in Jesus. It was a simple statement and thought. Just have faith, and we would have the power of Jesus too. The reality of having that complete faith was something I, and all of us, would struggle with for the rest of our lives. There would be moments of that clear and complete faith, but to make it consistent and lasting would elude me and everyone else. We talked about this matter often; none of us had a technique or secret to make that "faith of a mustard seed" permanent or lasting.

From that village at the foothills of Mount Hermon, we split up into a few teams for a short time to cover more towns as we continued to head north back to Galilee and my hometown of Capernaum. We would come together once week and spend a night together. To this day I am not sure how we actually did that. There was no master plan by Jesus when He broke us up into our groups and sent us out. It was as if we were part of a master plan already prewritten, guiding our movements. It was an amazing feeling for us. Imagine, we were in separate groups, wandering along different paths to the north and staying in different towns for a varied amount of days with no real agenda. Sometimes we stayed two or three days in a town and sometimes only one. Like some amazing force, once a week we came to a town, and during that day we all at different times arrived in that same town. We all laughed about it, in awe of Jesus and His power. It was like a weekly homecoming, and it helped us to grow closer together as a family, a family in Jesus.

During one of these gatherings, during dinner Jesus again told us of His eventual death. The news was all very upsetting; I wasn't about to open my big mouth like I had the last time. We had to accept the words of the Teacher. Curiously Jesus also again mentioned in that same sentence what He had told James, John, and me on the mountain. Although He would die, He would be raised from the dead. Of course, this statement did little to console us, since Jesus would first have to die to be risen from death. There was grief about this news, also mixed in with a bit of fear. What would we do without Jesus? And would we also be tortured and killed? The Jewish leaders saw us as a threat almost as much as Jesus was as we preached the words of Jesus and healed in His name. *Where was that "faith of a mustard seed"?* I wondered as a knot formed in the pit of my stomach at the thought of torture and death.

The looks of the others were the same as mine, anguish at the thought of the death of our Teacher mixed with fear and apprehension.

We continued north and all arrived in Capernaum somewhere around midwinter. There we stayed for some time; Jesus preached during the day and healed those had come to Him. We listened intently to all the Master's sermons, and at night over supper He revealed to us the deeper meaning of His sermons and parables. There was so much to learn. Jesus told a simple parable; its deeper meaning was so profound once revealed to us: the lost-sheep story, the being-like-a-child-to-enter-the-kingdom-of-heaven story, the forgiving-brothers-and-sisters-who-sin-against-us story, and so many more. It was a great period for all of us to be together and receive intensive learning from the Teacher.

# 16

## Spreading the Word

*Lord, do you want us to call fire down from heaven and destroy them?*
—James and John, the sons of Zebedee, also known
as Boanerges (sons of thunder) (Luke 9:54)

Winter turned to spring, and from spring summer was approaching. We were learning so much from Jesus, and the sermons and parables He taught in the temple square always brought about a fairly large-sized crowd. After a time, we noticed they were the same people. We got to know them better, and they became stronger disciples of Jesus, learning every day as we were and witnessing the miraculous healings. There were comfort and a feeling of steady peace by being with familiar faces in the safe haven of our hometown.

As summer approached, we all sensed that Jesus was becoming a bit anxious. Pushing harder every day, teaching us and others, He seemed a bit frustrated that all He was teaching wasn't sinking into us fast enough. And there was something else that was bothering Jesus at that time. It was almost with a sense of urgency that Jesus taught us.

We thought our slow pace of learning was frustrating Jesus (and it was) when the Teacher announced to us over dinner one evening that it was time to leave Capernaum and continue spreading the good news. Jesus's anxious mood turned to determination, and we all felt His energy. We were finally going to once again expand to the wider world. This news charged us all up, although with some apprehension, for we knew our Jewish leaders were firmly against Jesus's teachings of forgiveness, grace, and redemption without ritual sacrifice. Our base of firm disciples had expanded from the few of us to a great many people. Jesus told us to assemble the other firm followers and send them out to the neighboring villages to the south, for we would be slowly making our way toward Jerusalem. Jesus had a plan of a slow journey through the villages so He could take time to spread His message to as many people as He could. Over the next few days, we made preparations and packed up for what would be a long period of slow journeying through the countryside.

Summer was the best time to travel. The days were warm, and the nights were cool. As we made our way slowly southward, we sent out messengers to the next village to secure a place for us to stay and let the people know we would be coming their way. The Teacher even said for us to go to the Samaritan villages. He wouldn't leave any without them hearing His divine teachings, even the Samaritans. That was just another thorn in the side of our Jewish leaders; Jesus taught Samaritans and treated them the same as He did our people (that is, proper Jewish people). Jesus wouldn't hear of a divided Jewish people based on some thousand-year-old dispute over whose worship was the proper way or where the official place to worship God was—Jerusalem to the Jews and Mount Gerizim to the Samaritans.

Both Jews and Samaritans worshipped the same God, the God of Abraham and Isaac. The other petty disputes were distractions that brought division among us. As we made our way one night, we received a report that the village we intended on visiting next had told the messengers that they wouldn't allow us into their community since we were headed to Jerusalem; it was the wrong place to worship God. This news didn't bother me too much, and Jesus didn't seem so upset about it. It would take time to change people's thinking. For some reason James and John were outraged by this, and I thought I was the hothead. They went on a tirade about how much we did for the Samaritans.

At the town of Sychar, we stayed with their fellow Samaritans for days. Jesus taught them and healed their sick and lame. Now this refusal was a slap in the face. James and John over dinner asked Jesus, "Lord, do you want us to call fire down from heaven and destroy them?" The table went silent, and all looked to the Master. Jesus sat there, stone faced, and actually seemed to be contemplating the request. I sat there, astounded that Jesus would even give their request a moment of thought. Surely it was madness to destroy a whole town just because they had refused to let us stay there. Jesus then slowly got up and moved toward the two brothers, grasping them both on their shoulders. Jesus's face turned from a serious face of contemplation to that mirthful face and sly smile. Jesus said we had a new nickname for the two sons of Zebedee. From now on James and John would be called Boanerges (sons of thunder). We all had a good laugh, and again, I was thankful that this laughter episode wasn't at my expense. Jesus then proceeded to give us a lesson in tempering our passions and always remembering forgiveness and grace. Mixed in with his rebuke of James and John was a sense that Jesus had agreed with the "Thunder Brothers"—not about physical destruction but about something even more powerful. Eternal life would come only to those who believed in Him.

It was clear as we slowly made our way through the various villages that we still hadn't personally reached many people. Jesus wanted to go through them all and meet every person, but there wasn't nearly enough time for us to spend a day or two in each of the hundreds of small villages dotting the landscape. The Teacher decided to appoint seventy-two of the ones who had been faithful disciples to go into the towns two by two ahead of us to preach and heal. Just as He had given us the power to heal, Jesus placed His hands on each of the seventy-two and said a small prayer. Our Teacher then gave them the same instructions not to bring anything with them but to go into the towns and stay with them if welcomed. He gave them the power to heal the sick and the lame as He had given to us. Their faces showed the same excitement and nervousness we had experienced when we first set out, excitement that they would have the chance to preach the word to people as they had seen Jesus and us, the close disciples of Jesus, perform daily. And even more was that Jesus had given them the same healing powers.

The nervousness came with requirements. "Bring nothing with you" meant you were totally dependent on the goodness of others and the apprehension of healing people. Could they actually do it? We spoke with them afterward with words of encouragement. We told them their mixed feelings of excitement and apprehension were the same ones we had experienced when we first went out alone without Jesus, preaching

His sermons and healing the sick and lame. The matter was about faith. They needed to faith that Jesus had already ordained them and that they would be able to do all He had said they could do. Preach the good news; heal the ill.

With thirty-six pairs going out into the towns, the message was surely to spread to all the region. This time, however, Jesus was firmer with the ones going out. Jesus said that if they went into a town and weren't welcome, then they were to go into the streets and warn them that they were rejecting the kingdom of God. "Whoever listens to you listens to me; whoever rejects you rejects me; but whoever rejects me rejects him who sent me." The people of the region had experienced three years of Jesus's preaching, and most had heard of Jesus, and many had even seen and heard His sermons. From the words of Jesus, I remembered His previous warnings of His capture and death. Time was running out, and being nice to people who wouldn't accept His teachings was coming to an end.

As they filtered into the countryside, the reports from the seventy-two filled us with joy. The word was now spreading like wildfire. They said to Jesus, "Lord, even the demons submit to us in your name." They had faith, and their faith in Jesus was manifested in their powers of healing. Jesus had one of the biggest smiles I have seen yet upon hearing their news; He warned them not to get too boastful, for we all knew the trap of the evil one. He would seek to change our hearts, thinking we have the power to heal. No, that power only flowed through us and came from believing in Jesus and God, our Father. Jesus privately told us later, "Blessed are the eyes that see what you see. For I tell you that many prophets and kings wanted to see what you see but did not see it, and to hear what you hear but did not hear it." We instantly knew what Jesus was talking about. Jesus, our Teacher, was the foretold Messiah, the fulfillment of the prophecies and even more. Jesus, the Son of Man, was also Jesus, the Son of God. And we were witnesses; even more, we were part of the fulfillment of the prophecies.

From that time on, Jesus's teachings really ramped up, and we were making pace through the various villages, supported by messengers going ahead of us, setting up our next place of stay, and the seventy-two preaching the word. Healing brought more people to accept Jesus as a divine Prophet. The Teacher's preaching was so intuitive that even the experts in the Law couldn't deny it. As often as they had the opportunity, our Jewish leaders questioned Jesus and tried to trip Him up so the people would lose confidence in Him. The good Samaritan parable was always one of my favorites, for it showed that mercy, kindness, and caring were the manifestations of love. It was that simple. As one of the learned leaders questioned Jesus, He replied,

> "A man was going down from Jerusalem to Jericho, when he was attacked by robbers. They stripped him of his clothes, beat him and went away, leaving him half dead. A priest happened to be going down the same road, and when he saw the man, he passed by on the other side. So too, a Levite, when he came to the place and saw him, passed by on the other side. But a Samaritan, as he traveled, came where the man was; and when he saw him, he took pity on him. He went to him and bandaged his wounds, pouring on oil and wine. Then he put the man on his own donkey, brought him to an inn and took care of him. The next day he took out two denarii and gave them to the innkeeper. 'Look after him,' he said, 'and when I return, I will reimburse you for any extra expense you may have.' Which of these three do you think was a neighbor to the man who fell into the hands of robbers?" The expert in the law replied, "The one who had mercy on him."

What else could he say? The story was simple yet powerful. I heard later that the expert in Law who questioned Jesus had come to believe in Him.

We never knew when Jesus would give us a learning moment. He had the ability to take any situation and turn it into a word of wisdom for us to take in and remember. I remember one time when we were in the village called Bethany, located to the east of Jerusalem. A kind woman by the name of Martha opened her home to us to stay for a few days. Martha wasn't a wealthy woman, and there were the twelve of us, Mary, and Jesus staying at her place. That was a lot of people to take care of along with getting sleeping places ready and preparing dinner. Martha was whizzing around the house like a busy bee while Jesus was preaching to us in the outside courtyard.

Martha had a sister living with her, Mary, but Mary sat with us to listen to Jesus's teachings. Exasperated, Martha came to us outside and told Jesus, "Lord, don't you care that my sister has left me to do the work by myself? Tell her to help me!" I thought Martha was right. There was much to do, and Mary needed to help her sister out. I also felt a little bad for Martha, and we should all have helped her. Instead of agreeing with Martha and sending Mary to help her, Jesus smiled at Martha and said, "Martha, Martha, you are worried and upset about many things, but few things are needed—or indeed only one. Mary has chosen what is better, and it will not be taken away from her."

When I thought deeper, I realized Jesus was right again. Of course. Caring for our physical needs was important; however, there was nothing more important than learning spiritual truth. When there was opportunity, we needed to jump at taking the time to learn the word of Jesus. Everything else could wait.

Reluctantly Martha also sat down with us to hear the words of our Teacher. That meant we would eat late that evening and had to make our own bedding arrangements. The prize was the change in Martha. Her natural anxiousness to get things done to please people's worldly needs melted away into a deeper understanding of what was truly important in life. One needed to feed the spirit to have peace. All else was secondary.

Wherever we were and no matter how early we got up in the morning or how late we slept that evening, Jesus always took breaks during the day and went off on His own to pray. Normally, we were so exhausted from walking from village to village and managing the crowds—at times healing and preaching—that it was hard to do anything when we got a break except to sit and rest. Jesus, as exhausted as He looked or felt, wouldn't rest; He prayed. At times it was only once a day due to our hectic schedule, but the Teacher never failed to pray. We learned so much from Jesus, since He always explained His sermons and parables to us, so we understood what He meant and what truth He was trying to get across. We never asked Him about how to pray. I was a doer, an action man of sorts who was living his whole life on the seas in the fishing business, and now I was in the business of being a fisher of men, as Jesus had put it to us once. What was it like to take time to be still? What would I say, and how would I say it? It was as if we were in sync in our thoughts.

I was pondering this thought one day when we saw Jesus returning from His solitude of prayer. Mary spoke up and asked Jesus to teach us to pray. Jesus gave Mary a big smile and then motioned all of us to come together. We sat down, all facing the Teacher. He asked us to clasp our hands together and then recited,

> Our Father in heaven,
> hallowed be your name,
> your kingdom come,
> your will be done,
> on earth as it is in Heaven.
> Give us this day our daily bread.
> And forgive us our debts,
> as we also have forgiven our debtors.
> And lead us not into temptation,
> but deliver us from the evil one.

It was such a beautiful prayer. We asked Jesus to repeat it again and then several more times. All the while Jesus didn't show any frustration at repeating the prayer. He appreciated our earnestness to commit it to memory. From then on, to make sure we all had the prayer firmly rooted in our minds every morning, before or after breakfast, we all sat together and recite it. Hearing us recite the prayer every morning, Jesus called it "our disciples' prayer."

We continued to travel on a speed course through the various villages for the rest of the summer. Messengers were ahead of us, setting up our next place to visit, and the seventy-two were still in the field, "harvesting," as Jesus put it. And it was a harvest! So many more came, believing in Jesus by the retelling of His good news teachings and by witnessing His power through the healings performed in His name. For us it was our time of intense learning as we were with the Teacher every day. Jesus preached to the crowd during the day; then at night He told us the deeper meaning of His teachings and especially His parables. It didn't matter what day of the week it was; if Jesus had an opportunity to teach or heal, He did, even on the Sabbath, when we were forbidden to work. I am not sure which of the thirty-nine prohibited actions on the Sabbath prohibited healing someone. The Pharisees and Jewish elders always proclaimed that healing someone was "work" and therefore prohibited. I don't think there was anything else that made Jesus angrier at our esteemed leaders than when they tried to stop Him from healing someone who was in pain just because of some rule.

One Sabbath day, Jesus was preaching in a synagogue, and He healed a woman who had been crippled for eighteen years. Imagine eighteen years of suffering. And upon seeing her made whole again, all the synagogue leader could say was, "There are six days for work. So, come and be healed on those days, not on the Sabbath."

Jesus tore into him with a tirade. "You hypocrites! Doesn't each of you on the Sabbath untie your ox or donkey from the stall and lead it out to give it water? Then should not this woman, a daughter of Abraham, whom Satan has kept bound for eighteen long years, be set free on the Sabbath day from what bound her?" All His opponents were shamed by Jesus, and the crowd roared with joy from all the good Jesus was doing. Common sense and Jesus's good judgement once again beat up the naysayers.

On another Sabbath, we were invited to eat in the house of a prominent Pharisee. When I say we were invited, most times it was Jesus who was invited, and in turn Jesus invited us. Anyway, we were at the Pharisee's house along with a crowd of the village people. It was obvious that the elders were keeping a close watch on Jesus to see whether He would do anything against our Jewish laws so they could proclaim to the people that Jesus was a troublemaker, an instigator, a man who broke the laws God had set forth. As Jesus made His way through the house, greeting the people there in front of him, there was a man suffering from abnormal swelling of his body. Jesus asked the Pharisees and experts in the law, "Is it lawful to heal on the Sabbath or not?" They remained silent. Jesus was clearly disgusted by their lack of compassion. Taking hold of the man, He healed him and sent him on his way.

Jesus then turned to our learned leaders and asked them, "If one of you has a child or an ox that falls into a well on the Sabbath day, will you not immediately pull it out?" And they had nothing to say. I thought Jesus was going to explode on them. Their stony silence, full of righteous indignation at the rebuff from our Lord, spoke volumes about their cold hearts. They were all rules and no compassion. Jesus simply turned away from them, and throughout the rest of the evening, He poked back at them, showing the crowd how wrong the leaders were through a multitude of parables.

# 17

## (Start of Fifth Year with Jesus, Fall-Winter, AD 32)
# Eternal Life

*I am the resurrection and the life. The one who believes in me will live,*
*even though they die; and whoever lives by believing in me will never die.*
—JESUS, THE CHRIST (JOHN 11:25-26)

In cities, towns, villages, and even single homes dotting the landscape, we went with the Teacher, preaching and healing. His sermons took on much more force now that many had come to be followers, and many more were hearing the words of the Messiah. No longer were the teachings of Jesus only about forgiveness, compassion, and grace. He spoke more and more about warnings if they didn't change their ways. The consequences of not having forgiveness, compassion, and grace to our fellow brothers and sisters were to give up eternal life in heaven with God. Jesus's teachings were about helping, caring, and loving those around us. There was no more tolerance of greed, selfishness, and pride. He was proclaiming that the gates of heaven itself were now closing to those who didn't change their ways. This was causing more people who had once been fascinated and accepted the teachings of Jesus to divide, for those with wealth didn't want to give what they had to others, and Jesus was facing them squarely and telling them to share, care, and love or be forever lost in hell. For those who were suffering and had nothing in this world, all would be given to them in heaven, for what were we if we didn't help our fellow brothers and sisters in need? How could we justify our lives and what we had done in this world at the gates of heaven if we didn't care for others? By others Jesus didn't mean just family members or relatives.

The Teacher continued to heal the sick and lame as He preached and as more and more came to believe in Him as a great Prophet and the Messiah. It was during that winter that the Teacher performed such a great miracle that even the Pharisees and Jewish leaders had to admit that the works of Jesus were truly miraculous. We were in a small town north of Galilee when we received word from a messenger about Mary and Martha. Mary and Martha were sisters who were close to Jesus's heart, for it was Mary who had once poured perfume on Jesus and wiped His feet with her hair. They had true faith, love, and adoration for Jesus, and we all got along well with them. Whenever we were in the Bethany area, we stopped by their house. The messenger told us that Lazarus, Mary and Martha's brother, was very sick. We had many requests such as these from members of our followers, and normally Jesus, always full of compassion, at once sent one of us, His close twelve disciples and Mary, to go with the messenger. For very close friends and family, such as Mary and Martha, Jesus always went.

This time Jesus curiously said Lazarus wouldn't die and that his sickness would be used to glorify God's greatness. The messenger waited patiently; however, Jesus said no more, and we continued about our work in the village. For a whole day, the messenger waited, following us around, but there was no other news to bring back. No one was coming for Lazarus. The messenger, with deep concern and sadness in his eyes, finally turned and headed back to Bethany to give the news that no one was coming. Before he left, the messenger said he expected that by the time he got back, Lazarus would probably be dead, for he was very ill.

I felt very sad about Lazarus being sick and that we weren't going back to help him. I also felt a bit ashamed of myself since I also felt relieved to see him go; we were no longer welcome in the south. When we'd been in the Judea area just a few months ago, Jesus had been so confrontational with our leaders that they'd wanted to stone us. In fact, they had incited the crowd so much that there had been a few times when stones were thrown at us. Matthew suffered a broken arm, and many of us of had severe bruises. Now with Jesus's more forceful teachings, people either loved or hated Him. Perhaps *hate* wasn't the right word. *Fear* and *shame* were better.

People either loved Jesus or were ashamed and feared His words, since they spoke such basic truths about how we lived and went about our daily lives. There was no longer any middle ground, and Jesus said that as well. I remember once Jesus said, "Do you think I came to bring peace on earth? No, I tell you, but division. From now on there will be five in one family divided against each other, three against two and two against three. They will be divided, father against son and son against father, mother against daughter and daughter against mother, mother-in-law against daughter-in-law and daughter-in-law against mother-in-law."

It wasn't that Jesus was angry with anyone. It was just time for people to choose and either accept or reject the teachings of Jesus. This winter marked four full years since Jesus had first called us to be His disciples and the Teacher had started His ministry work. By now most people had heard either Jesus or the other seventy-two chosen ones. Most had seen or heard the miracles and healings performed in the name of God, the power of healing God had given to Jesus. It was time to decide plain and simple. The Jewish leaders knew this as well, and the divide grew as more and more came to believe in Jesus. Fear struck the hearts of the Jewish leaders that their traditions and structures of the elite were in trouble. What would Judaism and our Jewish culture look like if all turned to the teachings of Jesus? Or even half?

Two days passed since the messenger came to tell us of Lazarus being sick. It was morning, and we finished breakfast and said our disciples' prayer. Jesus also had His personal prayer time. Finishing, He approached us and said, "Let us go back to Judea." That feeling of relief I'd had when seeing the messenger leave came back to me, and I tried to hide my fear.

It was Judas who spoke up, warning Jesus about our recent incidents in Judea as a tinge of personal fear rose in his voice. Jesus looked at all of us and saw we all had the same concern on our faces. The Teacher always seemed to know our thoughts and had a compassionate look on His face when He said Lazarus had fallen asleep; we were going there to wake him up. It was then that James's brother John spoke up. "Lord, if he sleeps, he will get better." In other words, we should stay where we were and just let Lazarus get better by resting.

Jesus looked again at all of us to read our expressions. We all put on our best faces of concern and murmured that John had a good point and that we shouldn't bother Lazarus. The Teacher's look of compassion for us turned to His sterner look when we did or said something wrong. He could see through our thinly veiled concern for Lazarus and saw the fear for our own persecution. Jesus replied, "Lazarus is dead, and for your sake I am glad I was not there, so that you may believe. But let us go to him."

We didn't understand what Jesus was saying; by His monotone voice, we knew Jesus was obviously disappointed that we had put our fear ahead of helping one of our close friends. He directed us to pack up and leave immediately. Jesus left us to pack up, and when we were alone, Thomas spoke up and said what we were all thinking. "Let us also go, that we may die with him."

It took us nearly five days to travel to Bethany. We could have made the journey much quicker, but Jesus wanted to stop in several towns along the way to continue preaching and healing. We also were in no rush, so we didn't press Jesus about moving faster. As we approached Bethany, we saw there were many more people there than normal. Their faces looked worn and tired. Jesus was right. Lazarus was dead. Messengers had gone before us and alerted Mary and Martha that Jesus was coming.

Martha came to us. Her clothes were wrinkled, and it looked like she hadn't slept in days. With puffy eyes and tangled hair, she walked toward us slowly as if half asleep. Standing unsteadily before Jesus, Martha fell into His arms, and the Teacher gave her a warm hug.

After a moment Martha looked up and said. "If you had been here, my brother would not have died. But I know that even now God will give you whatever you ask." She then told us that Lazarus had died four days ago. There was a tinge of bitterness in her voice due to Jesus's tardiness, even though she knew that with Jesus Lazarus would be with God our Father in heaven and was at peace. Her bitter voice was tinged with some gratitude that Jesus had come to mourn with her and Mary.

Jesus said to her, "Your brother will rise again." We all knew our scriptures from our Pharisee teachers that the faithful would come back to life again.

Martha responded, "I know he will rise again in the resurrection at the last day."

Jesus clasped both of His hands on Martha's shoulder, looked into her eyes, and said, "I am the resurrection and the life. The one who believes in me will live, even though they die; and whoever lives by believing in me will never die. Do you believe this?"

Martha replied with the same words I had said once before. "Yes, Lord," she replied, "I believe that you are the Messiah, the Son of God, who is come into the world." Martha in her heart knew what I knew. Jesus told Martha to bring Mary. She left at once, nearly running into town.

A short time later, we saw a large crowd coming toward us from the distance. They were moving slowly, led by a woman wearing a plain and simple dark-colored, long tunic. It was Mary. Her face wrought with anguish, she approached. Instead of leaning into the Teacher for a hug of condolence, she fell at Jesus's feet. There were many people with Mary, and they also fell to their knees, hands covering their faces, which were full of tears.

Mary looked up at Jesus, tears streaming down her face. Now she wailed at the top of her voice, "Lord, if you had been here, my brother would not have died!" Her voice mixed with sadness and anger toward our Lord. She buried her face on the feet of Jesus, tears streaming down to the Teacher's toes and mixing with the sandy dirt. Those who were with her also wailed in sorrow. The moment was too much. Everyone was overcome with grief. Tears began to well up in my eyes along with those of the other disciples. Jesus also began to cry when He saw how much pain everyone felt at the loss of Lazarus.

He asked where Lazarus was buried, and Martha replied, "Come and see, Lord." Jesus slowly lifted Mary, and she fell into His arms, exhausted from lack of sleep and deep sadness. Andrew and I took Mary into our arms to steady her, and we made our way to the tomb of Lazarus. Martha was being consoled and was in the arms of our Mary (Magdalene). A large crowd followed us to the tomb. Everyone was sad. We heard some say the same thing we were thinking. Jesus had performed great miracles, even healing a man born blind. If Jesus truly loved Lazarus, why hadn't He come as soon as possible and healed Lazarus when he was alive?

Where was the compassion the Teacher talked so much about? Some even went so far as to say that perhaps Jesus had known Lazarus's sickness was too grave and that he couldn't be healed.

Lazarus's tomb was set at the base of a rocky hillside, the entrance covered by a large circular stone. Jesus called out to us to take away the stone. It was Martha who spoke up. "By this time there is a bad odor, for he has been there for four days."

Jesus took Martha into His arms and said, "Did I not tell you that if you believe, you will see the glory of God?" It took six of us, together with a large metal rod, to get the circular stone to start moving; once it moved, we got it to continue rolling until the entrance was fully open. Just as Martha had said, a foul odor exhaled out of the tomb, and the crowd backed up due to the repellant smell.

After a few moments, I thought the smell would get better; it never did. I wrapped a cloth around my face to help lessen the awful odor of death, as did everyone else. The smell didn't even phase Jesus. It was as if He were immune to the smell. The Teacher went to the entrance of the tomb, knelt in front of the opening, clasped His hands, and prayed silently. The crowd's talking and wailing lessened as everyone's focus turned to Jesus.

After a short time, when all was silent, Jesus, still kneeling, lifted His hands and said in a loud voice all could hear, "Father, I thank you that you have heard me. I knew that you always hear me, but I said this for the benefit of the people standing here, that they may believe that you sent me." After saying this, Jesus rose to His feet and stretched His hands toward the dark tomb. With authority He said in a loud voice, "Lazarus, come out!"

The silence was deafening. No one dared to say a word. There were no birds chirping; even the wind stopped suddenly, leaving only silence. Then it hit me all at once. A fragrant smell replaced the pungent odor coming from the tomb. Slight at first, the fragrance grew in strength until all the crowd smelled it, and I had smelled that sweet fragrance before. It was the same perfume Mary had poured on Jesus.

Just then a shape started to appear in the darkness of the tomb. A figure appeared, walking unsteadily, one slow step in front of another. The fragrance grew more powerful. I immediately motioned to John, and we went to the cloth-wrapped figure, grasping his shoulders so he wouldn't fall. Wrapped in linen from head to toe, a walking mummy appeared. Jesus then commanded us, "Take off the grave clothes and let him go." We started to unwrap the mummy from the feet first so it could stand upright without swaying from side to side; then came the body and lastly the head. And there he was. Lazarus was living, breathing, and smelling like Mary's perfume.

The deafening silence erupted all at once into deafening praise and worship. Jesus had brought Lazarus back from the dead! There was truly nothing the Master couldn't do. People were shouting, singing, and praising Jesus, the Teacher, great Prophet, and Healer. Many also shouted, "Messiah," and many more even started shouting what I had said just a short time ago. It was what Martha had said just earlier in the day. Jesus was the Son of God!

None there could deny the power of Jesus, and many more became followers. There were others in the crowd who were against the Messiah, whether because of fear, jealousy, loyalty to the Pharisees, or anger toward the teachings of Jesus, especially the rich. One cannot know the thoughts of men and women. Evil thoughts they were, and some of them went to our Jewish leaders to tell them all they had seen and describe how many more were coming to believe and following Jesus—and not just as a prophet. They saw Him as the Messiah, and many even shouted, "Son of God!"

The Pharisees called a meeting of the Sanhedrin and discussed their dilemma. It was the high priest Caiaphas who spoke up and said what all were thinking. "You know nothing at all! You do not realize that it is better for you that one man die for the people than that the whole nation perish!" He didn't say this on his own; as high priest that year, he had prophesied that Jesus would die for the Jewish nation—and not only for that nation but also for the scattered children of God to bring them together and make them one. From that day on, they plotted to take His life.

Word got to us of the leaders' plotting to take the life of Jesus and persecute His close disciples. Knowing we could no longer move freely through the villages, we traveled to a remote town called Ephraim.

Ephraim was a remote village, but Jesus's fame was so great by now that even people in the remote regions gathered in large numbers. There was truly no place where we could go and not be surrounded by the faithful. At least here in the remote areas, surrounded by people who truly loved the Teacher and were His devoted followers, we were safe from any schemes of our Jewish leaders to harm Jesus. From time to time, a Pharisee or two came to check up on us, to make sure they knew where we were, and to try to question Jesus; they were always looking for something they could proclaim as blasphemy or say Jesus was doing wrong. They also appeared to be at least somewhat comforted that here in this remote village, Jesus was contained and wasn't actively recruiting new believers. Perhaps Jesus would remain here, and over time His fame would wane, and He would become just another prophet in our history.

Jesus continued to teach in parables and confound the Pharisees while teaching us basic truths of what it meant to live a good live and what God really desired of us: hold God first in our lives, love our neighbor as yourself, forgive and forget, and always help others in need. These were simple words but seemingly impossible to follow.

I remember that one day a young, handsome, rich man came to Jesus and asked, "Teacher, what good thing must I do to get eternal life?" It was a fair question from the young man. He was known in the region since he had great wealth and was a devote Jew, following all our laws and traditions. He was well liked since many of our wealthy treated people as things and objects to further their wealth and serve their needs; however, this young man treated everyone well.

Jesus replied, "Why do you ask me about what is good? There is only One who is good. If you want to enter life, keep the commandments."

Ever pressing, the young man asked, "Which ones?"

The Master replied, "You shall not murder, you shall not commit adultery, you shall not steal, you shall not give false testimony, honor your father and mother, and love your neighbor as yourself."

At Jesus's response, the young man's face lit up, and he had a big smile. We all felt good for him since he was an honorable man, and we thought he would make a great disciple. Instead of stopping there, the young man pressed Jesus. Instead of just accepting the words of the Teacher, the young rich man wanted more. I guess this was true of all of us. No matter what we had, we wanted more. We wanted to be sure about our position in life and in the life to come. This may have been truer of the rich, since they so easily got whatever they wanted; their focus was always more on what they could have, not on what they had; they focused on what they could get rather than on what more they could give. Wealth tended to distort one's thinking and focus, so the young man asked the Teacher, "All these I have kept. What do I still Lack?"

Obviously, he didn't think he lacked anything else. He kept all the commandments and our laws. What more was there? Such was the pride of people. And it was then that Jesus lowered the thunder on him. What more must the young man do to attain eternal life and be a true follower of the Son of God? Jesus knew our weaknesses, thoughts, and hearts. The two were close together. Jesus placed His left arm on the man's shoulders. They locked eyes, and Jesus responded, "If you want to be perfect, go, sell your possessions and give to the poor, and you will have treasure in heaven. Then come, follow me."

I think I saw almost the full range of emotions in the young man's face. He went from a cheerful smile, knowing he lived all our rules and commandments, to sheer shock at what Jesus had asked him to do, to concern over what this meant for him and his worldly lifestyle, and to sadness and dejection, for so great was his wealth. He knew his riches were his greatest asset, and now he understood they were also his greatest weakness since he would never be able to do what Jesus had asked of him. For a moment I thought the man was about to cry; he just looked down at the ground, no longer able to look into Jesus's eyes.

The Teacher wasn't angry at the man. He held his shoulder with his left arm, never letting go, and then, reached up with His right arm, He grasped the other man's shoulder. There was silence for a moment, and then the man turned and slowly walked away. Jesus knew how hard it was for the man, for He told us over dinner about some of the trials He had gone through while living in the wilderness for forty days just prior to His call by God to start His ministry work. He spoke of how the evil one had come to tempt Him with riches and wealth beyond imagination. Jesus knew all the feelings we experienced. He knew the pull of earthly wealth and pleasures. It was a battle we faced every day.

When the man had left, Jesus turned to us and the crowd, and said, "Truly I tell you, it is hard for someone who is rich to enter the kingdom of heaven. Again, I tell you, it is easier for a camel to go through the eye of a needle than for someone who is rich to enter the kingdom of God."

It was a shocking statement. A camel through the eye of a needle? That was obviously impossible. If that was so difficult for a rich man, who could be saved? We asked Jesus this, and He replied, "Truly I tell you, at the renewal of all things, when the Son of Man sits on his glorious throne, you who have followed me will also sit on twelve thrones, judging the twelve tribes of Israel. And everyone who has left houses or brothers or sisters or father or mother or wife or children or fields for my sake will receive a hundred times as much and will inherit eternal life. But many who are first will be last, and many who are last will be first."

In later years, I would come to revisit all of Jesus's teachings, have them written down, and reflect and pray over them, for there were so many hidden truths in His words. At that time, however, my mind didn't work deeply, and there was little time for reflection between my brain and mouth. Thinking of only myself, I replied, "We have left everything to follow You! What then will there be for us?"

Jesus turned and locked His eyes on me and then on the rest of His band of disciples. His expression was of peace, and with a smile He told us we would be in heaven with Him, representing the twelve tribes of Israel. Any who had left home or family or experienced hardships in life for the sake of following Him would receive eternal life. We were instantly energized by His words. Yes! We would be great in heaven! We had given up all we had, and we would have eternal life with Jesus and God, our Father. In our exuberance over the words of Jesus, we all failed to understand or let sink in Jesus's words of "experience hardships." Those two words would come back to me time and time again.

We must hold Him first in our lives and have faith in Him. That was a very simple statement to live by; I had found that I failed miserably many times in my life, especially when combined with the Teacher's foretelling of experiencing hardships. I was also thankful for Jesus's teachings of grace, compassion, and forgiveness, for I had found myself needing those from our Lord so many times that I dare not try to count them all.

# 18

# The Final Journey

*We are going up to Jerusalem, and the Son of Man will be delivered*
*over to the chief priests and the teachers of the law. They will condemn*
*him to death and will hand him over to the Gentiles to be mocked and*
*flogged and crucified. On the third day he will be raised to life!*
—JESUS, THE CHRIST (MATTHEW 20:18-19)

Winter was turning into spring as we stayed in Ephraim. It was a welcome break from the intensity of the push Jesus had begun during the last summer. The Teacher continued to preach and heal every day, as we did as well, and there was time enough for Jesus to take long periods of prayer. His calmness belied a restlessness, and we saw it in His expressions and His continued pointed teachings on repentance.

Time was growing short. Our Lord had told us twice before of what future lay in store for Him: capture, torture, and death by the hands of our Jewish leaders. We knew this rest break, this time in our little hideaway, wouldn't last forever, and it came to an end sooner than I expected. Jesus announced during dinner on a cold, late winter night that we were to pack up since we were headed back to Jerusalem. We were going to travel back on a slow course and make it in time for the Passover celebration. Going back to Jerusalem concerned us, especially when it was clear our Jewish leaders had secretly proclaimed that they would kill Jesus. What would happen to us? What was even more troubling was that Jesus wouldn't talk about what would happen or where we were to go after Passover. It was if all plans ended there and then. Reluctantly, we packed up everything, and the next day we headed out on our slow journey back to Jerusalem. The joy of Jesus's proclamation that we were to sit over the twelve tribes of Israel in heaven was overshadowed by what it might take to get there. We put on our best faces and readied ourselves for the journey. Even more so than us, Jesus also readied Himself for what was to come.

About halfway to Jerusalem, Jesus took us (His inner twelve disciples and Mary) aside from the rest of the larger group of followers traveling with us; and for the third time in recent months, He told us what was to come. The Teacher said, "We are going up to Jerusalem, and the Son of Man will be delivered over to the chief priests and the teachers of the law. They will condemn him to death and will hand him over to the Gentiles to be mocked and flogged and crucified. On the third day he will be raised to life!"

Our hearts sank again to new lows. Immediately I thought of rebuking Jesus and saying we wouldn't let that happen to Him. We should protect Jesus from harm. Before my big mouth could blurt it out, I noticed Jesus was looking straight at me with very intense eyes. He knew my heart, and I chided myself, remembering the last time I had said something like that. It wasn't that Jesus was mad at me, for my intent was good. The issue was about temptation. Our words were like the evil one's words during Jesus's forty days in the wilderness, tempting Him to take the easy way out.

My mouth opened, but nothing came out. Jesus came up to me and put His hands on my shoulders, telling me to take comfort, for everything would be as God our Father had willed it to be. We must remain firm and strong. He said this loudly enough for all to hear and take comfort. We took some comfort in Jesus's words, but the uncertain future hung over us like a low, dark rain cloud. You could see it coming, and there was nothing to stop it.

We were a small, tight group, and going through the last four years together, we had become a family but were even closer than family. We'd witnessed so many miracles and gone through many rough times with the Jewish leaders, who'd incited the crowd to throw stones at us. We'd had no shelter or a place to sleep on many nights when we traveled around, preaching the good news of Jesus. We'd given up our family, businesses, friends, and relatives to be full-time disciples of Jesus. Many understood what we were doing just as many thought we were crazy. None who met Jesus, witnessed His power, and listened to His teachings could deny He was a great prophet and more than a prophet. Like all families, we had our internal disagreements, petty jealousies, and general annoyances with each other. We were only human after all.

One night as we were eating dinner as usual, Jesus told us the deeper meaning of what He had preached that day. The mother of James and John, also known as the "Sons of Thunder," came into the room; coming up close to Jesus, she knelt before Him. "Lord, I came to ask a favor of you."

James and John were sitting just across me, and I looked at them to see their expression and discern whether they had any idea what this was all about. Their faces showed no expression of either surprise or concern. Jesus asked her what she wanted, and she responded, "Grant that one of these two sons of mine may sit at your right and the other at your left in your kingdom."

What was this nonsense all about? Surely, she wasn't serious. We were all equal. I was sure Jesus would give her a stern rebuke. Other chatter around the table went silent. All eyes turned to Jesus. The Teacher, with a concerned look, was thinking about her request. Perhaps there was a parable about equality in the group or something like that. This rebuke was going to be a good one.

He turned to the woman and replied, "You don't know what you are asking." Turning to the Sons of Thunder, He looked directly at them and asked, "Can you drink the cup I am going to drink?"

What? Jesus was actually going to give these two hotheads their request? This was madness!

Excited because Jesus was actually thinking about their mom's request, the "Thunder Brothers" responded, "We can!" And Jesus looked upon them again but not with concern, almost with a sad and sympathetic look, for He knew, as we did much later, what it would cost to sit with Jesus.

He said, "You will indeed drink from my cup, but to sit at my right or left is not for me to grant. These places belong to those for whom they have been prepared by my Father." He then promptly left us to go off on His own to pray, and the mother of James and John also promptly got up and left.

We sat there in silence after finishing our dinner. I could take it no more, nor could the others. Even Mary was visibly upset with James and John. I spoke up. Looking directly at the two, I said, "We are all equal here at the table of Jesus. We all sacrificed our jobs, our family. We walk in danger every day with the Pharisees, who are trying to find a way to accuse and silence us. People throw rocks at us in villages. Brothers, we are all equal here. What madness is this that you would scheme with your mother to ask Jesus for you to be elevated over all of us?"

At once everyone else jumped in, his or her feelings coming out. The two tried to explain that they had known nothing about what their mother was going to ask Jesus. Mary then stood up and said to them directly, "Tell us, brothers John and James, that you will go to Jesus and withdraw you mom's request then." Silence again.

James and John looked uncomfortable due to Mary's angry stare, and all other eyes look upon them. They said nothing, so Mary left the table. Everyone else also got up in silence and left the two.

Later that evening, Jesus returned from praying. Seeing and hearing no one, He came to me and asked where everyone was. Normally we would still be finishing dinner, or all would be together in the courtyard, discussing the next day's travel and events. I was hurt that Jesus couldn't see what a blow it had been to us to have James and John elevated over us, especially me, His rock of the church.

I looked directly at our Teacher and told Him what had happened after He left. I was shaking with rage and hurt, and Jesus put both of His arms on my shoulders and looked at me with warm eyes. "Peter you will be the rock of my church and nothing will change that fact through all of history. We are all equal in the eyes of our father in heaven. What James' and Johns' mother ask of me is not mine to give and it will never will be." I was almost ashamed by my pettiness of being jealous and even more so that I was relieved to hear from Jesus that we are all equal and that I was still His rock. We preached Jesus's words of forgiveness, grace, and redemption every day; yet when confronted with our own inner desires, we immediately turned on each other.

The Teacher told me to call everyone back to the dining room. We all gathered with an obvious gap between us and the Thunder Guys. Jesus took His time and looked into each of our eyes. As He did, we knew exactly what He was thinking. How little had we learned about His teachings? No one dared lock gazes with the Son of God for too long, since His gaze looked directly into our hearts. Anger in the group turned to muted acknowledgment of our weakness, since all had wanted what the mother of James and John requested. We just had never asked Jesus in the open. We'd kept our inner desires for greatness deep within us, and now those desires were exposed.

Looking at us with a warm and gentle smile, Jesus said, "You know that the rulers of the Gentiles lord it over them, and their high officials exercise authority over them. Not so with you. Instead, whoever wants to become great among you must be your servant, and whoever wants to be first must be your slave—just as the Son of Man did not come to be served, but to serve, and to give his life as a ransom for many." He explained to us that to be great in heaven, we must be servants here on earth. Forget about positions or titles, for they meant nothing in heaven. Preach the good news, heal the sick and the lame, be servants to each other and to all who come into our lives; and we would inherit eternity with the Father and Himself. Jesus then got up and left us alone again as He had before. There was a brief uncomfortable silence.

I was the first to speak. "James and John, you are my brothers and family. Forgive me for being angered at you, for it was my own jealousy and inner desire that made me mad at you two."

James and John, visibly shaken, unexpectedly started to weep, and they wailed, "Forgive us, for we are the ones at fault. We should have rebuked our mother for asking such a thing, but when Jesus said it was possible, we were overcome with the evil one, who put pride and power in our minds!"

We all came together and with hugs and tears, and promised each other not to let anything come between us again. It was a powerful lesson, and looking back now, I am sure Jesus knew exactly what would happen since He always did; for we would need to be as one with all the strength and love as a single mind to do what Jesus was asking of us. We would all one day need all our strength to drink from the same cup Jesus drank.

We continued to make our way south to Jerusalem. Passover was closing in on us, and everyone was getting excited. The people who greeted us in the villages were visibly in the holiday spirit. It was Passover time, a time when we remembered and celebrated our freedom from captivity. All the times before, it had been a good time to celebrate and reflect, but this time it was different. Now Jesus walked the earth, and all had heard of His miracles and teachings; many were coming to have faith in Jesus as we had. The kingdom of God was near. He wasn't just a great man, prophet, and healer. Many now chanted, "Jesus, the Son of God!" The kingdom of God was here! Would this be our year of salvation? Freedom from our oppressors?

We could see the anticipation in the people's eyes, and far from joy, we could also see the fear in the eyes of our Jewish leaders. Rome wouldn't stand for this and would crush any rebellion with the death of many; even worse it would crush our rituals, religion, and very way of life. All would be lost. The anticipation grew and grew as we continued closer to Jerusalem. My personal dread, along with that of others, grew as well. Jesus's words about Him being captured, tortured, and killed filled us with fear.

It was a week before Passover, and we spent Saturday in Bethany, a town near Jerusalem. We were among our closest friends now, at the home of Simon the Leper, whom Jesus had healed. Mary, Martha, and Lazarus, the young man Jesus had brought back from the dead last year, were there as well. Jesus again talked of coming events of His burial when Mary had poured expensive perfume on Him. While others had been offended by the expensive perfume going "to waste," I had been happy that Jesus had had that moment of comfort and joy. He had given so much by serving others; it was nice to see Him being served. Judas didn't like that gift at all. It was only later that we found he had been taking some of the money for himself. That expensive perfume would have given Judas a nice pay day. Such were the temptations of this world.

Dinner was over, and it was getting late. Everyone wanted to talk to Jesus and us. It had been a while since we'd been in Bethany, and it was great catching up with friends. Everyone wanted to hear about the many other miracles of Jesus and some of His best parables. We could have stayed up all night, but it was getting late. Jesus stood up and faced us.

Everyone went silent. It was now the fork in the road. What would we do? Would we stay here in relative safety or enter Jerusalem for Passover? Jesus looked at us and told us to get a good night's sleep, for tomorrow we would enter Jerusalem. It was time!

There were many in the room who cheered on the news of our going to Jerusalem, and they shouted, "Hosanna in the highest!" They thought Jesus would deliver our people from that bondage of the Romans like Moses had so many years ago from our previous captures. Most departed quickly to get rest and prepare for our Savior to enter Jerusalem for Passover. Jesus had also left to pray and get ready. The noise quieted down, and only His twelve disciples and Mary were left in the room. There were no words of cheer or joy, just looks of concern, for we remembered Jesus words of His capture, torture, and death. Would this be the end of our mission? Dread for what was to come? Sorrow for what may happen to Jesus and fear for what may become of us? Would we also be hunted and killed?

Rest didn't come easily for any of us, and we all got up early the next morning. Jerusalem was only a few hours' walk away. As we started out on our last journey, Jesus told Phillip and Thaddeus to go ahead into the next village. There would be a donkey tied to a tree along with her colt. They were to untie them and bring them to Him. Most people would have asked Jesus how He could have known there would be a donkey and colt tied to a tree, but we were accustomed to believe in anything Jesus told us, having seen so many of His miracles. It was just a fact that there would be a donkey tied to a tree.

Off they went, and the two came back just as Jesus had asked, with a good-sized donkey and a colt. We were close to Jerusalem now, just outside the great city walls, and we were on the road approaching the main gate that led straight through the city to the temple. People lined the road on both sides and were shouting, "Hosanna to the Son of David!" and "Blessed is he who comes in the name of the Lord!" Hundreds of the faithful lined the road with cut branches and trees. Many even laid down their cloaks on the road.

It was an incredible scene I would remember for the rest of my life. There was so much joy and enthusiasm that our fear and concerns melted away in the shouts of joy. It would be years from now when I read our history from the book of Zechariah that I would learn that so much of what Jesus had done was foretold by our ancestors, that Jesus was the fulfillment of the prophecies. Zechariah 9:9 says, "Say to daughter Zion, 'See your king comes to you, gentle and riding on a donkey, and on a colt, the foal of a donkey.'"

Entering Jerusalem, we went down the main road and headed straight for the temple. A magnificent structure, the temple rose up ahead of us; it had been built over five hundred years ago by Zerubbabel. The first temple, constructed by King Solomon over one thousand years ago, had been destroyed by the king of Babylon, Nebuchadnezzar.

The beauty of the temple was drowned out by the noise and the smells. It was filled with livestock, merchants, and money changers. The long lines of people in front of the money changers' tables, waiting to convert various Greek and Roman coins to our Jewish money for the temple offerings, snaked around other booths, making it hard to walk. Others lined up in front of the livestock booths to pay for animal offerings, and it was obvious from the shouts and haggling that the merchants weren't giving fair exchange rates and were overcharging on the animals.

It got to be such a big business about fifty years ago that Herod the Great expanded the Temple Mount area, almost doubling its size. He added large areas to the north, west, and south of the pre-Herodian complex. Above the southern wall of the Temple Mount, he built a huge colonnaded structure called the Royal Stoa, a platform supported by pillars that created a covered walkway, a portico opening up more merchant area. This expanded area was called the Court of the Gentiles and wasn't considered sacred temple ground.

To ensure the merchants didn't defile the actual temple area, a low fence (soreg) had been erected to separate the inner sacred ground from the outer creation by Herod the Great. On the fence were banners clearly saying no stalls were allowed beyond. The inner courtyard was the holy ground of God Himself. As in all things, the greed of man knows no bounds, and during the big festivals. the temple priests conveniently closed their eyes, allowing merchants to set up shop beyond the fence line, and many openings were provided for easy access. Passover was the biggest festival of them all, and their area was sheer chaos.

As we walked past the outer courtyard, crossing the fence line onto holy ground, we heard a man and woman shouting at each other. The man was a seller offering doves. Poor people were still required to bring offerings to the temple, and if they had little money, they went to the booth to buy doves. The woman was pleading with the man; she was obviously in a bad way. She was an older woman, clearly a widow with no family since she was alone. Her worn clothes, the ends of her dress near her ankles, were tattered in many places and covered with dust and dirt. Her bare feet looked twisted since she leaned on a crutch made of an old wooden branch. In her outstretched hand was a single silver shekel.

The dove man, obviously unimpressed with the amount, didn't want to sell a dove for the token before him. She wailed that her husband and sons had been killed and that all she had was the single shekel. There was a long line of poor and equally downtrodden people behind her, and the dove man became so irritated with her that he came from behind his table and shoved her aside.

She fell to the ground, her only coin rolling off to nowhere. And to our astonishment, no one went to help the woman. Instead, the poor standing in line simply crossed over the woman to get to the table to buy their dove offering. The looks on their faces were ones of sad acceptance. That was just the way it was for them. The poor had no rights, power, or dignity. In the distance we saw our Jewish temple guards and some of the temple Pharisees. They had seen it all, and yet they made no attempt to help the poor widow.

I turned my head in shame, and great sadness welled up inside me. We had become worse than our Captors in the treatment of our own people in the name of greed. Looking to Jesus, we saw He too was caught up in the scene and had the same expression of shock and sadness; and then He had something more. The sadness in His face changed. A fire was lit, and His eyes burned with something I would say was close to madness. It was too much to bear for the Son of God to see His people treated worse than animals—and to do such a callous and heinous act in the house of God!

Jesus swiftly moved forward to an animal booth next to us and grabbed a whip. Moving fast, the crowd, knowing who the Teacher was, parted to let Him pass. Coming to the booth, Jesus overturned the dove man's table; coins splashed to the ground, and a few doves in cages on the table stumbled to the ground and broke loose. Instead of flying away, the doves hovered over Jesus, making a slow circle.

His anger still burning, the Teacher went to the other booths next to the dove man and overturned them as well. Angry vendors now shouted at Jesus. We quickly moved in and surrounded the Son of God, pushing away all who would dare come close to Him. The people backed off and encircled us. Fiery anger shone in the vendors' eyes, and tears of joy glistened in the eyes of the poor. Finally, there was one who would stand up and protect them.

The Pharisees and temple guards, seeing their well-run business being disrupted, quickly moved in to restore order. As they approached to arrest the disruptor, they held back when they saw it was Jesus. As angry as the vendors were, the crowd surrounding Jesus wouldn't let anything happen to their Savior. When the poor realized it was Jesus who was their champion, the amount of protection for us rose to new levels. The Pharisees saw it in their eyes and approached us with measured anger and caution. One of the Pharisees called out to Jesus, "Who are You to disrupt the temple activities. We make the rules and the law, not You."

Our Savior replied, "It is written. 'My house will be a house of prayer; but you have made it a den of robbers.'" It was a standoff between Jesus with the poor and the working people at His side and the temple elite and their money machine on the other. There was an uncomfortable silence, a calm before the arrival of a great storm. The Pharisees fidgeted, some with uncomfortable expressions as they briefly whispered to each other. Jesus was back to a calm face and relaxed posture. As if a hand of grace came over Him, He almost glowed with peace. We could feel the tension in the Pharisees, and at the same time, we felt peace radiating from Jesus as if it were a physical force.

The leader of the temple, Joseph Caiaphas, stepped forward and commanded the temple guards, "Make sure all vendors stay outside of holy ground." The holy men promptly turned their backs to us and retreated back into their inner sanctum, no doubt to lick their wounds at being put down by Jesus. But there was no greater danger than a wounded animal, and I was sure we hadn't heard the last of them.

The Teacher had now crossed a dangerous line. By confronting the temple high priest directly, affecting their precious livelihood, and clearly having the people at His side, He'd gone from agitator to a person who could possibly topple their power to control the people and their livelihood.

We went to the temple area every day during Passover week, and Jesus continued to preach and heal the sick and lame, all the while under the watchful eyes of our Jewish leaders. Some of them took turns to question Jesus and try to show the people they knew more than Jesus or waited for Him to say a wrong answer. The Teacher never made a mistake and always answered with truth and accuracy, at least, that is, as far as I knew, since the Pharisees never came back in response to Jesus's answers to their onslaught of questions. It was an amazing time. Every day thousands of people packed the inner and outer temple area, and the noise and commotion that came with selling and buying for the ritual sacrifices diminished as vendors and the people talked only in hushed tones and respectful whispers whenever Jesus was talking. Although the place was packed with people, the reduced trade was noticeable, with the people transfixed by the parables from Jesus. People lining up to be healed instead of buying animals or changing foreign money to Jewish coins.

Closer and closer we came to Passover, with the words of Jesus always in the back of our minds. Would it be today when Jesus was arrested? Tomorrow? As the week drew on, our nerves became more frayed as the crowd grew bigger. The faces of the Sadducees and Pharisees grew angrier as Jesus continued to rebuff them, drawing more and more to believe in the Savior. Would we be arrested as well? And have it all end for all of us in torture and death? My thoughts weren't my own since the concerned faces of others showed the same frowning faces whenever the temple guards drew too close to us.

# 19

# Slipping

*I tell you, Peter, before the rooster crows today, you*
*will deny three times that you know me.*

—JESUS, THE CHRIST (LUKE 22:34)

As the end of the week drew close, most of the people focused on the Passover meal, which began at sundown Thursday (which was also the beginning of Friday in our Jewish custom). It was the old covenant sacrificial meal of the Feast of Unleavened Bread. There was to be no leavened bread in any Jewish household. So strict was our custom that many gathered up all the leavened bread and gave it to their Gentile neighbors, only to buy it back again the next day. It was quite a business, and everyone took it as normal.

Jesus always told us He appreciated the rituals since they gave us time to reflect on the goodness and power of Father God. Through Moses's faith, God had brought our people to freedom. But being so strict as to give good bread to your neighbors and then pay them to get it back was going too far. There were people in need who could be helped instead of wasting time and money on such strict rules. Jesus was ever practical and always told us to focus on the basics. Love God. Love your neighbor. There was little else. Keep it simple. Too many rituals tended to complicate and dilute the meaning of the festivals.

Jesus wanted the Passover dinner to be a special time just for His closest friends. On the first day we arrived in Jerusalem, Sunday, He sent Andrew and me to acquire a private room big enough for fourteen people for Passover supper. Jerusalem was already bursting at the seams with people from all over the country and beyond for Passover week and even more so on Passover night. Jesus's directions were specific. He said to go into the city to the house of the famous metal pot maker, the man whose son Jesus had healed last summer. We had been there and remembered the man, for he had graciously allowed us to stay the week with him. We did as Jesus told us to do and took some time, wandering through the narrow streets. It was sensory overload with wall-to-wall people lining the streets, all moving in every direction and trying to find their way.

Vendors were at every corner, selling food and drinks. There were also those selling pottery and woven cloth to commemorate the festival. There were the smells, the loud noises, and people pushing from every direction. How in the world would we ever find the metal pot makers at home?

Walking down a side street, where there was less noise, we came to a four-way intersection with an ornately decorated metal poll. It was the sign for the man's shop. Thank God! When we knocked on the door, the old man opened it, and his eyes widened to see us.

He exclaimed, "Hallelujah! The Master has come back to us!" The metal pot maker and his entire family had become devoted disciples of Jesus.

We gave the words of Jesus to him. "The Teacher says, my appointed time is near. I am going to celebrate the Passover with my disciples at your house." Tears streamed down from the man's eyes, and he gave thanks to us for giving him such good news and promised that all would be prepared for us for the Passover meal.

The days passed too quickly, and here we were again at the metal pot maker's home. This time everyone was with us. It was Thursday, and the sun was waning low in the horizon. The pot maker and his family met us at the door and showed us to his upper room. And just as promised, all was prepared. The long table was adorned with our traditional food, spread nicely and set for fourteen. Pillows lined all sides with deeply woven rugs to cover the hard flooring. We embraced the man and his family, and they had time for a long talk with the Teacher. Jesus was in no hurry, and we all truly appreciated all His family had done to prepare such a meal for us. The bonds of brotherhood and sisterhood in Jesus were strong, and we all felt so alive. The city was bursting with life. Everyone was in a festive mood, and it was Passover day, in commemoration of the night when God had brought down His vengeance on our ancient oppressors and given us freedom. Even more than that, in this Passover we had Jesus! And He was in full force this week, preaching good news of redemption and forgiveness. Would a miracle happen on this Passover, and would the Romans fall tonight? This was the buzz in the city. The people were expectant. The temple leaders were concerned about Roman retaliation and tried ever harder every day to squash Jesus and His teachings but to no avail. Everything was coming to a massive finale.

I will never forget that dinner, and we all committed it to memory as much as we could. Before we ate, Jesus gave thanks to God for His goodness and for all He had given to us over these past four years. We were no longer a group of people following the teachings of Jesus. We were family now. We had left our old lives behind to become new. We were reborn and now belonged to the family of Jesus and God.

Jesus took bread, broke a small piece off it, and ate it. Then He broke it in half and passed it to each side. He also told us to take a piece of it and eat it as He did. As we did this, Jesus said, "Take and eat, this is my body." Then the Teacher took a cup, gave thanks, took a sip, and passed the cup to us, saying "Drink from it, all of you. This is my blood of the covenant, which is poured out for the many for the forgiveness of sins. I tell you, I will not drink from this fruit of the vine from now until that day when I drink it new with you in my Father's kingdom."

Later on, during the dinner, as we were all in good conversation, Jesus suddenly stopped talking, and a pale shade came over Him. Sweat poured down His face, and His body shivered. We thought He had eaten something bad or gotten a piece of food caught in His throat. After a short time, Jesus's complexion returned, and He was able to talk.

"One of you will betray me tonight."

"We will not!" We all exclaimed and we all gave Jesus our pledge of trust. Jesus remained silent. When Judas said, "Surely you don't mean me, Rabbi?"

Jesus responded, "You have said so." Immediately Judas left us. We had thought Jesus was sending Judas to buy more food or wine, since he was in charge of the money. It was only later that we found out the depths of His treachery.

Typical of our normal routine after a big dinner, we needed to stretch our legs and walk off the meal. As we strolled, Jesus started to sing our traditional Passover songs (the Hallel or praise in Psalms 113–118), and everyone joined in. It was when we sang Psalm 116 that I felt Jesus. The spirit in His voice rang with such passion that it made all of us hush our voices just a bit so we could better hear the passionate singing of the Teacher.

## Psalm 116

I love the Lord, for he heard my voice;
he heard my cry for mercy.
Because he turned his ear to me,
I will call on him as long as I live.
The cords of death entangled me,
the anguish of the grave came over me;
I was overcome by distress and sorrow.
Then I called on the name of the Lord:
"Lord, save me!"
The Lord is gracious and righteous;
our God is full of compassion.
The Lord protects the unwary;
when I was brought low, he saved me.
Return to your rest, my soul,
for the Lord has been good to you.
For you, Lord, have delivered me from death,
my eyes from tears,
my feet from stumbling,
that I may walk before the Lord
in the land of the living.
I trusted in the Lord when I said,
"I am greatly afflicted";
in my alarm I said,
"Everyone is a liar."

What shall I return to the Lord
for all his goodness to me?
I will lift up the cup of salvation
and call on the name of the Lord.
I will fulfill my vows to the Lord
in the presence of all his people.
Precious in the sight of the Lord
is the death of his faithful servants.
Truly I am your servant, Lord;
I serve you just as my mother did;
you have freed me from my chains.
I will sacrifice a thank offering to you
and call on the name of the Lord.
I will fulfill my vows to the Lord
in the presence of all his people,
in the courts of the house of the Lord—
in your midst, Jerusalem.

After a time, the songs ended, and we walked together in silence. We were headed east out of the city to the Mount of Olives, one of our holiest places steeped with rich history. David had ascended the Mount of Olives to flee Absalom's coup. Zechariah had also referred to it in his vision of future warfare against Jerusalem. In that apocalyptic time, the Lord will stand on the Mount; it will split in two, and our people will flee through this valley. This prophecy was the basis for the tradition that from the Mount of Olives God would redeem the dead when the Messiah came. It was holy ground.

All of us were lost in our thoughts. As we neared the Mount of Olives, we stopped for a quick rest. It was then that Jesus told us He would soon be arrested and that on this very night we would all fall away and scatter like lost sheep. This was nonsense! We had been through rough times with Jesus over the last several years, leaving everything to be His disciples. We wouldn't fall away. My heart was pounding, and I could feel my old friend, anger, boiling up within me.

I blurted out, "Even if all fall away on account of you, I never will!" I was hurt and angry, as were all, by the Teacher's lack of faith in us.

Jesus turned and looked directly at me with such penetrating eyes, and for a moment, I had to turn away but only for a second. Then I locked my eyes on the Son of Man. Jesus wasn't angry with my explosion. He put His hand on my shoulder and told me in a firm voice with a hint of sadness, "I tell you, Peter, before the rooster crows today, you will deny three times that you know me." He said this with such calmness as if it were a fact that had already happened. My knees instantly grew weak.

Gathering myself in the firmest voice I could muster, which was now a bit shaky, I replied with unsteady words. "Even if I have to die with you, I will never disown you!"

All the other disciples immediately said the same. Jesus kept His hand on my shoulder and looked at each and every one of us with a smile of thankfulness. His expression was more of one that said, *Thank you for your words. Even though I don't fully believe you, the gesture is well received.* Each of us came to Jesus and gave Him a hug and kiss. We were family, and times were about to get hard.

With our brief rest and anxiety-filled talks finished, we continued on; the mountain loomed ever larger. Our path took us to the garden of Gethsemane, located at the base of the Mount of Olives. It was a serene and quiet place. Jesus often liked to come here to get away from the noise of the city to pray. Set on a gentle upward slope, there was a fairly good-sized cave used for shelter and a work area to press the olives.

It was late at night, and there was no one there. Jesus told us to wait at the cave while He went a bit farther to pray. It was an ideal place to shelter, and Andrew quickly started a small fire to keep everyone warm. As Jesus turned to walk away, He called me and the Sons of Thunder, James and John, to accompany Him.

At first, I was a bit hesitant since the warmth of Andrew's fire beckoned my tired body. James and John took this request as Jesus wanting some protection, and their fiery zeal was on full display as they jumped up with their swords clanging on their waist belts. Jesus gave us three that look that said, *Why did I choose these three to come with me?* Dutifully we stepped in line behind the Messiah, me a bit cold. James and John's heads swiveled back and forth, looking for the enemy. Earlier, Jesus had said He would be arrested tonight, and the "Thunder Brothers" were ready for it.

We didn't go far from the cave when the Teacher told us to wait, and He went just a few steps ahead, wanting to be alone to pray and staying within earshot. It was obvious that just three of us weren't there for protection since we were so close to the others at the cave. We were there more to give Jesus company during this stressful time.

Sometimes Jesus prayed for just a few minutes and other times much longer. Tonight was one of those longer nights. It was cold, and we were away from the cave in an open area. The wind was blowing frigid air, and we huddled close together for warmth. Not thinking it would be a long walk, we hadn't brought our heavier clothes. Time seemed to pass by very slowly; my body seemed to slow down, conserving energy for warmth, and my eyes grew tired. Then I heard some rustling of bushes and a shout. Metal clanged on the ground.

I opened my eyes; the "Thunder Brothers" were stumbling forward awkwardly with their long swords, banging noisily on the hard ground. Jesus was there, standing in front of us with a frown, showing more disappointment than anger. "Couldn't you men keep watch for me for just one hour?" He blurted at us while turning His back. "Watch and pray so that you will not fall into temptation. The spirit is willing but the flesh is weak."

Ugh. We'd failed Jesus again! Before we could mutter some words of apology, He went walking away to pray again. John and James came close to me, and we started to pray, "Father God, give us strength to stay alert, to protect Your Son, and to give Him comfort in His time of need." We repeated this same prayer several times and then started to recite together the disciples' prayer Jesus had taught us. We said this several times as the cold creeped into our bones. Our prayers became softer, and before I knew it, my eyes became tired again. My spirit was willing, but my body was weak, cold, and tired.

I struggled to keep awake, looked over, and saw James and John struggling as well. Blackness engulfed me. Then the same metal clanged again. I jumped up this time, all my senses tingling. It was freezing cold, but sweat started to drip down my forehead. The noises were different this time. I could hear shouts from our other brothers. Andrew and Matthew's voice called out from afar. I stumbled forward into the arms of Jesus.

Jesus righted me and looked at me, James, and John as shadows moved close to the Lord. "Look, the hour has come, and the Son of Man is delivered into the hands of sinners. Rise! Let us go! Here comes my betrayer!" We moved quickly to the entrance of the cave, where the others were. In the distance a number of torches were coming toward us.

And there he was, in the front of the large crowd, Judas, our brother! Behind him were temple guards and just behind them a few temple priests and their servants. There were other people as well, those loyal to the Jewish leaders. More likely they had been paid to be there since most of the common people loved Jesus. As if on cue, the crowd stopped, and Judas kept walking toward us and Jesus.

I started to step forward to block Judas, but Jesus put His hand on my shoulder, whispering to me. His voice was soft with a deep sadness. "Let it be as it must come to pass."

Judas stopped directly in front of the Teacher, his face a blank mask. There was no emotion at all, as if all His feelings were spent, and there was nothing left of Judas but a shell. Our brother blurted out, "Greetings, Rabbi."

Jesus raised His arms open and replied, "Do what you came for, friend." Judas then stepped forward and kissed Jesus on His right cheek, and then he took a couple of steps back.

Then something strange happened to Judas, revelation of what he had just done. His blank face contorted. All at once Judas's face changed to fear, sorrow, and shame at the same time. Tears started to stream down his face, and he yelled, "Forgive me, Lord!" He quickly ran away.

The temple guards rushed forward with the high priest's servants. Pushing us aside, they grabbed Jesus roughly and started to bind His arms with rope. Jesus didn't resist as if He expected this to happen. Pushed to the ground, James and John were struggling to get up when one of the guards pushed me, and I tripped over James, landing hard on top of him.

Time seemed to slow down, and I felt as if I were moving in slow motion. It was always like that for me. In times of crisis and stress, it was as if the world around me slowed, and I vividly remembered all the details. I put my hands on the hard, cold ground to push myself back up. When I felt around, my hand came upon cold metal. James's sword! I grabbed it while pushing up with my other hand, springing forward toward Jesus and the men who were binding Him. When I moved forward, my arm rotated the sword in a high arch. There was a loud shrieking noise like the howling of a wild animal.

At first the noise didn't register with my brain, but then it hit me. That was *my* voice yelling.

The man just to the side of Jesus turned His face, becoming instantly white with fear as my sword rotated high in the air, looking to severe his head off. The man jerked back, instinctively trying to get away from the gleaming metal shape coming for him. Just missing him, the metal came down.

The man screamed in agonizing pain and fell to the ground. Red liquid poured from His face, and His white robes turned to red near His neck. It was a glancing blow.

With rage in my eyes, I started forward again, lifting the sword to finish the task, when Jesus stepped in front of me.

"Put your sword back in its place. For all who draw the sword will die by the sword!" The Teacher placed both of His hands on my shoulders.

My trembling body, rushing with energy from the intensity, seemed to instantly calm down.

My Lord then said, "Do you think that I cannot call on my father and he will at once put at my disposal more than twelve legions of Angels? But how then would the Scriptures be fulfilled that say it must happen this way?" It was as if all my anger and hate washed away, and the sword fell from my hands to the ground.

Jesus turned away and bent down to the bleeding man on the ground. With his right hand, the man clutched the place where his right ear should have been, and in his left, he held his severed ear. The Son of God whispered something to the man, took the severed ear, and with both hands laid on the man's head, He started to pray. The man, a servant of the high priest, slumped down for a second, and then his head jerked up. He looked directly at Jesus but not with agonizing pain as he had just a moment ago; he had a look of total peace, as if God Himself had touched the man. And it *was* God Himself.

The man's ear was completely healed! Jesus stood him up. The guards witnessing everything stepped back as well, completely amazed by what Jesus had done. Surely this was a holy man. They hesitated and wouldn't bind Jesus.

It was then that one of the temple priests stepped forward and ordered the guards to bind Jesus while stirring up the crowd, calling Jesus's miracle the work of a demon. The crowd began to yell, and the temple soldiers moved forward again to bind Jesus.

The Teacher then started to retort to the crowd, asking why they would put Him in chains. The crowd, whipped up in a frenzy by the temple priests, looked like they wanted to kill Jesus and everyone around Him.

Fear gripped my heart! My anger turned instantly into a depth of fear for my life that I had never known before. The faces of the other disciples showed the same. The angry mob moved closer to us, torches and clubs raised about their heads in angry arms. The guards surrounded Jesus to protect Him from the mob and started to lead Him away back to the temple. Unable to get their hands on our Lord, the mob turned to His followers for satisfaction. That was us!

There was nothing to do. We couldn't save Jesus from the soldiers. Jesus Himself had said not to. We could stay and be clubbed to death, become martyrs or heroes of the faith, or run. There was no time to think. It happened so fast.

The next thing I remember was my heart pumping. Sweat dripped down my face, and a noise came from my mouth I will never forget. I yelled, "Run!"

And just like that, we did as Jesus had foretold. We scattered like wild rabbits in all directions, leaving our Teacher to His fate, abandoning the Messiah, the Son of God. I tried to justify my actions. Jesus had told me to put down my sword. If I hadn't run and told the others to run, then we would all have been killed. Then what would have happened to the mission to spread the gospel of Jesus? These were all good thoughts. Deep down I knew Jesus would have protected us. Yes, we would have been beaten and injured, but His plans for us would have gone on.

It was the moment. It was fear. It wasn't having full trust and faith in Jesus that escaped me, leaving me only with self-perseveration. And if that wasn't enough, shame; and the night wasn't over yet.

We scattered like rats when they took Jesus, running fast enough that the mob lost interest. They had their man, and the people followed the arrested Jesus back to Jerusalem, heading to the main temple, where the high priest and the whole Sanhedrin were gathered. I could see the train of torches and followed from far behind. It was a long night; I no longer felt the cold, my senses working on high alert.

Sometime later that night, I was able to make it to the outer courtyard of the main temple. No one was being allowed into the sacred inner temple area, where they held the Teacher. My heart was full of sadness, and I prayed that they were just asking Jesus questions and no more. Guilt welling up inside me for running. I huddled along with the large crowds. Everyone knew what would happen, and people were slowly gathering in the courtyard. Fires were lit to keep warm, and talk was a hushed whisper. No one seemed to want to voice his or her allegiance to Jesus or to defend Him. There were those devoted and paid by the Jewish leaders to pick out any of Jesus's followers. These were dangerous times, and all knew what happened to those who didn't fall into line with the temple leaders: banishment from the Jewish community or even worse, according to the spreading rumors. There was no tolerance left, and all would be punished severely.

The cold was getting to me, so I moved closer to one of the fires for warmth. It felt good, the flames providing heat and warming my body. The fire did something else I hadn't realized until it was too late. It was also illuminating my face.

A young girl came up to me. She pointed her finger at me and, with a loud and accusing voice, shouted, "You also were with Jesus of Galilee!"

My heart raced and seemed to burst out of my body. In a moment of panic, I blurted out, "I don't know what you are talking about!" I got up quickly and turned to the crowd, moving away from the finger still pointing at me. I kept moving until I reached the outer gateway, and then again there was another voice. There were a different voice and a different finger but the same accusation.

"This fellow was with Jesus of Nazareth!"

Like a repeat of before, my answer came swiftly. "I don't know the man!" And I kept moving. And if my shame weren't great enough, a few people came to me later as I huddled in a corner, talking softly to a disciple friend.

Accusing words rang in the darkness. "Surely you are one of them. Your accent gives you away."

For the third time on that terrible night, my reply was automatic. "I don't know the man!" And then like thunder from the heavens, a rooster began to crow. Instantly, my thoughts returned to earlier that night when I had been a much bolder man, telling Jesus I would stand by Him and defend Him to the death.

The Teacher's only reply had been, "Before the rooster crows you will deny me three times." All had come to pass just as Jesus foretold. I was no better than Judas. In my shame, I remembered Jesus's other words that He would be tortured and killed. Everything was happening exactly as He had said it would. I ran as fast as I could away from the people, away from the temple, and away from the reality of what had happened and was to come to pass. Tears came of shame and sorrow for the fate of my Messiah, my friend, my brother, my Savior. What was to become of all of us now?

# 20

# Ignition

*I walk in the wilderness of life. This time I am not lost or alone.*
—SHI'MON BAR JONAH (PETER)

We slowly gathered together in the same upper room where we'd had our last supper with Jesus. The owner was a devote follower of Jesus, and we trusted him. How or why we were all drawn to this place was a mystery to us. When asked, each of us had the same reply. We had felt a pulling back to the place where we had last had supper with Jesus. There was a feeling of home and safety. The only other person who knew of this place was Judas, but John told us that Judas had hanged himself shortly after betraying the Son of God. It was hard to be too angry with Judas, for we had all fallen short for Jesus that night. We were more saddened to hear of Judas's death and said prayers for his soul. May God forgive him for what he did that night. May God forgive us for what we *didn't* do that night.

John sat with us later and told us about what had happened to Jesus that day and night: the public torture, the trial, more torture, the long road to the hill of skulls, the crucifixion. It was unbearable to hear. How could they have been so cruel to Jesus, who had nothing but heal others and spread teachings of love, grace, forgiveness, and hope? Where were His faithful disciples, His appointed apostles during the time when Jesus had needed us most for support? We were in hiding.

I was so ashamed. We all were. In my despair I was thankful that at least one of us had had the courage and strength to be there with the

Teacher every step of the way—and not just one of us but three. John; Mary Magdalene; and Jesus's mother, Mary, had stayed with our Messiah through it all. I could understand Jesus's mom being there, but Mary Magdalene and John? What courage! The three showed no frustration or resentment for our not being there with them, not being with Jesus.

To this day I thank John, Mary Magdalene, and Mary for their courage and support to Jesus. Whenever times get hard, I come back and remember their strength. Then I too am encouraged to have that same strength and even more than that, the same love for Jesus.

The long and solemn Saturday ended, and Sunday was upon us. The sun rose as it did every morning, showing her bright face over the horizon. Our mood, however, didn't reflect the dawning of a new day. We were held in the grief of the past. Our Lord and Savior, the Son of God Himself, was no longer with us. He'd been tortured, crucified, killed, and buried in a small tomb cut out of a rock hillside with a large stone rolled in front of the opening. We were thankful to hear that one of Jesus's disciples, a rich man named Joseph of Arimathea, had been able to get the body of the Teacher and bury Him in the tomb Joseph had originally made for himself.

Roman soldiers guarded the entrance, keeping watch lest one of the followers of Jesus should steal His body and falsely proclaim His rising from the dead just as Jesus had once foretold would happen. Our Jewish leaders were trying to stop any possibility that the words and works of Jesus could continue after His death. With our misery completed, what could be worse?

The door suddenly vibrated, and a creaking noise emanated from the large wooden rectangle. My heart raced, and my throat dried instantly. When the door slowly opened, a voice came from behind it.

"Friends, do not worry." It was our host.

The tension in the air immediately vanished. He walked in with some fruit. Our host, a cautious man, brought up the food in multiple trips at different times to thwart any onlookers of suspicious activities. Such was the world we lived in now. No leader, no agenda. Even with the brightness of day, it seemed like there was a dark cloud hovering above us, obscuring the light and hope, and leaving only uncertainty and fear. We thanked our host, gathering around that same supper table.

This time we ate in total silence. There was nothing to be said, each of us lost in his or her thoughts.

It was Mary Magdalene who first spoke, breaking the deafening silence. "Peter, Mary and I are going to the tomb to anoint Jesus." Mary Magdalene and Mary, the mother of James, had prepared spices to anoint Jesus's body but weren't allowed in the tomb since no work was allowed on the Sabbath. Before Peter could reply, Thomas spoke.

"Peter? You mean Shi'mon. Peter was the rock of the church of Jesus. I see only Shi'mon here today."

*Ouch.* That hurt deep. What could I say? I, Peter, Jesus's rock of the church, had denied knowing Jesus, not once or twice but three times in Jesus's hour of most desperate need. My head slumped down.

Mary, sitting next to me, blurted out, "Thomas, that is quite enough! I think we all have had our failings in the last two days. It there was one thing Jesus taught us, it was forgiveness and grace. I am sure He has forgiven you, Thomas. Please, do the same and forgive us for our failures."

Thomas got up and came over to us, kneeling to our sitting level. He looked at Mary, then turned to me. "Forgive me, Brother. It was harsh and wrong of me. Those aren't my words. You are the rock of the church of Jesus." We embraced.

There was so much pain among us all. How would we ever move forward? Mary Magdalene got up and motioned to Jesus's mother. They got the spices that were already neatly packed up in two small satchels and slung them over their shoulders. At the door Mary Magdalene looked back at me, and I gave her a warm smile and nodded. I was still their leader. And out the door they went.

The morning passed, with our moods and thoughts still lost in despair when it hit us. The room began to shake violently. We instinctively lowered ourselves and went to the nearest wall to brace ourselves. The walls shuttered and groaned, seeming to wave like palm leaves in the wind. It was the same shake we'd felt just two days ago. It was John who told us that the violent shake had happened on Friday at the exact moment when Jesus died on the cross. *What was this one?* we wondered.

No one dared to speak what was in our hearts. Hope. Was this the signal of the return of Jesus from the dead as He had foretold? As we anticipated the return of the two Marys, time seemed to slow down and move slowly. Much too slowly.

Later in the early afternoon, Mary Magdalene and Jesus's mother finally returned. They were breathless as they swung open the door, running in with excitement on their faces. Coming straight toward me, Mary Magdalene shouted, "Jesus is alive!" Excitedly, Mary Magdalene told us what had happened. Just as they had arrived at the tomb, a large shake had vibrated the entire hill, and the large stone blocking the tomb entrance had rolled away. Then there were flashes of light from the sky above; they were so bright like lightning, they'd had to cover their eyes.

She said, "When we looked again, there was a man sitting on the large entrance stone. His clothes were as white as snow, and hi whole body glowed. He told us Jesus wasn't in the tomb and that He had risen from the dead. The two Roman soldiers guarding the tomb had been so afraid that they'd run away."

Upon hearing this, I grabbed the man next to me (it was John), and I blurted, "Come and we will see for ourselves! Everyone else, wait here. We must still be careful."

We ran as fast as we could to the tomb. When we arrived, it was just as Mary Magdalene had told us. The stone had been rolled away, and the tomb was empty. We went inside, and on top of the rock table where Jesus had lain, there was only His graveclothes. But no Jesus! Could He really have risen from the dead?

I motioned to John, and we turned to head back as fast as we could. As we raced back into town, a realization struck me. The words of Jesus during our last supper together rang in my mind, and a picture of Jesus formed as clear as day, sitting in front of us, breaking bread, and drinking a cup of wine; and then there were His words. It was late in the day by the time we returned. Entering, John and I saw that dinner was all prepared, but no one had started eating yet. All were waiting for our report of what we had seen. I told everyone to sit around the table just as we had done for the last supper we had with Jesus. All sat silently and expectantly.

I said a prayer. "Lord, we thank You for everything You have provided for us. We thank You, Jesus, by whose word all things come to be." I then grabbed a piece of bread. Holding it up, I ripped off a small piece and ate it. Breaking it in half, I passed it on and spoke the words of Jesus. "Take and eat, this is my body."

After everyone took a piece of bread and ate it, I reached forward again and lifted a cup of wine. Taking a sip, I passed it on and again repeated the words of Jesus. "Drink from it, all of you. This is My blood of the covenant, which is poured out for the many for the forgiveness of sins. I tell you, I will not drink from this fruit of the vine from now until that day when I drink it new with you in My Father's kingdom."

After everyone had taken a sip from the cup, we prayed in silence. The fear was gone. The anxieties were gone. It was as if a covering of peace and contentment had come and covered us all. Our silence was broken by a loud thunderclap; a voice boomed from just behind me.

"Peace be with you!"

That voice! That beautiful voice! I couldn't see Him; looking forward at the faces on the opposite side of the table said it all. All the faces were a mixture of sheer happiness and awe, as if they couldn't believe what their eyes were telling them. Sheer joy!

A hand came down on my head. Turning, I too then saw Him, Jesus, our Lord! The Son of God Himself was among us again, risen from the dead in three days just as He had promised.

We all jumped up and rushed to our Messiah. Each of us gave our Messiah a long and warm hug and kiss on each cheek. I waited to the last. Just before me, Thomas came up to Jesus. "How do we know it's You, Jesus?"

Of course, our doubting Thomas. He didn't say the words with malice or distrust. It was just the way Thomas thought. He needed to see proof that it was Jesus and not just a lookalike. Jesus looked at Thomas and sighed. "Put your finger here, see my hands. Reach out your hand and put it into my side. Stop doubting and believe."

Dutifully doing what he was told, Thomas reached out. Then, dropping to his knees, he blurted, "My Lord and my God!"

Jesus responded with words I will never forget. "Because you have seen me, you have believed; blessed are those who have not seen and yet have believed." We'd had the privilege and blessing to have been witnesses to all of Jesus's miracles and still had fallen short in truly believing in Him, until now when we had seen Him risen from the dead.

I have taken this event to heart and truly admire the people I have since met, who have firm belief in the good news of Jesus, that Jesus is the Son of God, even though they haven't seen Him in the flesh as we did.

For the next forty days, Jesus stayed with us, teaching us more about the kingdom of God. We spent many glorious dinners together, just like the old days when we'd traveled and preached. But it was different now. Now eternity sat with us. The risen Jesus had conquered death itself to show us that His words were real. Heaven and eternal life were real. Jesus was real. Jesus was alive forever.

On that fortieth day since Jesus first came back to us, our Messiah brought His eleven apostles and Mary Magdalene up to the top of the Mount of Olives. We gathered around Jesus, and Mary asked, "Lord, are You at this time going to restore the kingdom to Israel?"

Our Savior looked on us with a contemplative look, not like He was searching for something to say as a reply but more like, *How should I say this in a way they will understand?* His reply was like a teacher to his students. "It is not for you to know the times or dates the Father has set by his own authority. But you will receive power when the Holy Spirit comes on you; and you will be my witnesses in Jerusalem, and in all Judea and Samaria, and to the ends of the earth." Then the clouds opened, and Jesus was elevated into the sky and disappeared.

We continued to strain our eyes to see whether we could still see the Son of God when two men dressed all in white suddenly appeared in front of us. They spoke in unison. "Why do you stand here looking into the sky? This same Jesus, who has been taken from you into heaven, will come back in the same way you have seen him go into heaven."

And they too, just like the Teacher, disappeared right in front of us. We were again alone, but this time it was different. There was no loss. No sorrow. No feelings of shame or regret. Instead, determination, hope, peace, and energy filled us. The others turned to me and asked, "What should we do next?"

I thought for a second, and then His words came to me. "Brothers and sister, remember what Jesus told us last week while eating dinner. 'Do not leave Jerusalem, but wait for the gift my Father promised, which you have heard me speak about. For John baptized with water, but in a few days, you will be baptized with the Holy Spirit.' We go back to Jerusalem and await the coming of the Holy Spirit into us."

We all came together in a group hug, lifted our eyes to the sky once more, and thanked Jesus for His eternal blessings in our lives. We turned and headed back to Jerusalem. As we walked down the side of the mount, a thought flashed across my mind, and I smiled.

*I walk in the wilderness of life. But this time I am not lost or alone.*

| No. | Page | Scripture | Chapter/Verse |
|-----|------|-----------|---------------|
| 1 | 14 | "I baptize you with water. But one who is more powerful than I will come, the straps of whose sandals I am not worthy to untie. He will baptize you with the Holy Spirit and fire." | Luke 3:16 |
| 2 | 14 | "Repent for the kingdom of heaven has come near." | Matthew 3:2 |
| 3 | 15 | "Look, the lamb of God who takes away the sins of the world! This is the one I meant when I said, 'A man who comes after me has surpassed me because he was before me.' | John 1:30 |
| 4 | 15 | "I saw the spirit come down from heaven as a dove and remain on him. And I myself did not know him, but the one who sent me to baptize with water told me, 'The man on whom you see the Spirit come down and remain is He who will baptize with the Holy Spirit.' I have seen and testify that this is God's Chosen One." | John 1:32–34 |
| 5 | 16 | "What do you want?" | John 1:37 |
| 6 | 16 | Andrew replied, "Rabbi, where are you staying?" | John 1:38 |
| 7 | 20 | "You are Shi'mon [he who listens to the word of God], son of Jonah. From now on you will be called Cephas [Peter, the rock]." | John 1:42 |
| 8 | 25 | "Woman," Jesus replied, "why do you involve me?" | John 2:4 |
| 9 | 25 | "Fill the jars with water" | John 2:7 |
| 10 | 26 | "Everyone brings out the choice wine first and then the cheaper wine as guests have had too much to drink, but you have saved the best till now." | John 2:10 |
| 11 | 30 | "Destroy this temple, and I will raise it again in three days." | John 2:19 |
| 12 | 30 | "It has taken forty-six years to build this temple, and you are going to raise it in three days?" | John 2:20 |

| No. | Page | Scripture | Chapter/Verse |
|-----|------|-----------|---------------|
| 13 | 31 | "Very truly I tell you, no one can see the kingdom of God unless they are born again." | John 3:2–3 |
| 14 | 31 | "no one can enter the kingdom of God unless they are born of water and the spirit. The flesh gives birth to flesh, but the spirit gives birth to spirit." | John 3:5 |
| 15 | 35 | A person can receive only what is given to them from heaven. You yourselves can testify that I said, 'I am not the Christ but am sent ahead of him.' The bride belongs to the bridegroom. The friend who attends the bridegroom waits and listens for him and is full of joy when he hears the bridegroom voice. That joy is mine, and now it is complete. He must become greater; I must become less." | John 3:27–30 |
| 16 | 39 | "Will you give me a drink?" | John 4:7 |
| 17 | 39 | "You are a Jew and I am a Samaritan woman. How can you ask me for a drink?" | John 4:9 |
| 18 | 39 | "If you knew the gift of God and who it is that asks you for a drink, you would have asked him and he would have given you living water." | John 4:10 |
| 19 | 40 | "I have food to eat that you know nothing about." | John 4:32 |
| 20 | 40 | "My food" said Jesus, "is to do the will of him who sent me and to finish his work." | John 4:32–34 |
| 21 | 42 | "Unless you people see signs and wonders you will never believe." | John 4:48 |
| 22 | 43 | "Go. Your son will live." | John 4:50 |
| 23 | 49 | "The time has come. The kingdom of God has come near. Repent and believe the good news!" | Mark 1:15 |
| 24 | 50 | "Come, follow me, and I will send you out to fish for people" | Matthew 4:19 |

| No. | Page | Scripture | Chapter/Verse |
|-----|------|-----------|---------------|
| 25 | 55 | "And you experts in the law, woe to you, because you load the people down with burdens they can hardly carry, and you yourselves will not lift one finger to help them." | Luke 11:46 |
| 26 | 56 | "Be quiet! Come out of him!" | Luke 4:35 |
| 27 | 56 | "What is this? A new teaching—and with authority! He even gives orders to impure spirits and they obey him." | Mark 1:27 |
| 28 | 58 | "Let us go somewhere else—to the nearby villages—so I can also preach there. That is why I have come" | Mark 1:38 |
| 29 | 63 | "I am willing. Be clean!" | Matthew 8:3 |
| 30 | 66 | "Friend, your sins are forgiven." | Luke 5:20 |
| 31 | 66 | "Why are you thinking these things in your hearts? Which is easier—to say, 'Your sins are forgiven' or 'Get up and walk'? But that you may know that the Son of Man has authority on earth to forgive sins." So he said to the paralyzed man, "I tell you, get up, take your mat and go home." | Luke 5:22–24 |
| 32 | 67 | "Follow me." | Mark 2:14 |
| 33 | 67 | "It is not the healthy who need a doctor, but the sick. I have not come to call the righteous, but sinners." | Mark 2:17 |

| No. | Page | Scripture | Chapter/Verse |
|---|---|---|---|
| 34 | 71-72 | Blessed are the poor in spirit, for theirs is the kingdom of heaven. Blessed are those who mourn, for they will be comforted. Blessed are the meek, for they will inherit the earth. Blessed are those who hunger and thirst for righteousness, for they will be filled. Blessed are the merciful, for they will be shown mercy. Blessed are the pure in heart, for they will see God. Blessed are the peacemakers, for they will be called children of God. Blessed are those who are persecuted because of righteousness, for theirs is the kingdom of heaven. Blessed are you when people insult you, persecute you and falsely say all kinds of evil against you because of me. Rejoice and be glad, because great is your reward in heaven, for in the same way they persecuted the prophets who were before you.<br><br>Jesus then looked right at us.<br><br>You are the salt of the earth. But if the salt loses its saltiness, how can it be made salty again? It is no longer good for anything, except to be thrown out and trampled underfoot. You are the light of the world. A town built on a hill cannot be hidden. Neither do people light a lamp and put it under a bowl. Instead they put it on its stand, and it gives light to everyone in the house. In the same way, let your light shine before others, that they may see your good deeds and glorify your Father in heaven. | Matthew 5:3–16 |

| No. | Page | Scripture | Chapter/Verse |
|-----|------|-----------|---------------|
| 35 | 74 | She sent for Barak son of Abinoam from Kedesh in Naphtali and said to him, "The Lord, the God of Israel, commands you: 'Go, take with you ten thousand men of Naphtali and Zebulun and lead them up to Mount Tabor. | Judges 4:6 |
| 36 | 75 | "Don't cry." | Luke 7:13 |
| 37 | 75 | "Young man, I say to you, get up!" | Luke 7:14 |
| 38 | 80 | "Simon, I have something to tell you." "Tell me, Teacher," he said. "Two people owed money to a certain moneylender. One owed him five hundred denarii and the other fifty. Neither of them had the money to pay him back, so he forgave the debts of both. Now which of them will love him more?" Simon replied, "I suppose the one who had the bigger debt forgiven." "You have judged correctly," Jesus said. Then He turned toward the woman and said to Simon, "Do you see this woman? I came into your house. You did not give me any water for my feet, but she wet my feet with her tears and wiped them with her hair. You did not give me a kiss, but this woman, from the time I entered, has not stopped kissing my feet. You did not put oil on my head, but she has poured perfume on my feet. Therefore, I tell you, her many sins have been forgiven-as her great love has shown. But whoever has been forgiven little loves little." Then Jesus said to her, "Your sins are forgiven." | Luke 7:40–48 |
| 39 | 80 | "Your faith has saved you; go in peace." | Luke7:50 |
| 40 | 85 | "For six days work is to be done, but the seventh day is the day of Sabbath rest, holy to the Lord. Whoever does work on the Sabbath day is to be put to death." | Exodus 31:15 |

| No. | Page | Scripture | Chapter/Verse |
|-----|------|-----------|---------------|
| 41 | 85 | The Lord said to Moses "The man must die. The whole assembly must stone him outside the camp." | Numbers 15:35 |
| 42 | 86 | "Look! Your disciples are doing what is unlawful on the Sabbath." | Matthew 12:2 |
| 43 | 86 | "Haven't you read what David did when he and his companions were hungry? He entered the house of God, and he and his companions ate the consecrated bread—which was not lawful for them to do, but only for the priests. Or haven't you read in the Law that the priests on Sabbath duty in the temple desecrate the Sabbath and yet are innocent? I tell you that something greater than the temple is here. If you had known what these words mean, 'I desire mercy, not sacrifice,' you would not have condemned the innocent. For the Son of Man is Lord of the Sabbath." | Matthew 12:3–8 |
| 44 | 88 | "Get up and stand in front of everyone." | Luke 6:8 |
| 45 | 88 | "I ask you, which is lawful on the Sabbath: to do good or to do evil, to save a life or to destroy it?" | Luke 6:9 |
| 46 | 88 | "Stretch out your hand!" | Luke 6:10 |
| 47 | 89 | "If any of you has a sheep and it falls into a pit on the Sabbath, will you not take hold of it and lift it out? How much more valuable is a person than a sheep! Therefore, it is lawful to do good on the Sabbath." | Matthew 12:11–12 |
| 48 | 89 | "Stretch out your hand!" | Luke 6:10 |
| 49 | 91 | them "a wicked and adulterous generation." | Matthew 16:4 |
| 50 | 91 | "For as Jonah was three days and three nights in the belly of a huge fish, so the Son of Man will be three days and three nights in the heart of the earth." | Matthew 12:40 |

| No. | Page | Scripture | Chapter/Verse |
|-----|------|-----------|---------------|
| 51 | 93 | A farmer went out to sow his seed. As he was scattering the seed, some fell along the path, and the birds came and ate it up. Some fell on rocky places, where it did not have much soil. It sprang up quickly, because the soil was shallow. But when the sun came up, the plants were scorched, and they withered because they had no root. Other seed fell among thorns, which grew up and choked the plants. Still other seed fell on good soil, where it produced a crop—a hundred, sixty or thirty times what was sown. Whoever has ears, let them hear. | Matthew 13:3–9 |
| 52 | 93-94 | When anyone hears the message about the kingdom and does not understand it, the evil one comes and snatches away what was sown in their heart. This is the seed sown along the path. The seed falling on rocky ground refers to someone who hears the word and at once receives it with joy. But since they have no root, they last only a short time. When trouble or persecution comes because of the word, they quickly fall away. The seed falling among the thorns refers to someone who hears the word, but the worries of this life and the deceitfulness of wealth choke the word, making it unfruitful. But the seed falling on good soil refers to someone who hears the word and understands it. This is the one who produces a crop, yielding a hundred, sixty or thirty times what was sown. | Matthew 13:19–23 |
| 53 | 97 | "Quiet! Be still!" | Mark 4:39 |
| 54 | 98 | "Why are you so afraid? Do you still have no faith?" | Mark 4:40 |
| 55 | 100 | "What do you want with me, Jesus, Son of the most high God? I beg you don't torture me!" | Luke 8:28 |
| 56 | 104 | "My little daughter is dying. Please come and put your hands on her so that she will be healed and live." | Mark 5:23 |

| No. | Page | Scripture | Chapter/Verse |
|---|---|---|---|
| 57 | 105 | "Who touched my clothes?" | Mark 5:30 |
| 58 | 106 | "Daughter, your faith has healed you. Go in peace and be freed from your suffering." | Mark 5:34 |
| 59 | 107 | "Why bother the Teacher anymore?" | Mark 5:35 |
| 60 | 107 | "Don't be afraid. Just believe." | Mark 5:36 |
| 61 | 108 | , "Why all this commotion and wailing? The child is not dead but asleep." | Mark 5:39 |
| 62 | 109 | "Talitha koum!" which means, "Little girl, I say to you, get up!" | Mark 5:41 |
| 63 | 112 | "The harvest is plentiful, but the workers are few. Ask the Lord of the harvest, therefore, to send out workers into his harvest field." | Matthew 9:37–38 |
| 64 | 112 | , "Do not go among the Gentiles or enter any town of the Samaritans. Go rather to the lost sheep of Israel. As you go, proclaim this message: 'The kingdom of heaven has come near.' Heal the sick, raise the dead, cleanse those who have leprosy, drive out demons. Freely you have received; freely give." | Matthew 10:5–8 |
| 65 | 112 | Take nothing for the journey—no staff, no bag, no bread, no money, no extra shirt. Whatever house you enter, stay there until you leave that town. If people do not welcome you, leave their town and shake the dust off your feet as a testimony against them." | Luke 9:3–5 |
| 66 | 126 | "It is not lawful for you to have your brother's wife." | Mark 6:18 |

| No. | Page | Scripture | Chapter/Verse |
|-----|------|-----------|---------------|
| 67 | 126-127 | When the daughter of Herodias came in and danced, she pleased Herod and his dinner guests. The king said to the girl, "Ask me for anything you want, and I'll give it to you." He promised her with an oath, "Whatever you ask I will give you, up to half my kingdom." She said to her mother, "What shall I ask for?" "The head of John the Baptist," her mother answered. At once the girl hurried to the king with the request. "I want you to give me right now the head of John the Baptist on a platter." Herod was greatly distressed, however, because of his oaths and his dinner guests; he didn't want to refuse her. So he immediately sent an executioner with orders to bring John's head. The man went, beheaded John in the prison, and brought back his head on a platter. He presented it to the girl, and she gave it to her mother. | Mark 6:22–28 |
| 68 | 128 | "They do not need to go away. You give them something to eat." | Matthew 14:16 |
| 69 | 129 | "We have here only five loaves of bread and two fish." The Teacher replied, "Bring them here to me." | Matthew 14: 17 and 18. |
| 70 | 131 | "Come." | Matthew 14:29 |
| 71 | 132 | "Peter, you of little faith. Why did you doubt?" | Matthew 14:31 |

| No. | Page | Scripture | Chapter/Verse |
|-----|------|-----------|---------------|
| 72 | 133 | "For Moses said honor your mother and father, … but you [the Pharisees] say that if anyone declares what might have been used to help their father or mother is instead given to God then you [the Pharisees] no longer let them do anything for their mother or father." He went on to say in our defense, "Nothing outside a person can defile them by going into them. Rather, it is what comes out of a person that defiles them." | Mark 7:10–15 |
| 73 | 136 | "My time is not yet here; for you any time will do. The world cannot hate you, but it hates me because I testify that its works are evil. You go to the festival. I am not going up to this festival, because my time has not yet fully come." | John 7:6–8 |
| 74 | 141 | "With joy you shall draw water from the wells of salvation." | Isaiah 12:3 |
| 75 | 142 | "Lord, save us! Lord, grant us success!" | Psalm 118:25 |
| 76 | 142 | "The wind blows wherever it pleases. You hear its sound, but you cannot tell where it comes from or where it is going. So it is with everyone born of the Spirit." | John 3:8 |
| 77 | 143 | "Let anyone who is thirsty come to me and drink. Whoever believes in me, as Scripture has said, rivers of living water will flow from within them." | John 7:37–38 |
| 78 | 144 | "I am the light of the world. Whoever follows me will never walk in darkness, but will have the light of life." | John 8:12 |
| 79 | 145 | "Who do people say the Son of Man is?" "Some say John the Baptist brought back to life. Others say Elijah. And still others, Jeremiah or one of the prophets." "But what about you? Who do you say I am?" | Matthew 16:13–15 |

| No. | Page | Scripture | Chapter/Verse |
|-----|------|-----------|---------------|
| 80 | 145-146 | "Blessed are you, Simon son of Jonah, for this was not revealed to you by flesh and blood, but by my Father in heaven. And I tell you that you are Peter, and on this rock I will build my church, and the gates of Hades will not overcome it. I will give you the keys of the kingdom of heaven; whatever you bind on earth will be bound in heaven, and whatever you loose on earth will be loosed in heaven." | Matthew 16:16–19 |
| 81 | 146 | "Get behind me, Satan! You are a stumbling block to me; you do not have in mind the concerns of God, but merely human concerns." | Matthew 16:23 |
| 82 | 148 | "Lord, it is good for us to be here. If you wish, I will put up three shelters, one for you, one for Moses, and one for Elijah." | Matthew 17:4 |
| 83 | 148 | "This is my Son, whom I love; with him I am well pleased. Listen to him!" | Matthew 17:5 |
| 84 | 149 | "Lord, have mercy on my son," he said. "He has seizures and is suffering greatly. He often falls into the fire or into the water. I brought him to your disciples, but they could not heal him." | Matthew 17:15–16 |
| 85 | 149 | You unbelieving and perverse generation. How long shall I stay with you? How long shall I put up with you? Bring the boy here to me." | Matthew 17:17 |
| 86 | 154 | "Lord, do you want us to call fire down from heaven and destroy them?" | Luke 9:54 |
| 87 | 156 | "Whoever listens to you listens to me; whoever rejects you rejects me; but whoever rejects me rejects him who sent me." | Luke 10:16 |
| 88 | 156 | "Blessed are the eyes that see what you see. For I tell you that many prophets and kings wanted to see what you see but did not see it, and to hear what you hear but did not hear it." | Luke 10:23–24 |

| No. | Page | Scripture | Chapter/Verse |
|---|---|---|---|
| 89 | 157 | "A man was going down from Jerusalem to Jericho, when he was attacked by robbers. They stripped him of his clothes, beat him and went away, leaving him half dead. A priest happened to be going down the same road, and when he saw the man, he passed by on the other side. So too, a Levite, when he came to the place and saw him, passed by on the other side. But a Samaritan, as he traveled, came where the man was; and when he saw him, he took pity on him. He went to him and bandaged his wounds, pouring on oil and wine. Then he put the man on his own donkey, brought him to an inn and took care of him. The next day he took out two denarii and gave them to the innkeeper. 'Look after him,' he said, 'and when I return, I will reimburse you for any extra expense you may have.' Which of these three do you think was a neighbor to the man who fell into the hands of robbers?" The expert in the law replied, "The one who had mercy on him." | Luke 10:30–36 |
| 90 | 158 | "Lord, don't you care that my sister has left me to do the work by myself? Tell her to help me!" | Luke 10:40 |
| 91 | 158 | "Martha, Martha, you are worried and upset about many things, but few things are needed—or indeed only one. Mary has chosen what is better, and it will not be taken away from her." | Luke 10:41–42 |

| No. | Page | Scripture | Chapter/Verse |
|-----|------|-----------|---------------|
| 92 | 159 | Our Father in heaven, hallowed be your name, your kingdom come, your will be done, on earth as it is in Heaven. Give us this day our daily bread. And forgive us our debts, as we also have forgiven our debtors. And lead us not into temptation, but deliver us from the evil one. | Matthew 6:9–13 |
| 93 | 160 | "You hypocrites! Doesn't each of you on the Sabbath untie your ox or donkey from the stall and lead it out to give it water? Then should not this woman, a daughter of Abraham, whom Satan has kept bound for eighteen long years, be set free on the Sabbath day from what bound her?" | Luke 13:15–16 |
| 94 | 160 | "Is it lawful to heal on the Sabbath or not?" | Luke 14:3 |
| 95 | 161 | "If one of you has a child or an ox that falls into a well on the Sabbath day, will you not immediately pull it out?" | Luke 14:5–6 |
| 96 | 165 | "Do you think I came to bring peace on earth? No, I tell you, but division. From now on there will be five in one family divided against each other, three against two and two against three. They will be divided, father against son and son against father, mother against daughter and daughter against mother, mother-in-law against daughter-in-law and daughter-in-law against mother-in-law." | Luke 12:51–53 |
| 97 | 165 | "Let us go back to Judea." | John 11:7 |
| 98 | 166 | "Lazarus is dead, and for your sake I am glad I was not there, so that you may believe. But let us go to him." | John 11:14–15 |
| 99 | 166 | "Your brother will rise again." | John 11:23 |

| No. | Page | Scripture | Chapter/Verse |
|---|---|---|---|
| 100 | 167 | "I am the resurrection and the life. The one who believes in me will live, even though they die; and whoever lives by believing in me will never die. Do you believe this?" | John 11:25–26 |
| 101 | 167 | "Lord, if you had been here, my brother would not have died!" | John 11:32 |
| 102 | 167 | "Come and see, Lord." | John 11:34 |
| 103 | 168 | "Did I not tell you that if you believe, you will see the glory of God?" | John 11:40 |
| 104 | 168 | "Father, I thank you that you have heard me. I knew that you always hear me, but I said this for the benefit of the people standing here, that they may believe that you sent me." | John 11:41–42 |
| 105 | 168 | "Lazarus, come out!" | John 11:43 |
| 106 | 169 | "Take off the grave clothes and let him go." | John 11:44 |
| 107 | 170 | "Why do you ask me about what is good? There is only One who is good. If you want to enter life, keep the commandments." "Which ones?" He enquired. Jesus replied, "You shall not murder, you shall not commit adultery, you shall not steal, you shall not give false testimony, honor your father and mother, and love your neighbor as yourself." | Matthew 19:17–19 |
| 108 | 171 | "All these I have kept. What do I still Lack?" | Matthew 19:20 |
| 109 | 171 | "If you want to be perfect, go, sell your possessions and give to the poor, and you will have treasure in heaven. Then come, follow me." | Matthew 19:21 |
| 110 | 171-172 | "Truly I tell you, it is hard for someone who is rich to enter the kingdom of heaven. Again, I tell you, it is easier for a camel to go through the eye of a needle than for someone who is rich to enter the kingdom of God." | Matthew 19:23–24 |

| No. | Page | Scripture | Chapter/Verse |
|-----|------|-----------|---------------|
| 111 | 172 | "Truly I tell you, at the renewal of all things, when the Son of Man sits on his glorious throne, you who have followed me will also sit on twelve thrones, judging the twelve tribes of Israel. And everyone who has left houses or brothers or sisters or father or mother or wife or children or fields for my sake will receive a hundred times as much and will inherit eternal life. But many who are first will be last, and many who are last will be first." | Matthew 19:28–30 |
| 112 | 174 | "We are going up to Jerusalem, and the Son of Man will be delivered over to the chief priests and the teachers of the law. They will condemn him to death and will hand him over to the Gentiles to be mocked and flogged and crucified. On the third day he will be raised to life!" | Matthew 20:18–19 |
| 113 | 175 | "Grant that one of these two sons of mine may sit at your right and the other at your left in your kingdom." | Matthew 20:21 |
| 114 | 175 | "You don't know what you are asking." | Matthew 20:22 |
| 115 | 175 | "Can you drink the cup I am going to drink?" | Matthew 20:22 |
| 116 | 175 | "We can!" | Matthew 20:22 |
| 117 | 175 | "You will indeed drink from my cup, but to sit at my right or left is not for me to grant. These places belong to those for whom they have been prepared by my Father." | Matthew 20:23 |

| No. | Page | Scripture | Chapter/Verse |
|-----|------|-----------|---------------|
| 118 | 177 | "You know that the rulers of the Gentiles lord it over them, and their high officials exercise authority over them. Not so with you. Instead, whoever wants to become great among you must be your servant, and whoever wants to be first must be your slave—just as the Son of Man did not come to be served, but to serve, and to give his life as a ransom for many." | Matthew 20:25–28 |
| 119 | 182 | "It is written. 'My house will be a house of prayer; but you have made it a den of robbers.'" | Luke 19:46 |
| 120 | 186 | "The Teacher says, my appointed time is near. I am going to celebrate the Passover with my disciples at your house." | Matthew 26:18 |
| 121 | 187 | "Take and eat, this is my body." Then he took a cup, and when he had given thanks, he gave it to them, saying "Drink from it, all of you. This is my blood of the covenant, which is poured out for the many for the forgiveness of sins. I tell you, I will not drink from this fruit of the vine from now until that day when I drink it new with you in my Father's kingdom." | Matthew 26:26–29 |
| 122 | 187 | "You have said so." | Matthew 26:25 |
| 123 | 189 | "Even if all fall away on account of you, I never will!" | Matthew 26:33 |
| 124 | 190 | "I tell you, Peter, before the rooster crows today, you will deny three times that you know me." | Luke 22:34 |
| 125 | 191 | "Couldn't you men keep watch for me for just one hour?" He asked Peter. "Watch and pray so that you will not fall into temptation. The spirit is willing but the flesh is weak." | Matthew 26:40–41 |
| 126 | 192 | "Look, the hour has come, and the Son of Man is delivered into the hands of sinners. Rise! Let us go! Here comes my betrayer!" | Matthew 26:45–46 |
| 127 | 192 | "Do what you came for, friend." | Matthew 26:50 |

| No. | Page | Scripture | Chapter/Verse |
|-----|------|-----------|---------------|
| 128 | 193 | "Do you think that I cannot call on my father and he will at once put at my disposal more than twelve legions of Angels? But how then would the Scriptures be fulfilled that say it must happen this way?" | Matthew 26:52–54 |
| 129 | 196 | "Before the rooster crows you will deny me three times." | Matthew 26:34 |
| 130 | 201 | "Peace be with you!" | John 20:19 |
| 131 | 201 | "Put your finger here, see my hands. Reach out your hand and put it into my side. Stop doubting and believe." | John 20:27 |
| 132 | 201 | "Because you have seen me, you have believed; blessed are those who have not seen and yet have believed." | John 20:29 |
| 133 | 202 | "It is not for you to know the times or dates the Father has set by his own authority. But you will receive power when the Holy Spirit comes on you; and you will be my witnesses in Jerusalem, and in all Judea and Samaria, and to the ends of the earth." | Acts 1:7–8 |
| 134 | 202-203 | 'Do not leave Jerusalem, but wait for the gift my Father promised, which you have heard me speak about. For John baptized with water, but in a few days, you will be baptized with the Holy Spirit.' | Acts 1:4–5 |

# About the Cover Artist

Ju Oshiro is a professional artist who has lived in multiple countries (Korea, Spain, Italy, Turkey, United Arab Emirates) and in multiple States in the USA (Texas, Arizona, California). Her works have been showcased for competition in such venues as the 2014 the Scottsdale Artist Academy's Best & Brightest. Her paintings placed in the 2014 Portrait Society of America's 2014 member's only competition as well as being a finalist in the Art Renewal Center's (ARC) 2014 – 2015 world-wide ARC Salon competition.

Ju studied at the Scottsdale Artist Academy, the Watts Atelier, Los Angeles Academy of Figurative Art, Florence Angel Academy, and is completing her master skills at the Russian Academy in Florence Italy.

The cover painting is 50cm by 40cm oil painting on archival linen.

# About the Author

It has been a blessing to spend a lifetime living and working in the USA, Europe, Middle East, and Asia as an engineer. Over the years I had the honor to meet and serve with many full-time missionaries; gaining an appreciation of the joy, challenges, and hardships they face on a day-to-day basis. Brothers and sisters in Christ who have dedicated their lives to spreading the Good News of Jesus and serving others physically and spiritually.

In prayer the Lord directed me to go back in time to write about the first missionaries. Back to the very beginning. Back to the "Ignition" of our Christian faith.

Writing this book has been a long road for me personally in my walk with Christ. I pray that reliving the experiences of our first brothers and sisters will help you as it has helped me to ignite my faith in Jesus as our Lord and Savior.

Printed in the United States
By Bookmasters